A BULLET IS CHEAPER

A BULLET IS CHEAPER

❖

MARTIN PORYLES

TABLE OF
CONTENTS

CHAPTER
1

Harry Rosen was in a world of trouble. He'd lived through the first bombing of the World Trade Center, 9/11, the Yankees losing to the Red Sox in 2004, and now the past weekend.

His Saturday bets were a disaster, and Sunday was even worse. On Saturday, he bet six college football games and lost five. On Sunday, he was sure he would make it up with the NFL. He bet eight games and lost six. Harry now believed that NFL stood for "No Fucking Luck." At a thousand a game, it was an ugly weekend. The phone was going to ring, and it was going to be his bookmaker, Big Tim Cassidy, who would want to pick up the $9,100 Harry lost. Betting money you didn't have was one thing. Losing it and not being able to pay was another. Harry didn't have the money, and that was not something he wanted to tell Big Tim.

Harry walked twenty-two blocks up the dimly lit avenue until he arrived at his office. He was breathing heavily by the time he walked up the one flight of stairs. He flipped the light switch on. Two rows of bare fluorescent lights lit the space. He waddled behind his desk and squeezed the 260 not-so-tightly-packed pounds on his five-foot-six-inch frame into a coffee-stained chair. Sitting at his desk, he started fidgeting with his cell phone. Harry had been sweating since the last game ended the previous evening, and even in the cool fall air, his shirt was damp. He propped up the cell phone against the computer on his cluttered desk and stared at it, knowing the call was coming. It was 5:30 a.m. on a Monday morning.

He was a real estate broker who worked from an office in Manhattan. Depending on how you viewed it, it was either on the Upper East Side or Spanish Harlem. There was a big difference. The Upper East Side a rather tony, upscale neighborhood, while Spanish Harlem was, well, Spanish Harlem. The two communities were separated by 96th street, the Upper East Side to the south and Spanish Harlem to the north. It wasn't like Rio Grande that separated Texas from Mexico, but it might as well have been.

Harry's office was on 105th St., and Harry always lied, "It's only seven blocks." It was actually nine blocks.

The number of Starbucks indicated just how upscale a neighborhood was. The only Starbucks in this neighborhood was fifteen blocks away.

The office was up one flight of stairs and above a fried chicken joint that held the permeating stench of a long-dead fish.

There were six metal desks, three against each wall, with an aisle between them that led to Harry's office. The desks served the purpose of filing cabinets, stacked with files and papers. It was a lit match and an oily rag away from arson.

The location did not attract a superior sales staff or any foot traffic. Most people who did wander in were looking for the restaurant bathroom or dining room, which shared the same floor.

Despite the location, lack of qualified personnel, and absence of any conventional marketing efforts, he managed to do well enough financially to support his lifestyle and gambling losses.

"Tim, that fucking prick, fuck him," he mumbled under his breath. "I should start placing these bets on one of those Internet websites." That would have been an alternative for Harry, except for the fact that you needed a credit card that wasn't maxed out.

There was no reason for him to be in the office this early, except for the fact that he didn't want to spend one more minute than he had to with his wife of twenty-three years. Harry hated her more than George Bush hated broccoli. And his wife, Debbie, felt the same way about him. She did not have a job and never had, unless one considered babysitting during her school years as employment. Her fierce desire not to work prevented her from divorcing him. She would have, except for the fact that he had no money and his business sucked. Debbie would walk away empty-handed.

Years ago, she had taken out a two-million-dollar life insurance policy on her loving husband, so every night Debbie prayed for two things, first that he would get hit by a crosstown bus, and second that Harry would go quickly. And not to the hospital either. Straight to the afterlife. Maybe she would be able to sue and get a nice settlement from the city. Until then, she got her marital bliss by breaking his balls.

His bookmaker, Tim Cassidy, lived in Gramercy Park. It was a most desirable neighborhood and actually had its own park, which was fenced, locked, and private. Tim's apartment was on the third floor, facing north toward the park, giving him a pastoral view by city standards, and sunlight, another coveted commodity for city residents. Only certain buildings surrounding the park had access, and those residents received a coveted key to the park. Tim had one.

Tim Cassidy made a nice living off the vig, the ten percent of each losing bet. When someone bet $1,000 and won, they got $1,000. When they lost, Cassidy got $1,100. Harry's bad luck was going to help pay for Tim's annual winter trip to St. Martin. With the football season not over until early February and the NCAA basketball tournament starting in mid-March, it gave him a terrific stretch of about a month to spend days on the beach with his wife, Casey. She would bring an armload of magazines to page through. He would bring Ray-Ban sunglasses with dark lenses to surreptitiously check out the topless women.

Tim only vacationed in places that had casino gambling. He wasn't much of a player, but it was a great place to scout for clients. If someone was playing blackjack or shooting craps, chances were they'd bet on a sporting event. That was his first encounter with Harry.

A few years back, Tim was hanging around a craps table at a casino in St. Martin, making ten-dollar bets, when he heard a booming voice.

"Give me a marker for twenty-five hundred." A marker was an IOU the casino took from bigger players.

Harry signed the marker, got the chips, and announced, "The dice are now hot. The H train is here, and now is the time to get on board."

"What's the H train?" Tim asked.

"I'm the H train on a direct route from rags to riches. But looking at this table, it's more like from doing not so bad to buying a third home."

The comment drew some laughs, and the crowd around the table grew larger and more animated. Players started throwing chips on the table and yelling out their bets to the dealers.

Harry dropped two hundred on the pass line. He carefully placed one die on the table with the six showing and stacked the other on top with the one facing up. He then stared at them momentarily as if trying to psychically control the outcome. He picked them up and tossed them in an arc toward the end of the table. When the dice stopped rolling, they showed a four and a three.

"Seven. Winner. Seven. Pay the pass line," the stickman called out. It drew a cheer from the crowed table. Tim, as he was accustomed, was betting with the house against the shooter.

Tim said to Harry, "Nice roll, but you just cost me ten bucks."

Harry threw two five-dollar chips at the dealer and said, "Here's a ten-dollar hard eight for Mr. Down-on-His-Luck," pointing at Tim. He then repeated his ritual by stacking the dice on the table and staring at them. This time he picked up the dice and rolled a pair of fours. "Eight the hard way," came the call from the stickman, and again it brought a roar from the table of believers. It could have been a revival meeting. And Harry Rosen was the preacher.

Tim picked up the chips, added them to his modest stack, and told him, "Thanks for the bet."

"You're costing me money. Who's got time for small talk? I'm working here."

Tim picked up his chips. "You're too strong for me, H-Train. Good luck."

Tim retreated to the economic safety of the bar and the comfort of Johnny Walker. Old-school. No single malt or trendy whiskey. He felt like he was living in the wrong era. The music on his phone was quintessential 1950s: Louis Armstrong, Ray Charles, Frank Sinatra. Newspapers, real newspapers, were better than digital media by his way of thinking.

He was old-school in another way: there was nothing wrong with having a girlfriend as long as your wife didn't know and the girlfriend didn't care.

Tim's last girlfriend didn't care because of an American Express platinum card and an apartment in the West Village. His next one wouldn't care either, or else she wouldn't be his next girlfriend. If nothing else, Tim was honest to a fault with them. No "my wife doesn't understand me" or "we're on the road to a divorce" stories.

The bar was empty except for a thirty-something woman, and the bartender was paying very close attention to her.

Tim looked very little like the fifty-two years he'd been on this planet. He had all his hair, and in a crew cut no less, with no gray. He managed to keep his weight to about 175 pounds on his 6'1" frame despite his diet. Breakfast: blueberry muffin. Lunch: BLT with French fries. Dinner varied, sometimes a sirloin, sometimes a filet mignon, and occasionally a chicken parmigiana if he wanted to eat Italian. Maybe just thinking about going to the gym was what kept the weight off.

While he was staring at the ice cubes in the bottom of the empty glass, he looked up to summon the bartender and saw H-Train, whose name he would soon learn was Harry Rosen, in the mirror behind the bar. He was pale-skinned, wearing shorts with a Hawaiian shirt that was a size too small. Tim turned on the stool. "Thanks again for that bet. I've got enough to buy you a drink."

"I'm happy for you. I've got enough left to buy a Rolex. And not the stainless-steel submariner, either. More like the rose gold Daytona."

"I wouldn't know one from the other, but you're in the right place to buy one. There are a ton of stores in Philipsburg hawking them."

"You want to know the difference? One is entry-level, kind of like the first car you buy from your uncle with 150,000 miles on it. You give him five hundred for it and drive around showing it off like it's the Hope Diamond. The other is like a vintage Corvette that sits covered in the garage. Like Janis Joplin sang: 'you know you've got it if it makes you feel good.'"

"That Alec Baldwin line, 'My watch cost more than your car.'"

"I don't know what kind of car you drive, but if I can find a guy that wants to do some cash business, the watch will probably cost me around twenty thousand."

"Save the tax and tariff."

"That and maybe enough to get something for my wife. Like a 1974 Ford Pinto with bald tires."

"Worst, most dangerous car ever to roll off an assembly line."

"Wouldn't be the worst if she got rear-ended and the car went up in flames. Just sayin'."

"What are you drinking, H-Train?"

"I'll have a gin and tonic. Bombay," Harry called to the bartender.

Harry stuck out his hand. "I'm Harry Rosen."

Tim shook it and introduced himself. "I'm Tim Cassidy. Most people call me Big Tim."

"If you care to invest some money in real estate, I can put you into some really terrific deals," Harry offered.

"I'll keep that in in mind, but my business requires that I keep a lot of cash on hand."

The bartender put fresh drinks on the bar and said, "My friend over there might be interested in some company," while pointing to the woman sitting at the other end of the bar.

Big Tim said, "Thanks, but my wife is here. That would be hazardous to my health."

Harry said, "Why not just offer me a kidney stone? Like I don't have enough trouble."

The bartender retreated without earning his cut. Probably a free roll in the hay. Unless some other drinkers, preferably a winner, appeared, the bartender was going to go home horny and broke.

Harry finally tired of talking about himself and asked, "So, where are you from, and what do you do?"

"Are we on a first date here?" Tim responded with a chuckle.

"Number one, you're not my type, and number two, if my wife did let me date, I think I could do better than you."

"I'm from New York City, Gramercy Park. I'm a bookmaker.

And so it was that Harry met Big Tim.

CHAPTER
2

TIM CASSIDY WOKE up and got ready for the day on Monday morning at 9:00 a.m., about an hour after his wife went off to work. It was pretty ironic that she was an attorney and he was gainfully engaged in an illegal activity.

Casey Cassidy, whose given name was Karen, had her initials joined together to form the nickname shortly after they wed twelve years ago. She was twenty-two when they met. Casey was a red-headed knockout then and had retained her good looks throughout the years. Her appearance served her well professionally, since adversaries would rather try to fuck her than fuck with her.

It also didn't hurt that Casey was incredibly smart. She finished high school a year early and with enough college credits to start college as a sophomore. She finished college two years later and law school three years after that, top of her class. It did not take long for her to be considered one of the top divorce attorneys in New York.

Tim loved his wife but wondered about two things: was she screwing around, and why was he?

Shortly after they met, Casey moved into Tim's apartment on Perry Street in the West Village. He helped her with her law school tuition. He saw this as prepaid legal fees in the unlikely event of an arrest. Tim also made sure Casey always had a few bucks in her pocket for emergencies, like a trunk show at Hermès. When she passed the bar exam, they married and moved to Gramercy Park.

Tim kept the place on Perry Street.

Dressed in a pair of jeans, black tee-shirt, and tweed sport jacket, Tim left the apartment and headed up Third Avenue. He grabbed a *Daily News* and the *Times* from the corner store and continued on to the bagel shop two doors down.

"Buenos días, Señor Tim," said the counterman as he packed a blueberry muffin and black coffee into a paper bag.

"Hola, Señor Nick. You know, your Spanish is better than my English."

"Hey, if I can't speak Spanish, how am I going to speak with the help? Besides them and us old Greeks, no one else is willing to work these hours."

"And your Greek is better than mine."

"I didn't know you spoke Greek."

"I can't. Not a word."

"I've been speaking it for sixty-six years." Nick laughed. "Muffin and a coffee, $3.25."

Tim left a five-dollar bill on the counter, picked up his breakfast, said thanks, and walked toward the door.

"Hey, Tim, I like the Jets this Sunday."

"You like the Jets every Sunday."

"They play the Bills this week, and I don't think the Bills could beat the Sisters of the Poor."

Tim shrugged and said, "I'm not so sure the Jets could either." He continued, "How did you do last week?"

"You owe me fifty."

"Way to go. I'll take your word for it." Tim reached in his pocket, found a fifty-dollar bill, and handed it to Nick.

"Thanks, big guy. I'll call on Friday about the Jets.

"Okay. See you tomorrow."

Tim really didn't care to take any small bets. His clients were mostly the Wall Street crowd. These guys were gambling with stocks and bonds all week and couldn't give it a rest. They needed more action. Basketball, hockey, hell, if they could bet on professional wrestling, they would. Tim thought that if they picked stocks as successfully as they picked winners with him, their investors would be losing their shirts. They lost often and paid quickly. They were such great clients that for Christmas they could count on a box of Cuban cigars (Cohibas that he got from a guy who got them from a guy who got them from South America) and a bottle of Johnny Walker Blue.

He would rather collect from someone who could afford to lose than someone who would have to do without because of a loss. Tim would often tell Nick after a loss that they could settle up later and wait for him to pick a winner so no money changed hands. He always paid up immediately if Nick had a winner.

Big Tim turned the corner and headed to the back office of the garage that housed his limousine company. He didn't work it. That's what his cousin Mike was for. He kept the cars clean and running, booked the jobs, hired the drivers, and likely skimmed some money for himself. Tim needed a business as a front to launder his illegal profits, and as long as there was enough money left to pay the bills, Big Tim was happy.

He sat down and read the sports section of the *News* and the editorial section of the *Times* while he ate his muffin. After that, he got to work tallying up who won, who lost, and how much over the past week.

It was a pretty typical week, with almost as many winners as losers and no extraordinary amounts — except for Harry Rosen. "Nine thousand, one hundred dollars." He said it each time he checked and rechecked his figures. He finished his coffee, checked his watch, and decided ten thirty was not too early to call.

Harry's phone finally rang, the caller ID confirming the nightmare. He had spent the last five hours trying to figure out how to deal with this.

"Hey, Big Tim, how's it going?" Harry answered with his happy voice.

"For me, a lot better than you."

"You know, I've been a little busy here. Haven't even checked the scores."

"When you do, you're gonna find nine thousand, one hundred reasons to be upset."

"That number can't be right. Tell me you're kidding."

"I'm as serious as a heart attack."

"Give me the chance to check it out, and I'll get back to you."

"Harry, cut the crap. You owe me the money. I lose, I pay you. You lose, you pay me. It's very simple."

"Come on, Big Tim. You know I'm only breaking your stones."

"No problem. We can settle up on Wednesday. Want to get some lunch?"

"Sure, sounds great. Where do you want to meet?"

"P.J. Clarke's, on 3rd and 55th."

"Like I don't know where it is. Good choice. How about one o'clock?"

"I will see you there."

Harry hung up the phone wondering how he was going to come up with all that money in the next two days.

CHAPTER
3

D EBBIE ROSEN WOKE up Monday morning, like every other morning, and looked on the other side of the bed. When she saw that Harry wasn't there, she checked the answering machine to see if this was her lucky day. *Crap.* No messages. She put a dark roast coffee pod in the coffee maker and grabbed a donut out of the always-stocked box on the counter. She picked through the three-day pile of mail, looking for the Nordstrom catalog. It was one of her favorite passive-aggressive tactics. Let the mail accumulate and force Harry to deal with it. Maybe when he saw the bills, he would stroke out.

The apartment was the same building she grew up in on the Upper East Side of Manhattan, a fabulous building on a fabulous block. It was a classic five: two bedrooms, living room, dining room, kitchen, and bathroom. In 1947, when her parents first moved in, their initial lease was for an astounding amount at the time: $44 a month. Thanks to it being a rare prize for New York City real estate — a rent-controlled apartment — modest limits were placed on rent increases, bringing the current rent to $637 a month. At that rate, given that comparable apartments in the building were more like $4,000, the landlord wasn't going to do any maintenance. With Harry being Harry, he wasn't going to spend a dime on anything unless he could wear it, eat it, drive it, or bet on it. The garage where Harry parked his Mercedes cost more than his rent. So did the lease on the car.

Debbie had wanted out of that apartment for years. Harry always had a good reason at the ready: "Where can we find another place like this, and at this price?"

She would prod, "You know the owner would pay us a fortune to move out. Apartments this size are selling for one and a half million in this building." One thing everybody in New York knew was the value of their own real estate, and most everyone else's too.

"More like two million, if the cheap bastard spent a few bucks on it."

"So maybe he gives us a million and we could move out."

"To where? To what? Some crappy one-bedroom on the West Side? And then we end up with a maintenance cost about triple our rent."

"Suppose we buy a small house in New Jersey."

"Stop talking like a crazy person. I could have you committed for even thinking that."

Debbie did some quick, easy math and figured that two million from the insurance policy on his life plus a million from dumping the dump she'd hated since adulthood would put her on the beach in Boca Raton. She missed the middle part of her life that most baby boomers experienced: leaving the city. It was a traditional pattern.

You were born in the city, even though The City was really only Manhattan, despite what everyone in the other four boroughs thought. Staten Islanders were more like from New Jersey.

After you reached school age, your parents then moved to the great white suburbs. God forbid you would have to go school with *schvartzes,* German for black and Yiddish for the 'n' word. That was the part Debbie missed. She was stuck in the city as teenager. Instead of getting a ride to the mall with a few bucks to spend, she got a token for the subway and a stiletto to hide inside her sock. If some bastard tried to rob you, you could say that your money was in your shoe. You'd reach down, grab the stiletto, and stick them if they didn't run fast enough.

When the kids were grown, it was then expected that you move to Boca Raton. That was where she would finally rejoin her brethren of baby boomers. If only.

Harry's phone rang again. In his sweetest voice, he answered, "Well, good morning sugar, you sleep okay?" He presumably hoped a good-natured greeting would defuse any hostility.

"I slept fine, thanks. Did you pay the Nordstrom bill?" she asked as she stared at the unopened envelope containing that very same item.

"Of course. Don't I pay all the bills? Yours, mine, and ours."

"That's good, darling, because I saw a few things in their catalog, and I'm heading over there."

"Debbie, it's the middle of winter. You know the real estate market is quiet until spring. What's so important you can't wait a few months?"

"I want to start putting together a few things for St. Martin. We *are* going this year, aren't we?"

"Only if you can swim that far. Things are a little tight right now."

"You say that every year. And thanks for reminding me. I need a few new bathing suits too."

"Whatever." He hung up.

Harry was glad that he kept up the premiums on her life insurance policy. Half a million bucks. If she knew about it, she'd kill him first.

That would change his life. Not just for the material things it would buy — Harry had plenty of those — but for the tranquility it would bring. Maybe he could give the policy to Big Tim. Harry would tell him he could take her out and keep the insurance money. Two problems solved, and worth every cent.

CHAPTER

4

SOON ENOUGH, WEDNESDAY morning rolled around and Tim was sitting in the overstuffed chair sipping on his first coffee when he heard Casey stirring in the bedroom. He got up and went into the kitchen to pour one for her. She walked into the living room dressed in low-cut sweatpants and a white tee-shirt that barely seemed to cover her breasts. Casey was as sexy and seductive as ever.

The night before, they played a double-header. About fifteen minutes after the first lustful romp, Casey said, "Hey, bartender, set up another round. I'm not ready to call it a night."

Big Tim was lying on his side with his elbow propped up and his hand supporting his head. He replied, "Hmm. I think you've had enough."

She cuddled a little closer, rubbed her hands over his butt, and purred. "Come on. Just one more. It's not like I'm asking you to go vegan."

Casey shook her flaming red shoulder-length hair, then gave him a big smile and playfully squeezed his ass. "And just how is the the real Big Tim this morning?" Unlike the night before, she settled for one turn at bat.

"Baby," Tim said, "you wore me out, but I am very, very happy. You're not going to write a review for Page Six in the *Post* are you?"

"No. But if I did, it would say that Big Tim was incredible between the sheets and on the floor. He gave nothing short of a world-class performance. And there was absolutely nothing short about him."

"You bring out the best in me. Care for some coffee?"

Big Tim spent the rest of the morning puttering around the apartment. He picked up his iPad and searched the Internet for flights to St. Martin. Harry Rosen was going to provide enough for the trip. Maybe even an extra week. If Casey couldn't get the extra time away, it might provide him the opportunity to make spring break just a little more interesting for a future girlfriend. At that moment, he thought of himself as a complete idiot. He had a gorgeous, super sexy, and attractive wife that had no intimacy problems. And yet he felt compelled to seek out extramarital relationships. *Why do I do this?* he thought. *Viagra, maybe?*

Big Tim left the apartment with enough time to walk up Third Avenue to P.J. Clarke's, where he was meeting Harry for lunch. It was sunny, and he hoped the cool late autumn air would invigorate him. There was no doubt about the fact that age was taking its toll on him. He should have had a spring in his step and a smile on his face after going at it again this morning with his wife. Instead he was in a fog and walking at a pace where slow would be an overstatement. If he were in a race with a three-legged turtle, the turtle would be the favorite.

He reached the restaurant, walked into the bar, and saw Harry sitting there.

"Harry, how're you doing?"

"Not bad for a guy my age. I can still pee without any pain. Although it does take about fifteen minutes."

"Spare me the details. Don't they have a pill for that? I'll probably be there soon enough myself."

"I take fourteen pills a day as it is. Add my wife, and it's fifteen."

"Biggest pill of all, huh?"

"If you look in the dictionary for the word miserable, you'll see her picture. What about you Tim, still married?"

"I am. She's a successful attorney and an absolute knockout. I don't think she's reached her sexual peak yet."

"My wife reached hers about three years before we got married."

"Let's get a table. I skipped breakfast this morning and am really hungry."

"Breakfast is the most important meal of the day. You gotta eat breakfast, big guy."

"My wife had other ideas," Tim said as he got off his bar stool and started walking towards the hostess standing guard before the dining room lest anyone take just any table.

Harry followed and said, astonished, "Holy fuck. People really do that in the morning too?"

The hostess seated them at a small, uncomfortable table that could have been almost any of them. Fortunately, the table next to them was empty, so there would be enough privacy to conduct their business.

An attractive young server came over to their table to leave menus and take their drink order. That seemed the pattern at restaurants these days, followed by the day's specials before you ordered and a pitch for coffee and dessert after you finished.

Harry spoke up. "Sweetheart, do you have any tonic water?"

"I'm certain we do," she answered.

"That's wonderful, dear. Bring me a gin and tonic. Bombay gin."

Big Tim ordered sparkling water.

As she started to walk away, Harry called her back and said, "Listen, I'm feeling a little guilty being the only person having a mixed drink at the table, so instead of the gin and tonic, leave out the tonic. Just bring a lime with the gin."

Tim picked up the menu and smiled. Harry was loud and obnoxious and devoid of an edit button between his brain and mouth. Because of that he was crude but entertaining to laugh at if you could look past many of the politically incorrect portions without being embarrassed. Harry seemed unaware that the days had passed when you could describe people in ethnic terms that were now considered insensitive and hurtful.

The server returned with their drinks and wanted to know if they would like to hear the day's specials. Big Tim wanted to hear more about her on a very personal level. By the end of lunch today, he thought she might be a candidate for his intimate companion during his third week away this winter.

She was tall and thin, with light brown skin, Latina, he thought. Full chested and an unfashionably small butt. Curly, shoulder-length hair and dazzling smile beneath a nose that had a slight bump. She was much more appetizing to Tim than anything on the menu.

"Sure, I'd love to hear the specials." Knowing full well what his lunch order was going to be, he added, "By the way, I eat here often and don't recognize you."

"I just started here."

"This is my friend Harry. I'm Tim, and please don't judge me by my friends."

"Nice meeting both of you. I'm Isabella."

"Isabella. What a pretty name," Tim thought out loud. "Has anyone ever said that you look a lot like Penelope Cruz?"

"That is so flattering. Thank you."

Harry broke in to this match dot com conversation and asked, "So, Izzy, what's good here?"

"Izzy? You know her like a minute and a half and she's already Izzy? Don't you still call your wife Mrs. Rosen? Isabella, excuse my friend. What he lacks in decorum he makes up for in rudeness."

"I don't mind it at all. Almost everybody calls me that. The raw bar is very popular."

With that suggestion, Harry ordered a half dozen oysters, shrimp cocktail, and a lobster, "not too big maybe like a pound and half." Tim asked for a BLT and side of fries.

After Izzy disappeared, Tim glanced around, saw they had some privacy, and said, "So, Harry, what have you got for me?"

"About that...I'm a little bit cash-poor right now."

"I'm not sure I understand what you're trying to tell me."

Harry quickly added, "I'm not trying to stiff you. I know we can work this out."

"We don't work this out. *You* work this out. And with $9,100. And before we leave here."

"Tim, I have a real estate deal closing on Thursday. My end is like twenty-five thousand, so it's no problem paying you then."

"Harry, tell me that's a fucking joke, because if it isn't, I'll be pretty goddamn pissed off."

"Tim, there's no need to get all worked up. I have a solution that you'll be very happy with."

"Does that solution include $9,100 in cash?"

"Even better," Harry said as he removed the Rolex from his wrist and held it up for Tim to see. "I bought this for like twenty grand. It's a rose gold Rolex Daytona. Why don't you keep it for two days? If I don't close my deal and come up with the money, the watch is yours." With that, Tim got even more agitated. "What am I, a pawn shop? Just go hock your fucking watch and pay me my fucking money."

Harry caught a short respite from Big Tim's temper as Izzy reappeared with their lunch. She placed Tim's plate in front of him and struggled to fit Harry's order, which needed one small plate for the shrimp cocktail and two much larger plates for the rest of his order. He inspected the feast fit for a gourmand, saw the lobster with a small container of melted butter, and asked, "Sweetheart, you don't serve corn on the cob with the lobster?"

Izzy calmly told him that he could order a side off the menu, and she would be glad to bring him the corn or any other he preferred.

Very impressive, Tim thought. She didn't loose her cool and turned the situation completely around from a potential argument into an opportunity to pad the check. Izzy was becoming irresistible to Tim, like a stick to a Golden Retriever.

"No need to go through the trouble. I just thought there'd be corn on the cob, a baked potato, something."

"Okay, then. You're all good?

"You know what, I'll have a baked potato."

Now looking at Tim she asked, "How about you Tim, anything else?"

"All good here."

She left, and somewhere between the oysters and the shrimp, Harry once again pursued his offer to Tim. "So you don't like my idea of using the watch as collateral?"

"Harry, we will meet again on Friday. I don't want any collateral or stories. I want my money."

"Not a problem. My deal is rock-solid and already scheduled to close. This lobster is amazing. How's your sandwich?"

After he finished his amazing lobster, and the shrimp, and the oysters, Harry tore off the lobster bib, looked at the watch he had placed back on his wrist, and told Tim about an appointment he was already late for. And would he mind getting the check? Lunch was great, and thanks a lot, but he had to run.

"I will see you on Friday, Harry."

"Without a doubt. Call me in the morning and let me know when and where."

Harry got out the door and started walking uptown on Third Avenue. A previous trip to Chinatown and the twenty bucks he spent to buy the knockoff watch was truly a waste of time.

Tim had barely finished half of his sandwich in the time it took Harry to wolf down his dinner for two. He sat there contemplating whether he wanted to finish the rest of his lunch or chase Harry out the door and grab him by the throat. His homicidal thoughts disappeared when Izzy came by to bus the table. Jesus, she was gorgeous.

"What happened to your friend?"

"He wanted to beat it before you got here with the check." Then he quickly added, "Excuse me. This may seem a little out of bounds, but I think you're incredibly attractive and would be honored if you would meet me for a cup of coffee or something stronger."

Izzy looked Tim square in the eye, deliberated for the briefest of moments, and said, "You know, there's something interesting about you. Let's do it."

Containing his elation, Tim asked for her number and heard her say that he could friend her on Facebook and send a message. "Isabella Ramirez, you'll find me."

"Izzy, with all due respect for modern communication, I'm only about six months removed from a pager, and I miss pay phones. Is there another way to reach you? I'm not on Facebook."

"Then how do I know you really exist?" she said with a short laugh. "Anyway, I live downtown. There's a Starbucks on First Avenue near Third Street."

They settled on meeting the following morning at ten, which would give her the built-in excuse that she had to get to work. And Tim barely enough time to get there, especially if his wife got frisky.

CHAPTER
5

DEBBIE ROSEN WOKE up on Thursday happy, as always, to find Harry had already left for work. *How did I end up married to Harry?* she thought. *I wasn't drunk. I wasn't pregnant.* Days before the wedding, her mother had presciently suggested that both of them were going to wish they were dead.

As Debbie was drying herself off after a long, hot shower, she took a look in the mirror for a self-assessment and decided that aging had been kind to her. Very little gray in her hair, still slim, with only a little sag. Nothing some silicone and Botox couldn't fix. It would be the perfect gift for her fiftieth birthday.

She opened her closet to pick out some clothes, noticed a slinky, low-cut black cocktail dress that had been in the closet for years, and decided to try it on. God forbid Harry should take her someplace where she could wear it. All in all, she decided she looked good enough to do much better than her husband. As an afterthought, she concluded that if she were bald, obese, and flat-chested, she could still do better. She would save the dress for another day and another man.

What a great day to go shopping. It was midweek and midday, so the only people likely to be in the stores were the housewives of Long Island. *Nordstrom, here I come!* During the short walk down the street to the garage, Debbie had an indescribable feeling of excitement. She felt good about herself and imagined her future without Harry. That was the only part she still had to work out. Without Harry.

At the garage, a polite hello and a five-dollar bill to the attendant got the car to her right away. She got in and saw the empty coffee cup and a crumpled-up napkin with crumbs inside. Debbie pressed the button that powered down the driver's window and handed the cup to the garage attendant to dispose of.

Harry was sitting in his office when the phone rang. A look at the caller ID brought about a heavy sigh. "Hi, honey, what's cooking?"

"What's cooking? I'll tell you what's cooking. I just picked up the car and it's like sitting in a pig sty. What's wrong with you?"

"I'm very busy right now. I've got a closing in a little while and have to get going. What's wrong with the car?"

"There's a dirty coffee cup and crumbs all over the car," she said.

"And this is worth the aggravation?"

"The only thing aggravating is you. It's bad enough you were eating in the car. If you're hungry, go to a diner. For like the millionth time: don't eat in the car."

"I was late for an appointment. I'm sorry. I shouldn't have done that." He was about as insincere as one could be. He was only sorry that he got caught.

"That's not the point. Why do I always have to clean up after you?"

"All right, Debbie, you're right. It's my fault. I'm sorry. I have to go. By the way, where are you going?"

"All of a sudden I'm accountable to you. Like I work for you. I can't have a life?"

"I didn't mean it like that. It was just a question."

"I'm going shopping. To Nordstrom in Garden City. And I hope the car can make it back. It's almost out of gas."

"You can't stop and fill the tank?"

"I'm not going pump gas. Who do I look like to you?"

"Honey, you'll stop in New Jersey. They're full-service there. They pump the gas for you."

"New Jersey? Maybe this is news to you, but Garden City happens to be in the other direction. On Long Island."

"So you'll go to the full-service island. Are you going to worry about spending an extra ten bucks to fill the tank? I think the last time you worried about spending money, Nixon was president."

"Goodbye, Harry. And by the way, would you do me a favor? On your way home, drop dead." Debbie ended the call.

She stared out the windshield and said to herself, "Full service. I could use some of that, and not at the gas pump either."

She arrived at Nordstrom with a wallet full of credit cards, knowing that the Nordstrom bill had not been paid, with the goal of enjoying any remaining purchasing power, starting with a spa treatment that included a manicure, pedicure, facial, body wrap, and massage. She felt wonderful, especially because the charge went through without incident. This inspired her to make an appointment for hair and makeup in the salon after lunch. This day was going to be as much full service as she could get.

Her indomitable spirit, as well as the credit card not being rejected after her makeover and purchase of a variety of expensive cosmetics, pushed her to continue to the shopping portion of the day. It was in the swimwear department that a watershed moment in her life occurred.

CHAPTER
6

C ASEY CASSIDY HAD a meeting on Long Island. She arrived at a luxury office building where her opposing council plied his trade. To her that meant the building was probably the equivalent of a dump by Manhattan standards, and her adversary might be good enough to get hired by a law firm that would occupy a dump in Manhattan. She was escorted into the conference room and made a point of standing there holding her coat arm's-length from her body until one of the people sitting at the table offered to hang it up for her. This was going to be cake.

She sat down and politely declined the coffee they offered, saying, "This isn't going to take that long."

Her opposition smiled. "I'm glad to hear that. My client has every desire to treat his soon-to-be-ex-wife reasonably."

"My client feels exactly the same way. Which is why she is prepared to settle for the Manhattan residence, the second home in Southampton, seventy-five percent of the previously disclosed liquid assets, and twenty-five percent of his gross income for the next fifteen years. And she gets the Range Rover too. He can keep all of his businesses."

"Just a tad excessive, don't you think? My client is prepared to offer..."

She cut him off. "I really don't care what your client is offering. This is not an opening bid. This is where we settle. It appears that my forensic accountant noticed forty-three irregularities that may be construed as fraudulent. Hypothetically, if he used the postal service to perpetrate these frauds, he could do twenty years on each one. And as I am sure you are aware, with just a fraction of that, we get the whole enchilada."

With their faces turning about as white as the polar ice caps, the counter was, "We will consult with our client and get back to you."

"You do that. And think about what a criminal legal defense is going to cost, and how much is going to be left to pay your fees." More silence.

More squirming. Casey said, "Oh, no. Don't tell me you didn't get a substantial retainer?"

"We don't have the authority to settle for those terms."

"Call your client and get it, because I am not going to make another trip out here or waste any more time on this. Ask someone to bring me a Perrier with a slice of lime and go find a telephone so you can have a 'come to Jesus' with your client."

"Ms. Cassidy, I'm not sure that we have Perrier, or a lime."

"For fuck's sake, just call your client so I can get out of this Third World country."

Casey took out her iPad as they left, and before she could read her emails, they returned to let her know they had a deal.

"I'm glad to hear that." She reached into her briefcase and produced the stipulation with the now-settled terms. Passing it across the table, she said, "I'm glad we were able to get this done so amicably."

"If this was amicable, I would hate to see your contentious side."

"Yes, you would." She put on her coat, picked up her bag, and left them all standing there, shell-shocked.

Casey decided to venture out to do some shopping before heading back to the city. Nordstrom was conveniently located nearby, so why not check out the summer collection?

February was right around the corner, and so was her annual trip to the Caribbean. Once again, she would try to convince Tim there were other islands besides St. Martin. Her powers of persuasion were insurmountable, except in this regard. In the past she had suggested St. Barth ("too quiet"), Anguilla ("way too quiet"), and Curaçao ("too far; it's like going to Venezuela"). Casey got the hint and gave up the fight. It was a losing and inconsequential battle.

Debbie thought it was a mirage when she looked in the mirror. She never looked good in bathing suits, but this one seemed not so bad. The slight bulge in her tummy looked less so, and her slightly less-than-generous breasts seemed more so. Debbie's insecurities about her physical appearance had nagged at her throughout her life. Maybe it was that very thing that first drew her to Harry. He was never critical of her appearance, and because of that she looked past all his other shortcomings.

The only other shopper in that department, a younger and incredibly attractive woman, said, "You really look fabulous in that." Considering the appearance of the woman making the statement, Debbie's interest in purchasing the item rose. It was $695, but if she did look that much better, why not? *What the hell. I'm not paying for it anyway.*

"Why, thank you. I'm never really sure if I'm too old or saggy even to wear a bathing suit," Debbie said.

"You shouldn't be self-conscious about that. I moved past that years ago. Let the twenty-somethings worry." With that, Casey walked toward a rack, picked up a fishnet cover-up, and handed it to Debbie. "Seriously, I would get this and wear it without the top of that two-piece. You'll turn heads."

"Oh my god. I could never do that." Debbie blushed.

"Of course you could, and believe me, you'll be amazed at how good you'll feel getting all the attention."

"I could see how you could get away with that. I mean you're so much younger and in such better shape."

"Are you buying that for a winter vacation? You could definitely do that in South Beach if you're going to Florida."

"I'm going to St. Martin. I could wear it there. If I have the nerve."

"Wow. That's incredible. I'm going there as well. You will be surprised how quickly you overcome that uneasiness. It's like when you want to go for a swim. You're at the shoreline up to your ankles, thinking how cold the water is, until you jump in. Then it's totally refreshing."

Debbie took all this in and decided she might actually enjoy the attention. The possibilities had her fantasizing about someone who was young and trim, educated and interesting, fawning and attentive. Someone to get a couples' massage with in a tent on the beach at dusk. Someone who wasn't Harry.

She said, "I am really so glad I met you. I'm Debbie."

"Glad to meet you, Debbie. I'm Casey. Listen, I'd love to hang out and chat a bit more, but I want to get back home to the city. My husband doesn't know it yet, but it's date night."

"I have to get back there myself. I live on the Upper East Side. Where do you live?"

Casey knew better than to draw any conclusions from that, but she was spending the day shopping at Nordstrom, and you couldn't get there by public transportation. It wasn't likely you would get a Zipcar or an

Uber to get here. So she had a car and lived on the Upper East Side. The makings of a terrific client.

Date night. Debbie tried to imagine what that might be like. Not with the man in the massage tent from her earlier daydream, but with Harry. Her skin went cold.

"My husband forgot date night existed, if he ever knew at all."

"And you you're okay with that?"

"Not really. I often think about him reaching an immediate and untimely death."

"We really should talk. I may be able to help you."

"Are you a therapist?"

"I provide the best therapy women could ever want or need. I'm a matrimonial attorney." Casey reached into her jacket pocket and handed Debbie a business card.

Debbie Rosen then smiled the biggest smile and asked if she could give Casey a hug. Casey spread her arms apart, and while in her grasp she let Debbie know that everything was going to work out just fine. She did not mention the part that always followed — *provided she had enough money for the retainer.*

CHAPTER
7

H ARRY GOT TO his office on Thursday morning and started to put together an invoice for his fee. He did the math, rechecked the figures, and filled in the amount due: $23,750. Let the selling broker, whom he'd dubbed the crazy Israeli, prepare his own invoice. This was going to be an easy end to an easy deal.

The recently deceased Esmeralda Ramirez had lived in her Harlem brownstone for practically her entire adult life. She and her husband bought the home in the early 1950s, raised five children, and both retired after spending almost forty years working for the City of New York, he as an engineer on a subway train, she as a teacher. Pensions, savings, social security, and the Depression-era view of debt ("if you can't afford to pay for it in cash, don't buy it") took them through a comfortable retirement. They traveled and doted on their children and grandchildren. Life was good to them. With an estate of about a million dollars in stocks and bonds and a brownstone that would sell for almost another million, life was going to be a little better for each of the Ramirez children. Exactly how their parents would have wanted it.

Harry reached out to the heirs after reading the obituaries. He expressed his condolences and of course mentioned that after they were ready get past the sadness, he would be glad to help them expeditiously dispose of the property. There was a high demand, and he could think of several clients that would likely be interested.

None of the children had any interest in moving back into the property after moving out to the suburbs. They remembered not only the happy times inside the house but also the drugs, gangs, and fear outside the home. Their experience shaped their opinion of life in New York City, despite recent depictions of the gentrification that brought the likes of Starbucks to 125th Street. Westchester and New Jersey were just fine with all five of them, thank you very much. So it came to pass that they gave the listing to Harry, who told them it would not be out of the realm of possibility to get a million for it.

Within a matter of days, Harry got a call from another realtor, Ezra Ben Solomon. Could he show the property to his clients? Maybe tomorrow? Early? He met them the following day at 8:00 a.m. and listened to them speak to each other in what he thought was Russian. It could have been Polish or Ukrainian. It didn't matter to Harry. Every language from Eastern Europe was Russian, much like every language from Asia was Chinese.

Harry was on his way back to his office after listening Gorbachev and Khrushchev or whatever their names were carry on about whatever they were carrying on about. It was a waste of fucking time as far as he was concerned. His phone rang, and after a small prayer that concluded with the phrase "please don't let this be my wife," he checked the caller ID. He was grateful it was the crazy Israeli. "Ezra, what's up? Your clients like what they saw?" Indeed they had, and after Harry let Ezra know that he would present the offer, it had as much chance of success as there was of peace in the Middle East. "Talk to Igor and Nikita. Let them know I think I can sell this at $950,000."

"Igor and Nikita." Ezra laughed. "You're a funny guy, Harry. I'll let you know."

Harry was climbing the stairs to his office after struggling to get out of the small backseat in this poor imitation of a taxi, wondering *whatever happened to Checker cabs?* when the phone rang once again. *Can I get lucky twice this morning?* he thought before checking the phone's display. Indeed he could. It was the crazy Israeli again.

"Hi, Harry," Ezra said, and without taking a breath added, "we can make a deal at nine-fifty."

"That is great news. Understand I am dealing with an estate, so I need five people to get to yes. Just be a little patient with me."

CHAPTER
8

T HURSDAY MORNING ARRIVED and brought with it a clear sky and a bright, warm sun. Tim woke up and looked at the clock radio on his nightstand. It had been there for years, refusing to be replaced by any recent technological advancement. The analog display showed the time at nine as the all-news AM radio station started to tell him about fires, murders, traffic tie-ups, and the weather.

Casey had already left. She gave him all he could handle the night before and then some. He rolled out of bed and headed to the coffee maker. On his way, a thought entered his still-unclear head, and he blurted out, "Holy crap." He had just remembered his date with Izzy.

Maybe it wouldn't be so bad if he no-showed. His life was pretty damn good. Izzy might make it so much better. She was incredibly attractive. On the other hand, she might make it much more complicated. Much more given the fact that his wife was a divorce lawyer and ironically one that he had put through law school. Maybe she would cut him a break if it got that far. *Not likely,* he concluded. Contentment and fear lost this battle with youth and beauty. Tim decided to get ready and head out the door to meet Izzy.

It was amazing that he owned a car service with a small fleet but had to call Uber for a ride. It made him wonder about the future prospects for his business. If he didn't need a legitimate front and a way to launder his illegal bookmaking profits, he wouldn't even bother with it. Tim didn't have a childhood dream to own a car service; a very unlucky former client got in over his head and sold him the business at a significant discount.

Tim went to the curb, checked his iPhone, and saw the car was one minute away. This was one of the few concessions to modern technology that warranted his admiration. He put his phone back in the inside pocket of his sport jacket. Even though the temperature was going to be a delightful mid to high sixties, according to the forecast, he was wearing a jacket. Lightweight and linen, it was perfect for the weather. He felt a little uncomfortable if he didn't wear one.

The Uber arrived, and a ridiculously quick ride brought him to the Starbucks where he was to meet the fabulously gorgeous Izzy. He ordered a coffee and found a table amongst the young crowd with their iPads and laptops busily cranking out screenplays, books, or Facebook posts. He was totally out of his element and having second thoughts about seeing Izzy until she walked in. She saw him waved, smiled, and walked over to the small table where Tim was seated. He got up, smiled back, and gave her the air kiss as he touched his cheek next to hers.

"What are you drinking?" he asked, and then added, "I hope you weren't expecting a champagne cocktail."

She laughed. "I wonder if they would ask what size and write my name on the cup. I'm going to settle for a cappuccino."

"Be right back. I'm sure they'll be able to manage that."

Tim placed and paid for the order, returned to the table, and asked, "So, just who is Isabella Ramirez?"

"Great question. I've met her, and can tell you that she grew up in Westchester. Went to Boston College. She's taking a gap year in New York and moved into a two-bedroom apartment with three friends. She got a job in a restaurant and one day you'll read about her in *Variety*."

"She's going to be an actor?"

"No, she's going to play the washboard in a zydeco band. Of course she's going to be an actor."

"Well, that's a good thing, because I never cared much for zydeco."

"Unfortunately, that acting job is going to have to wait. My father insisted that first I become a lawyer, then I can do anything I want." She paused to take her first sip of the cappuccino. "I'm taking a gap year because I figured I'll be working like crazy the next three years and want to think of this year as the good old days."

"I'm sure it'll be nice to have a lawyer in the family."

"The last thing my family needs is another lawyer. There's my father, an aunt, brother-in-law, and two first cousins."

"Your Thanksgiving dinners must be like meeting of the Bar Association."

"Worse than that. Some of them are Dallas Cowboys fans. They make it awful for the rest of us, especially if they win. Of course, when Dallas loses, which almost never seems to happen, they get it back pretty good."

Izzy took another sip of the cappuccino. "I'd like to ask a question of this mysterious older gentleman who has probably never heard of Adele or Sam Smith: just who is Tim Cassidy? Is he producing or directing a play or movie in which he has the perfect role for me, in which case I would be much more interested in him, but not enough to go to bed with him." She added the last phrase as a sex repellent.

"I'm not sure if that question is going to make me regret never being in therapy or make me consider it. To answer your question, I never refer to myself in the third person, I do know the two singers you mentioned, but I'm also old enough to know Aretha Franklin is better than Adele and Sam Smith will never be Frank Sinatra." He picked up a package of sugar and emptied it into his double espresso. After a quick gulp he added, "I grew up in Brooklyn, live in Gramercy Park, and full disclosure, with my wife. I own a small business and have never wanted to produce a play or movie."

"With your wife, huh?"

"Yes. With my wife."

"Well that's refreshing. An honest man."

"You can't cheat an honest man."

"W.C. Fields. Brilliant actor. I would have loved to play his daughter in that movie. Just to work with him must have been amazing. But does that mean an honest man can cheat?"

"Any man can cheat. The question is, will they? Statistically, about two out of three men do cheat. Just to put that in perspective, it's about the same percentage for women."

"So the odds are that you have cheated or will cheat."

Tim laughed. "Well, I know something about odds, and they are not always what they seem. For instance, in my case the odds might be lower. My wife is a matrimonial lawyer."

It was Izzy's turn to laugh. "Does this mean you could be sort of like the gay friend I don't have, except without the sense of fashion?"

"I didn't say the odds were zero, just lower. There's no such thing as a sure thing. And are you saying I have no sense of fashion?"

"You do have a sense of fashion, it's just that it's from like 1968, except you're not wearing bell bottom jeans."

Tim looked down at his pants, slowly looked back up, and said, "I must have left them in the closet. And I so wanted to make a good first impression."

She pulled her cell phone out of her back pocket and asked Tim for his phone number, and almost as soon as he finished saying it, he received the tone that told him he had a new text.

"You made quite an impression. When you check your texts, you'll see my phone. Don't worry, I won't call you. I wouldn't want to see you in court opposite Mrs. Tim."

"It's Cassidy. Mrs. Cassidy, wife of Mr. Fashion Plate of 1968, Timothy Joseph Cassidy."

"Timothy Joseph Cassidy, you are a very interesting man. Candid about your marriage, yet there is a mystery about you. I find it compelling enough to want to see you again. Gotta run."

Tim sat there watching her leave and wondering himself why he was so forthcoming with her. Did he want to start a truly honest relationship? Did he sense that perhaps it was time to cut loose from Casey? Or was he just plain stupid?

He had other girlfriends during his marriage with whom he had shared details of his personal life, but he had the feeling that if Izzy asked where his safe was, he would tell her the combination. He felt as if he were in ninth grade, trying to work up the courage to ask her to go steady.

CHAPTER
9

A WALKTHROUGH IS the last time a buyer looks at a property before they own it. Typically, the next owner wants to make sure that they are getting everything they're supposed to and that the property is in good working order and broom-clean, to use the contractual term.

The building was vacant, and the sellers entrusted Harry to handle that task for them. The buyers and their real estate broker met to do this Thursday morning, just prior to the closing. The two Russians or Ukrainians or Bosnians or whatever they were walked through every room on every floor, flushing every toilet, opening and closing every door, and looking at the wiring behind several of the electrical outlets. Before leaving, they spoke to each other at length in some language he didn't understand. Then they spoke to their broker in a language Harry should have understood but didn't: Hebrew. Their conversation was animated and loud, looking and sounding like a foreign version of a panel of Democrats and Republicans on a cable news talk show.

The crazy Israeli pulled Harry outside as the two Russians glared at both of them.

"Harry, do you understand Hebrew?"

"No."

"Then I will interpret what they said in not so many words. They are getting cold feet."

"They're getting cold feet now?" Harry looked at his Rolex, the real one. "We're closing in twenty minutes. They're getting cold feet? There's a Duane Reade on the way. I'll buy them each a pair of sweat socks."

"I'm serious. I don't think they'll close."

"Listen to me. You just get them to the attorney's office, and when we get there I will give them ninety-five thousand reasons to close. One for each dollar of the deposit they will lose."

"I'm in this with you. Who needs to work for free, right? I'll get them there."

Most people in that position may have been panic-ridden, but Harry being Harry, he figured that these buyers were just looking for an edge, a weakness, an opportunity to exploit. By the time he reached the subway, any trepidation he may have had was starting to abate. By the time he got off the train, he was feeling himself: egotistical, animated, and so confident and self-assured that most New Yorkers would have mistaken him for a Parisian, and most Parisians would have mistaken him for a New Yorker. The other seven billion or so people in the world would have thought him a cartoon.

Harry arrived at the law office where the closing was to take place. It was one of those big, fancy law firms with a big, fancy office in one of those big, fancy buildings. His demeaning feelings masked his envy.

That could have been me was what he really thought. If his father had lived long enough. His father passed away when Harry was in high school. He had to start working after that to help his mother. At first it was after school, and after graduation it was full-time. That is if you defined "full-time" as twelve hours a day, six days a week.

"Mom, why don't you sell this place?" he would ask daily.

She always answered, "It makes us a nice living." Her concept of "nice living" was no vacations and one day off each week. She thought life there was a paradise.

God, he'd hated working in that candy store. He'd hated haggling with the vendors. He'd hated arguing with older customers over the price of gum. He'd hated hearing "I remember when it was a penny." The only good thing, or so he'd thought at the time, was that there he met the most beautiful woman he'd ever seen. At least the most beautiful that would have anything to do with him. Thus his romance with Debbie began.

His mother's pleading with him to "go to school and make something of yourself" rang hollow. If he left her alone to work in the store, it would be a betrayal to her like no other. There was guilt, and there was Jewish guilt. Criminal guilt would get you a finite prison sentence. Jewish guilt got you a lifetime of therapy without resolution.

Several years later, his mother passed away. Item one on his list was to get rid of the business and figure out a future. His father had had the foresight to buy the building. "In this country, they won't take it away from me, and besides, I should pay rent to a landlord?" So after years of collecting rent and paying off the mortgage, Harry became the owner of a building that contained a store and three apartments.

Harry sought out the realtor who was in a similar building just down the street. After conveying his desire to sell the building, the realtor told him he thought maybe he could get a hundred fifty thousand for it. Harry responded, "You're kidding, right?" He would have been happy to walk away with enough to pay the first month's rent and a security deposit for a new apartment. The realtor, not sure how Harry meant the statement, told him, "Look, I can list the apartment for half a million, but if you want to sell it, you'll get the market value. In my opinion that's a hundred fifty, maybe a little more, maybe a little less." Harry could not contain his enthusiasm. The realtor continued, "And you should know that my commission for handling this is six percent."

Harry did the math and calculated the realtor would earn nine thousand. Harry had earned about that much in the previous year. His destiny came to him. This became his career path.

He walked into the lobby, gave a security guard seated behind a desk his ID, and had his picture taken. Harry passed through a turnstile and took the elevator up to the law offices of Fancy and Schmancy or whoever the hell they were.

By the time he arrived in the conference room, it was already standing room only. All five of the Ramirez family siblings were there, accompanied by their lawyer. The two Russians were there with their lawyer and the other realtor. Add to that the bank attorney and title closer and it left Harry standing in a corner next to a plant. Both he and the plant had a glorious view of the East River.

"Good morning, everyone. Shall we get started? Hopefully we do this quickly and painlessly," the attorney said in a cheery voice as he started to pass documents to the attorney for the Russians.

At that point, the Russians spoke to each other in their native tongue for few moments. Harry had been forewarned and sensed what was coming. It was a matter of who going to cave in to whom. The lawyer, who was speaking with them in Russian, finally turned to speak. He directed his statement to the lawyer for the seller. "My clients inspected the property earlier and found the amount of work required does not warrant their investment at the price in the contract. If you will consider a counteroffer of seven hundred thousand, they are prepared to close."

The only response from the attorney on the other side of this deal was "interesting." Harry was about to go ballistic when he added, "Would you excuse us, please?"

Here it comes, thought Harry. The negotiation starts now. The Ramirez team, led by their lawyer, left the room.

They gathered in another conference room, and the lawyer opened the conversation. "Rafael, as I recall, you speak Russian, don't you?"

Rafael Ramirez did in fact speak Russian. He had majored in international relations at Harvard and thought learning the language would give him a leg up, especially with a law degree, which he earned there as well. Such was the connection that brought the owners of a brownstone in East Harlem to a Park Avenue law firm.

Speaking to the lawyer, Rafael said, "You have a terrific memory. Here's what they said in essence: they thought there was an additional hundred thousand dollars of work required that they did not anticipate. They would be willing to go through with the deal at eight-fifty but wanted to see if they could get it for seven."

He added, "I think we should tell them they could buy it for the contract price or not buy it at all." Rafael then looked at his siblings and asked for comments.

His youngest sister, Carmen, spoke up. "I would prefer to find another buyer than do business with them."

"Any dissenting opinions?" he asked once again.

As all of the siblings agreed, they rose, and followed the lawyer back to where the rest were anxiously waiting. Brad, their attorney, announced that his clients were perfectly content to honor the contract as written.

The attorney for the Russians blustered that unless some relief on the price was made, his clients would have to walk away from the deal.

Harry was watching this like a car wreck in slow motion.

Brad, with his Ivy League polish and calm, suggested they could all save a lot of time by honoring the terms of the contract or leaving his office.

The Russians looked at each other, then looked at their lawyer, and finally looked across the table at the sellers and said, "Are you absolutely sure that is what you want to happen?"

Rafael Ramirez looked at his siblings and answered in flawless Russian, "Just so you understand clearly, there is nothing to negotiate."

Something like that would have embarrassed almost anybody. Anybody except these two. In a manner that bordered on threatening, one of them snarled in a comical accent, "You think you're so smart. Turn down our offer and you see what happens. Nobody offer as much money, especially if something happen to property while you wait forever for better offer."

The second Russian piled on. "I love the American expression, 'shit happens.'"

There was what seemed an interminable silence in the room until one of the Ramirez brothers put his hand inside the pocket of his suit jacket and laid a badge on the table that identified him as a deputy inspector in the NYPD. He then revealed his gun. "This is a Glock with a magazine capacity of fifteen, and it can fire those fifteen bullets in a matter of seconds. Part of my job is to make sure that shit doesn't happen. I am going to ask you in English, and if you want my brother can translate it into Russian: do you think anything is going to happen to our property?"

Clearly shaken, the two Russians said they understood and that if anything happened it wouldn't be because of them.

"You do understand that if anything does happen, you will be the primary suspects."

With that, the Russians and their attorney started speaking to each other in Hebrew. They elected to ask for their deposit back and pass on the deal.

The attorney spoke for them. "Do any of you happen to speak Hebrew?" This evoked some laughter all around and a "no" from the Ramirez side of the table. "Firstly then, please excuse my clients for what may be construed as crude language and rude behavior. They have no ill intentions and were merely negotiating in a foreign manner. Secondly, they feel you have a terrific property and will have no difficulty selling it to someone else. Having said that, would you please refund their deposit?"

Rafael Ramirez responded in Russian. "We will get back to you on that. We are not obligated under the terms of the contract to make any such refund. However, we will consider that after we do sell this to someone else. And this, comrades, gives you an interest in seeing that nothing bad happens to the property."

They looked at their lawyer and translated the Russian into Hebrew. After what seemed like a brief but heated discussion, the lawyer spoke. "Thank you." And then to Harry: "I hope you can get this done quickly. I'm sure that you and everyone else in this room is very anxious for you to succeed. Especially my clients."

Harry may have experienced a first in his life: an inability to verbally respond. He had a vacant look in his eyes and could only nod.

The room started to empty when one of the Ramirez clan asked Harry to stay. They wanted a private word with him. *Oh, crap,* Harry thought. *First I lose the sale, now I lose the listing. What else could go wrong?* Oh yeah, he couldn't pay Big Tim tomorrow, and there was no telling what he would do. He might actually have to pawn the Rolex. Maybe he'd get lucky, get hit by a cab on Park Avenue, end up in the hospital, and be able to sue somebody. *I should be so lucky,* he thought.

Speaking for the group, Rafael said, "Harry, we think you did an excellent job. Our research indicated that we maybe would get about eight-fifty for the property. When you told us nine, we thought you were being a little aggressive and considered it the nature of your work. Then you brought us an offer for nine-fifty. We hope you will keep working for us and bring us the best offer you can, as close to eight-fifty as you can, and as quickly as you can."

It didn't take Harry long to regain his composure. "You know I'm compelled to present any offers I get. I'm going to start making some calls. Let's see what happens." He added, "And you know I'm the guy that's going to make this happen," with bravado even beyond the typical for him.

"We are sure you are. Thanks for all you've done so far. Hopefully the next offer is a real one."

With that he left the office. The bad news was Harry didn't make a dime today. The good news was the sellers were not blaming him. The bad news was Tim was looking for his money tomorrow.

CHAPTER
10

DEBBIE ROSEN COULD not have been more excited. This was the day. Today she was starting on the path to liberation. Her personal freedom march. She dressed smartly and left the apartment with a bounce in her step. No bus or subway today. She was going to walk to her divorce lawyer's midtown office.

There were so many ways to sprinkle "divorce lawyer" into conversation.

"My divorce lawyer says…"

"According to my divorce lawyer…"

"Here's what my divorce lawyer is going to do…"

It sounded much like Forrest Gump listening to Bubba talk about shrimp.

Debbie arrived at the tower where her divorce lawyer's office was located. She walked into the elevator and asked a question to the captive audience: "Does anyone know if Mrs. Cassidy's office is on the 44th floor? I don't want to be late for my appointment. She's my divorce lawyer." It was the first time she'd said that in public. It felt even better than she'd imagined. Maintaining decorum, no one answered. She got off the elevator, approached the reception desk, and proudly asked the receptionist for Mrs. Cassidy.

"May I tell her who you are?"

"I am soon to be the ex-Mrs. Rosen."

"Please have a seat. I'll let her know you're here."

Moments later a man, no, not a man, an Adonis, a god, appeared and introduced himself. "I'm Matt Bernstein, Mrs. Cassidy's associate. Please come with me."

I'd love to, Debbie thought. He was tall and thin, but not in a sickly sort of way. More like a swimmer. Matt looked to be in his late twenties or early thirties, with short, dark hair and movie star good looks. No, movie stars could only wish they looked like him. *Bernstein,* she thought. *Probably Jewish too.*

They walked down an aisle with cubicles on one side and offices on the other. As she followed, her mind wandered to exotic places and erotic things. Was this what she'd been missing out on? Was this what she could look forward to? She thought some more and decided she wouldn't need a Caribbean island. She'd play grab-ass with him in the vegetable aisle of a grocery store.

They got to the end of the row of offices, and at the corner office, Matt knocked gently on the door while pushing it open. Casey stood up, smiled, and walked around her expansive desk to give Debbie a hug.

"Hello, Debbie. It's so nice to see you. I love what you're wearing, by the way."

While Debbie had dressed smartly, Casey had dressed almost provocatively, in a black knit woolen dress that clung to every curve. Debbie thought that with Casey and Matt, this could have been the set for a telenovela, except they weren't speaking Spanish.

"Oh, thank you. You look fabulous yourself."

"You're too kind. I'm glad you could make it in, and I hope we can make your life better. Divorce is nothing more than addition by subtraction. When you lose your spouse, you lose all the unhappiness that he's causing. It may be difficult at first, but within a short period of time you'll gain or regain the things that make you happy."

"I've been miserable for a long time. I'm really glad I met you."

"That's not something people usually say about lawyers. Maybe you haven't heard, but we have a very bad reputation. Everyone hates us, until they need us and then find out we're not so bad. Maybe even lovable."

Casey added, "Let's talk about your situation. Is your husband unhappy? Would he contest the divorce?"

"Harry, my husband, is a miserable man, but I don't think he thinks he's miserable. Would he contest the divorce? Maybe."

"If it's uncontested, it's not a complicated, time-consuming or expensive process. We can negotiate a settlement, draw up a separation agreement, and then file for divorce. It gets complicated with children or disagreements over support and the division of assets."

"We have no children. He's a real estate broker and owns his own business. We don't have much money in the bank."

Casey hid her rapidly declining enthusiasm. "Would you tell me what 'not much money' means to you? Do either of you own any real estate?"

"We have about ten thousand dollars in the bank and don't own any property. Although we live in a rent-controlled apartment and the landlord would love to buy us out. Maybe for a million dollars."

And just like that, Casey's enthusiasm returned. "Have you discussed your feelings with your husband?"

"No. If he can't bet on it, he's not interested."

"You should let him know where you stand. If he is agreeable, I can act as a mediator for you both. If you sense any hostility, I will represent you exclusively and promise you a vigorous and thorough advocacy."

"What does that mean, exactly?"

"It means he can put his clothes in a Hefty bag and leave. It means we are going to ask for an alimony check every month. It means we're going to ask him to sell his business and split the proceeds with you or buy you out for the fair market value of the business. It means we're going to ask that you get the car, and he gets the monthly payments. I don't play fair. I play hard, and I play to win for my clients."

Debbie pictured a cash register that was shaped like a bust of Harry that cried *ouch* every time she pressed a key to open the till. "I hope he doesn't want to mediate," she said. "I want to hear him cry and beg and see him squirm."

Casey saw her opening and went for it. "If that's your preference, I am now representing you exclusively. But you should know what to expect in terms of fees. I will need a retainer of five thousand dollars. As far as third-party fees, we will need a forensic accountant to determine what he has and what it's worth, and our time for legal and investigative work will likely run the total to about forty thousand. More if it ends up in court before a settlement is made. That's the bad news. The good news is that we are going to ask him to pay those fees."

"In that case, I really don't care. It's Harry's problem," Debbie replied with a smile.

Casey added, "Just so you know, it doesn't always go our way. If that's the case, you will be responsible for the fees, and if Harry can't pay, you may have to sell the apartment to raise the money."

"I'm going to sell it anyway after he's out of my life."

Casey responded, "Matt will draw up a retainer agreement and handle the preliminary work. Is that okay? He has great credentials and does great work."

"That's okay with me. How long will that take?"

Matt had been sitting quietly, making notes. He chimed in that he would get started on it, and perhaps she could stop by on Monday?

Debbie's mind had switched into another dimension. She imagined their next meeting much differently. It wasn't in the office. It was in a hotel room with candles. And champagne. And condoms. *Fuck the condoms,* she thought. *I could make love with him once and die happy.*

Her mind returned to the business at hand and answered, "Monday will be fine. The sooner the better."

Matt smiled and got up from his chair. "I'll see you soon then. May I show you out?"

Both women then got up, and Casey approached Debbie. She let her know that she was there for her and to call any time for any reason. With that they hugged. Casey then told Matt to return to her office after he showed Debbie out. "There are a few details we have to tend to."

When Matt returned to Casey's office, he pretty much anticipated the drill. It was going to be what he thought of as her version of a victory lap. She was sitting in her chair with her arm bent upward at the elbow, a red thong hanging down from a finger.

"Well, Matt, I need you to check on something under the desk. You don't mind, do you?"

He supposed he could make a case for sexual harassment, but he didn't exactly hate being her boy toy. No, he actually lived for it. Maybe one day she'd dump the old bastard she was married to and he'd be hers. Matt was going to once again prove how much he wanted to please her.

It was only a few minutes before she regained her composure. Casey reached into her desk drawer and took out a cigar. Matt was back on his feet to light it for her.

"Good work, Matt. Make sure you put this on your time sheet as billable."

She puffed on the cigar as Matt left the office and thought, *One day I have to have a Cuban.*

CHAPTER
11

TIM CLIMBED THE steps to Harry's office and wondered if the odor from the restaurant was toxic. He wished he'd had a surgical mask. Maybe he could make this quick. Say hello, get his money, and get out. Avoid the small talk and skip lunch.

He didn't call first, and he didn't knock when he got to the door. Tim walked in, looked around, and spotted Harry. He walked through the rows of empty desks and into the office.

When Harry heard the footsteps in his office, he was prepared to yell about the bathroom being out the door and down the hall, until he looked up.

"Hey, Tim. Great to see you. Thanks for coming."

"Likewise, Harry. Business good?"

"Unbelievable."

"Then we can settle up and I can get back to my business."

"For sure. Sit down and eat something. They make the best chicken in the city downstairs. I thought you'd want some." Harry opened the cardboard lunch boxes.

Tim thought about that for a nanosecond and told Harry that he was watching his cholesterol and trying to cut down on fried foods.

"Why? You think you're going to drop dead from eating some chicken? It happens to be very good for you. And these potatoes? Delicious. Here, try them with some gravy."

Tim looked into the box once again and realized that being rational or polite with Harry was futile. As nicely as he could manage, he said, "Harry, that may be good for you, but I prefer a healthier lunch. Besides, I really don't have that much time this afternoon."

"You're in a hurry? What, you got a boss that says you have to be back behind your desk in an hour?"

"Believe it or not, you're not my only client."

With feigned indignance, Harry answered, "I'm a client? Tim, come on, after all this time I thought we'd be friends."

"You know what they say. If you want a friend, buy a dog."

"So I'm a client. What we do is strictly business."

"Strictly business."

"Unless we're having lunch or sitting in a bar or going to a casino."

"It's all business, Harry."

"I gotta tell you something. A few days ago, we're having lunch and I see you put a move on that cute waitress. I'm thinking 'what kind of guy is this?' He's got a wife, and without batting an eye he sees a cute girl and makes a play. Me? Guys go to jail for murder and get out in less time than I've been married. And you know what else? I've never so much as thought about another woman the entire time."

"What's your point?"

"My point? Just before you got here I get a call from my wife. She's throwing me out and wants a divorce."

"I'm sorry to hear that."

"You should at least try one of these biscuits. They're fabulous."

"I see how much you're broken up over it."

"Hey, the hell with her. She has no idea right now how big her loss is. It'll take her ten minutes to figure out how good she had it. Let's see her try to get a nickel from me."

Tim figured her loss was at least two hundred and fifty pounds. And not the British currency.

"I'm sure you have lots of other things to deal with right now, so let's settle up and you can pay attention to those."

"Can you believe the nerve of that bitch, after all these years? I gave her everything. Never cheated. Not once. And it's not like I didn't have any opportunities. So now, all of a sudden, she thinks she can do better? Well, good fucking luck to her! I am going to go nuclear on her, and she'll be lucky to get enough to buy a can of cat food by the time I'm finished."

Tim had no interest in listening to Harry rant. He wanted to collect his money and then tell Harry to lose his phone number. Tim figured the next time Harry owed him any money, he'd have to hear about how "I had to pay my ex, so I'm a little short." Bad debts were a big expense and a bigger aggravation.

"Harry, if anyone can work himself out of a tight spot, it's you. But I didn't come here to watch you eat lunch. I'd like to collect my money."

"I can't believe I'm hearing this. I invite a friend over for a pleasant lunch and find out he's not a friend. 'Give me my money, give me my money.' Listen to yourself. You should relax. You're going to get your money, but first sit down and eat something."

Harry bit into a piece of chicken and asked, "Did I tell you how good this is? Here, have a drumstick. You'll love it."

"Enough is enough. You'll give me my ninety-one hundred, and I'll be on my way, and you can enjoy your chicken in peace."

Harry's delay tactic wasn't working. Shit. Now he had a war on two fronts: one with his soon-to-be-ex-wife and one with his bookmaker.

"Tim, there's no reason to be upset. I was just trying to be hospitable. I'm sorry you took it the wrong way." He picked up a piece of chicken with one hand, and with the other he stuffed a biscuit into a jacket pocket. "Come, let's go get your money. I have it around the block."

It was difficult for Tim to hide his impatience. "You knew days ago when and where we were meeting. You couldn't bring the money here? I'll tell you what: I'll wait here and you go get it."

"Stop being such a putz. You'll come with me. What, you think I'm gonna have somebody take you out? It costs more to get someone killed than what I owe you."

"So you thought about it?"

"Yeah, but not for you. For Debbie."

"Jesus. What's wrong with you? You can't do something like that."

"Fifteen grand and it's over. I know plenty of people."

"You'll meet plenty more in jail if you do anything that stupid."

"Hey, screw her. She gets cute with me, and she's shark bait off the Jersey Shore."

Tim stood up and told Harry, "Let's go. I really don't want to know anything about this."

Both of them headed out the door and down the steps, with the odor of fried chicken spiced with who knows what in the air. It reminded Tim of the women that sprayed perfume as you walked into a department store — except in there the aroma wasn't with you for two blocks.

It didn't take long to arrive at the vacant building with a "For Sale" sign prominently displaying Harry's name and phone number hanging out front. Harry walked to the front door, unlocked it, and implored, "Come on in. You have to see this place."

"Does it have ninety-one hundred of my money?"

"It certainly does," Harry replied.

"Then let's go."

"Look at this place. Three huge bedrooms in each apartment, the same on all three levels. Nice little garden in the back."

"That's great if I'm looking to buy the place, but I'm not."

"You know what this place is worth?"

It was bait no one in the city of New York could resist. Like everyone else, he knew what every piece of property was worth. Real estate consumed New Yorkers the way fans at a Super Bowl party consumed chili.

Tim surveyed the interior as he walked from the doorway into the apartment. "Probably needs a little updating," he said, "but a place like this around here, I'd say about a million three if you spent a few bucks on it."

"I had this in contract with a couple of smart asses at nine fifty. They figured they'd put about a hundred fifty in and then flip it for one point four."

"So what happened? Sounds like they were going to make some money."

"Go figure. The sellers have principles. The jerks try to renegotiate the contract price at closing, and the sellers tell them to get lost."

"What does this have to do with me?"

"Here's the best part. They tell me that they thought eight-fifty was a fair price for the property and asked me to get as close to that as quickly as I can. It's a great deal at eight-fifty, and maybe they take a little less. It's an estate sale with five heirs, so if they took fifty less, it's only ten thousand each. And there's no mortgage. They all walk away with decent money anyway."

"Are you suggesting that I buy this?"

"It's a great opportunity for us. I could flip this property as is for nine-fifty. There is so much real estate porn on TV that every jerk with a checkbook thinks it'll be the easiest money they ever make."

"How do you mean 'us'?" Tim asked; he was now the fish on the line that swallowed the bait.

"You put up the money, I do the rest. Hire the contractors to modernize this place, resell the place and everything in between. We'll probably make about half a million, and split it fifty-fifty."

"I'm putting up all the money?" Tim replied incredulously.

"Yeah."

"And you get half the deal? Harry, explain to me how that makes sense."

"I found the deal, and without that you get nothing. The better question is why should I give you an even split?"

"That's the most ridiculous thought I've ever heard."

At this point Harry thought he'd solved two problems. He was going to get the property sold and be able to pay off Tim. Maybe even make a few bucks to boot.

"What's so ridiculous? You don't like making money? Maybe you're like a communist? What's wrong with you? You don't want to make a quick and easy quarter of a million?"

Tim couldn't believe the chutzpah of this guy. Maybe he should just ask Harry to pay him off and walk away. But Tim was not immune to the herd mentality, and the herd were buying properties in New York City like kids bought ice cream in the summer.

He thought the pitch was solid, and the venture would ultimately be profitable, but he also knew that dealing with Harry Rosen was risk in itself.

"Harry, just pay me what you owe me and I'm on my way. Keep the half a million for yourself."

"I can't believe you're going to walk away from this deal. I thought we were going to be partners."

"You think too much. Especially if you thought I was going to finance this whole venture and give you half the profit."

Fish hooked. Harry was going to close this deal. "You know, maybe you're right. I was being greedy. So tell me what you think is fair, and maybe I can work with it."

On the walk back to Harry's office, Tim agreed to offer eight hundred for the property. Harry would get his commission from the seller and then pay off his gambling debt. Tim would renovate the property, list it for sale with Harry, and pay Harry a ten percent commission on the sale.

Tim declined Harry's invitation to finish lunch. "You're sure? I got a microwave in the office. I heat it up for like three or four minutes and we're eating. You'll love it even better than right out of the box."

Each of them thought through their own prism that they had made the deal of the century, Harry because he was putting up no money and going to make twice the typical rate for his efforts, and Tim because he essentially was going to make, by his thought process, a big, quick score.

Harry dutifully called the seller and conveyed the offer. Offer accepted. Contract to follow.

He walked over to the microwave, put the cardboard box that contained what was supposed to be Tim's lunch inside, and then punched a few buttons. He impatiently waited while the timer counted down. After he heard the microwave sound a ding, he withdrew the box and bit into a chicken leg. No one was in the room to hear Harry say, "I can't understand that guy. This is as good a lunch as you can get in this city."

Events of the day had sharply turned to Harry's advantage. He guessed that chickens probably came from farms upstate or who knows where, but the city, he was convinced, was full of pigeons.

CHAPTER
12

I T WASN'T LOST on Tim that he owned a limo service and was again taking an Uber. It was also the catalyst that would drive him to sell the business. He smiled to himself.

Before he got out of the car, he passed the driver a five. His world did not have a no-tipping policy.

As he approached his office, he saw Mike and yelled over, "Have you got a minute?"

"Sure, boss, what's up?"

Both men sat down and Tim asked, "How much cash can you get your hands on?"

"Is there a problem? I can help out a little bit, I guess. What do you need?"

"No, there's no problem. Another opportunity has come my way, and I am going to devote my time and attention in that direction. The reason I asked was to see if you had enough to buy me out."

For the second time that day, Tim negotiated a business deal. They agreed that all in the pot, Mike would pay him three hundred thousand dollars. From both vantage points they each thought they'd robbed the other blind, Tim because he saw the handwriting on the wall for the demise of the business, and Mike because he could now expand the drug delivery and escort services he was providing with Tim's cars.

They shook hands and agreed to settle up in a few days. The nice thing about buying a business for cash was the lack of formality. No financial statements or representations. No bankers or accountants.

"Do you think your lawyer wife will handle all the paperwork?" Mike wanted to know.

"Let's just get someone from the yellow pages."

"Yellow pages?" Mike quizzically asked.

"Never mind. We can google one," Tim said tersely. They shook hands, thus sealing the deal, and agreed to settle up in the next week.

Tim left the garage and smiled at the almost comical turn of events. Earlier in the day, Harry was scrambling to come up with the money he owed him, and just hours later Harry was off the hook and Tim was in fundraising mode.

Years earlier, in what seemed like a different era, banks would lend money on real estate to almost anyone who had air in their lungs. Not one to miss the party, Tim obtained a line of credit for his West Village property. The bank didn't care what he paid for it, only what it was worth. Nor did they care what he did for a living or how much he made. So he signed on the dotted line for the half-million-dollar credit line, and incurred no closing costs. The bank was nice enough to take care of those.

He had used the line sparingly. On two rare occurrences, there had been lopsided action and the bettors had been right. In time, he always recovered and paid the line off.

The quick mental math held that he would have enough to buy the property and make the improvements but leave him short on working capital in the event of a black swan. This was something he was willing to chance.

Casey briefly hesitated before answering her cell. She liked to sort out her thoughts, which were who was it, and why were they calling? Caller ID provided the answer to the first question, but the second was a mystery. Why would her husband be calling?

"Hey, big boy," she answered in a throaty kind of voice.

"Hi, Casey. I'm working on something and may need some legal help."

"Does it involve a felony?"

He heard the question and the laugh that followed. "Nothing criminal. Let's have dinner tonight. How about The Old Homestead? Eight o'clock?"

"Inspire me, Tim. Tell me it's a date night."

It was his turn to laugh. He told her there was some business he needed to discuss, but beyond that anything could happen.

"Oh, you're such a tease."

"The weather's nice, and I should be home early enough for us to walk there."

"I am not going to walk there wearing shoes that have a four-inch stiletto heels."

"Now who's being a tease? See you later."

He hit the icon for the red button on his phone to end the call and scrolled through the contacts until he saw the entry named "Izzy." A momentary pause and a tap on her phone number, and two rings later he heard her voice. "Hey, what's up?"

It produced a moment of slight anxiety, much like a teen asking someone out for their first date. This was incredibly unusual, given his stone-like nerves and the risks he took during the regular course of his business. He took the phone away from his mouth, inhaled slowly through his nose, and then exhaled. Regaining his composure, he answered.

"I think a better question is what's up with you?"

"Don't you know it's impolite to answer a question with a question?"

"Is that right?"

"Didn't you ever hear of Emily Post?"

"Who is she?"

"You're kidding, right?"

"Okay, this round of *Jeopardy* is over. You need not answer in the form of a question any longer."

"So, are you calling to ask me out for lunch at some exotic restaurant? I'm off tomorrow."

Tim, not being prepared for the directness, was practically at a loss for words. He regained his composure and answered, "As a matter of fact, I was."

"Well, that's too bad for you, Mr. Cool." She paused and added with superb theatrical timing, "Because I'd prefer a diner."

Tim played along and told Izzy that he was disappointed, but if she insisted it would be okay with him, as long she didn't order anything with kale.

"A day without kale is a sacrifice so great, I would do it only for you and Ryan Gosling." Another pause. "And maybe just about anyone else. Don't tell anyone I hate that stuff, or they'll take away my millennial membership card and ban me from every hipster neighborhood in Brooklyn."

They agreed to meet at the same Starbucks and then catch a ride to "this incredible diner" that Tim knew by the airport. He was sure they didn't serve kale.

CHAPTER
13

Harry was finishing the last of the chicken. He was amazed at the deal he'd just pulled off. His excitement came to a screeching halt when he remembered that Debbie wanted a divorce. Maybe she wasn't serious. Maybe she was bluffing or using this to get him to agree to move to New Jersey.

"Only one way to find out," he muttered to himself as picked up the phone to call her.

"What do you want, Harry?" she said instead of hello.

"I just wanted to see if we could talk this out. You know, clear the air."

"There's nothing to talk about. I've made up my mind. We're done."

At that moment, Harry had to make a decision. He could try to get her to change her mind and continue his hellish existence with her, or admit defeat. His ego would not accept the fact that she'd initiated this, and even though ultimately his life would be better with a breakup, Harry was going to try to change her mind. It should have been him telling her they were through, and it wasn't.

"Maybe we could get counseling. I've got a lot of time and money invested in you, and it would be a shame to just walk away."

Debbie yelled, "What am I? A piece of property you own? You arrogant, egotistical son of a bitch, do us both a favor and never call me again. And do yourself a favor too: drop dead!"

The last sound Harry heard was the click telling him the call ended.

"If she thinks that's the way this ends, she's nuts," he announced to the empty office.

His hatred and anger led him to make the decision he had only fantasized about for many years. His thoughts brought him to the darkest of dark places. For Harry it was just a solution to a problem, like back-spacing over a typo. *She told me to drop dead. Let's see who turns up dead.*

He pored through the stack of files on his desk until he found the file labeled "Ramirez." It didn't take long until he found the phone number for Boris whatever his last name was, one of the two Russians that backed out of the original deal on the property.

His first call was to Rafael Ramirez to confirm that he would refund the deposit. Armed with this, he then proceeded to call Boris.

"Hello, is this Boris?"

"Who's this?"

"It's Harry Rosen. I'm the other realtor from the property in Harlem that didn't close."

"Why are you calling me?" Boris said with both brevity and contempt.

"I'm calling with some not so bad news for you. I sold that property to someone else. The price was a bit less than you were in contract for, so the seller agreed to refund most of your deposit."

"How much is 'most'?"

"I practically had to put a gun to his head, but he agreed to seventy-five thousand."

"How about I come to your office and I put a gun to your head if I don't get back one hundred thousand? Ninety-five deposit plus five interest."

Fuck this commie piece of shit if he thinks he's going to intimidate me, Harry thought to himself.

"You think that's going to get you anything? I broke my balls to get you even that much. I'm helping you out. Otherwise, let your lawyer handle this and fight it out. See how long it takes and how much you get."

There was a long pause before the Russian answered in a voice so quiet Harry strained to hear. "You know people get killed for a lot less money than that."

That told Harry all he needed to hear. Boris was the guy who could solve his Debbie problem. But would he?

"Maybe we should talk this out. You'll stop by my office. Maybe we'll get some lunch? You like chicken?"

"No chicken, just talk about my hundred thousand. I come by tomorrow at eight o'clock in the morning."

"I'll see you in the morning. Let me give you the address..."

Boris cut him off. "I know where you work, and where you live too."

And that was what made Harry very nervous.

CHAPTER
14

C ASEY WAS AT home by the time Tim got there. She was dressed and
walking out of the bedroom when he walked in.

"Jesus, you look just amazing," Tim said in a voice that conveyed the
awe he felt looking at her.

She was wearing a low-cut black dress, and, as she'd mentioned earlier,
a pair of red shoes with what he assumed were the four-inch stiletto heels.

"Thank you, but my name isn't Jesus. And I've never seen a painting of
him wearing black."

"Or shoes with four-inch stilettos," Tim added.

"They're actually four and a half inches. An extra half inch can make a
big difference."

"You are talking about the shoes, right?"

"Of course I am. What did you think?"

Tim answered, "The same as you." It was a version of foreplay for her.

If all the pieces fell into the right places, he wasn't sure if he would be
in bed with Casey tonight thinking about Izzy or in bed with Izzy tomorrow thinking about Casey.

They left the apartment and got to the restaurant. It was the last vestige
of the meat packing district. The meat processors were long gone and
replaced by the likes of trendy restaurants, expensive apartments, and, of
course, an Apple Store. Only the name of the neighborhood and a restaurant, The Old Homestead, remained.

The hostess led them to their table, and when the waiter appeared,
Tim ordered a bottle of champagne.

"What's the special occasion?" Casey asked.

"It doesn't have to be a special occasion to drink champagne, does it?"

"No, it doesn't. But add it to the dinner date and it sure looks that
way."

"Well, there is a celebratory reason. I sold my business."

"I didn't know a bookmaker had a business that was salable."

"Not that one — the car service."

"Oh, and you need legal help with that?"

"No. That's taken care of. Mike is buying me out. I bought a piece of property in Harlem that I am going to flip. I need to figure out how to deal with this legally, given my primary source of income." If he ever got arrested for illegal gambling, it likely wouldn't result in a felony after a plea bargain, but if he had a run-in with the IRS for tax evasion, he'd be wearing an orange jumpsuit.

The waiter brought the champagne, popped the cork, and poured a small amount into the flute for Tim to try. After sipping it, Tim asked the waiter, "Has anyone ever said they didn't care for it and to take it back?"

The waiter, a serious sort, replied, "Nobody ever. Not in my twenty years."

"Well, I'm not going to be the first."

With that, the waiter filled both flutes and placed the bottle in an ice bucket.

Doing what could charitably be described as a very poor imperson- ation of Humphrey Bogart, Tim lifted the glass and said, "Here's looking at you, kid."

Not to be outdone in the classic movie category, she replied, "We'll always have Paris." Casey then proceeded to down half of the pour in one swallow.

"So let me guess. Mike is paying you in cash, and because let's just say the source of this cash would be suspect to the IRS, you are going to record the sale of the business for far less than he is paying you." She paused. "How am I doing so far?"

"Right on target."

"And you don't have enough legitimate money to close this deal, and the people you are buying from won't take a satchel full of cash. Still on target?"

"Bullseye."

"You're going to need a partner. Someone you can trust and with the resources you need to close the deal."

Tim didn't learn anything he already didn't know but thought it was a good way to broach the subject with his wife. They didn't really pry very much into each other's professional lives, but he guessed that both thought the other was doing just fine.

By this time the waiter had reappeared and took their orders, lobster for her, steak for him. He picked up the menus and left.

"Maybe you're interested?" Tim asked.

"Wow, that's subtle. Tell me about the deal."

He recounted the deal to her, sparing no detail. He kept her interest by starting with the premise that he thought there was about a half million to be made. Before he finished, the food appeared.

Casey, not being inoculated against the real estate fever that seemed to go on in perpetuity in New York City, was genuinely impressed. so much so that she actually offered to put some of her own money into the deal, which as every sharpshooter in that game knew was something you did only as a last resort.

The fact that they were husband and wife didn't change a thing. Business was business. She ripped a claw off the lobster that the waiter had placed in front of her, jabbed a fork in, and extracted the meat with one stroke. She dipped it in the melted butter and before she took a bite pointed the fork at Tim.

"The deal is fantastic. I think you're on to a winner, and of course I'll help you pull it off. Here's how we can make this work. I'll form a corporation in which we'll be equal shareholders. You put in the half million from your credit line, give me the three hundred thousand in cash, and I'll put in three hundred thousand from my personal account. I will use the cash you gave me to pay for the improvements." She took what might be described as a vicious bite of the lobster on her fork.

Tim sensed that, like the lobster, he was getting gouged. Unlike the lobster, he was getting eaten alive. "Tell me that I understand what you're saying. You're putting up three hundred, I'm putting up eight hundred, and we're splitting the deal evenly."

She smiled and answered, "That's exactly right."

"Give me a reason why I shouldn't just go to a loan shark and borrow the money."

Casey finished off the fork full of lobster in a most seductive way and told him, "That's easy. Because when we get home tonight, I am going fuck you hard. A loan shark is just going to fuck you over."

"Good point."

Casey knew she had him but didn't want to leave an open wound. "I'm not going to charge any interest on the money I'm putting in, and besides, half of everything I have is yours, and half of everything you have is mine."

Tim laughingly responded, "Unless we're in divorce court."

She raised up her flute of champagne and said, "Here's to a long, happy marriage."

He obligingly clinked her glass and added, "But not so much for everyone else, lest it be bad for your business."

Casey flashed a brief smile and took a long swig.

They finished off dinner with a glass of port. Casey stood up and told Tim to take care of the check and get a car while she went to the ladies' room.

The night of drinking left them both with a light buzz, and the thought of a big payday, courtesy of an out-of-the-blue real estate deal, kicked her libido into high gear.

When they got back to their apartment, she showed him why going to a loan shark would not have been as good. Make that great. He only thought about Izzy a little.

CHAPTER

15

T HE NEXT MORNING, Casey arrived at her office and summoned Matt Bernstein. He was wearing a classic gray pinstripe suit with a white shirt and a red tie. *Adorable,* she thought, *but not today.* She wanted to know if Harry Rosen's plea of poverty to his wife was real. She would search to see if he had any bank accounts or other property that her client didn't know about.

"Matt, I want you to dig into the finances of Harry Rosen. What does he own, what does he owe? The usual stuff."

"I anticipated that you would want to know that, boss, so I checked the property records, and it turns out he owns the building his business operates from. Chicken franchise on the ground floor, his business and additional seating for the chicken place on the second floor, two apartments on the top floor."

Boss. She liked that.

Matt continued, "There are no mortgages or liens, and best of all, it's deeded to Harold and Deborah Rosen."

"Anything else?"

"I checked some market data that indicates a value in the range of three million."

Casey was ecstatic both for her client and herself. A bigger settlement would mask her padded fee. "Matt, it looks like you're going to have to put more time into this."

She picked up the phone and dialed Debbie. "Hi, Debbie, it's Casey," she said as if they were best friends getting ready to idly chat.

"Oh, hi, how are you?" was the chirping response.

"I'm really great, but super busy, partly due to the work on your case. I'm going to need some time with you, but like I said, I am really stretched for the next week. Would it be okay if my associate, Matt Bernstein, I believe you met him, sat down with you?"

Debbie managed to contain herself and told her lawyer that wouldn't be a problem.

"Good. I'll have him call you. Take care, and we'll talk soon."

CHAPTER
16

WHEN HARRY GOT to his office the next morning, the door was open and Boris Volkov was sitting in the chair behind Harry's desk. His partner, Igor Kilimchuk, was seated in another chair turned toward the door. This gave Harry a full view of these two guys, who looked the size of football players, only bigger.

With a little swagger and in an attempt to control the situation, Harry said, "I thought we were meeting for lunch? Are you guys on like Moscow time?"

Boris answered, "You funny guy. You should be on television."

Igor added, "I don't think he funny. I think he a clown. Sad and pathetic. Maybe we should put him out of his misery?"

"Maybe, but then we don't get the hundred ten thousand he owes us."

That got Harry's attention, and sensing that he could turn the threat into a negotiation, told them, "Look, the property is in contract for eight hundred. You guys were supposed to buy it for nine-fifty. So they figure they'll return seventy-five to make up for part of the loss. And do you want to fuck with that cop?"

"So we take seventy-five from them and forty from you," Igor calmly replied.

"I don't know how they teach math in Russia, but everywhere else in the world that comes to one-fifteen, not the ninety-five you're out of pocket."

"Schools in Russia very good. Legal system in USA much better. Here you get money for pain and suffering. So we get money and you avoid pain and suffering." Igor looked Harry square in the eyes with a look that gave not the slightest hint of emotion. It was as if he would be glad to kill Harry where he sat and then walk over to the deli and order breakfast without giving Harry or the murderous deed a second thought.

"I got enough pain and suffering. Her name is Debbie, and she wants to be my ex-wife. So I don't know which is worse: the last twenty years of living in hell, or living without her, with no money or place to live. You could kill me now, and I come out ahead, but you're the ones who suffer, because you get nothing."

Boris, who had been letting his partner do all the talking, chimed in. "We don't care about your problems. We want our money. You figure out how to pay."

"If my wife didn't have everything tied up, believe me, I'd be glad to make you guys whole."

"Your wife is reason we don't get money?" Igor said quickly, grasping the problem and causing Harry to almost jump up and high-five them both.

"She is the cause of all this. Maybe you can fix it?"

"We can fix."

Boris said, "We want the ninety-five plus another twenty-five. No need for math. Ninety-five and another twenty-five."

Harry thought better than to grouse about the price. He did ask, "Can you make it look like an accident?"

"You watch too much television. It gets done. It's over. It doesn't matter how. Since you watch so much television, you know first person they look for is you, and you say anything about us, there goes the rest of your happy life with money, house, and no wife."

The two Russians got up and headed out the door. Harry walked to the window overlooking the street and watched them get into a van and drive away.

Settling back in behind his desk, he opened the file drawer. Riffling through the files that were in no apparent order, he found the one labeled "Insurance." Within the file were paid receipts, cancellation notices, reinstatement letters, the auto policy for a 1997 Buick LeSabre traded in long ago, and the grand prize: the life insurance policy on Debbie. There was the policy value in black and white: five hundred thousand dollars. He broke into his happy dance, which was nothing more than a poor parody of the Macarena.

CHAPTER
17

T IM WAS WAITING outside of Starbucks when Izzy arrived. He got an air kiss and a bro hug. Not exactly what he was hoping for. "I hope you weren't waiting long?"

"No, just long enough to buy a panhandler a grande skinny latte and a croissant."

"That is one high-maintenance panhandler."

"I should have just given him the dollar he asked for. It's my own fault. I told him I'd rather give him food than money and asked him what he'd like for breakfast. Go figure."

"Probably why he ordered the skinny latte. Those croissants are filled with calories."

Tim grabbed his phone and tapped it a few times. Minutes later, a car pulled up to take them to a diner by LaGuardia airport. He liked to think of it as the Airport Diner, with its neon sign and the outline of an airplane interspersed. The sign was still there, although unlit, and the original owners, he guessed, were happily back to whichever Greek Isle they may have been from, at least for the winter.

It seemed as if the first generation of immigrants, wherever they were from, had a romantic notion of returning to their homeland. Of course, almost all eventually remembered why they left and why they could never go back. They raised families here and realized their dreams here, something that would have been impossible almost anywhere else in the world. Boatloads came at the turn of the twentieth century, believing the streets were paved with gold. They and the country both prospered. It was the American dream. The belief and the dream still held a hundred years later.

They were seated in a booth and handed menus about the size of a newspaper and almost as long. Izzy said, "There's no way a menu this size doesn't have an item with kale."

"They may have it listed, but I'd bet they'll take the order and then come back from the kitchen to tell you they just ran out."

Izzy laughed. "I'd like to order a kale salad just to see if you're right, but if you're not I wouldn't want to get stuck eating it. I've heard that if you do you get an irrepressible urge to buy a plaid shirt and get a tattoo."

It was Tim's turn to laugh. He was going to stick with a BLT, thank you very much. Izzy opted for scrambled eggs.

"I have to tell you some fantastic news. I was going to bootstrap it through law school, you know, some scholarship money and then some loans and savings from what I earn this year. My father calls me last night to tell me that my grandmother's estate is going to be settled shortly, and he thought that her legacy would be for me and my sister to earn advanced degrees. According to my father, he and his siblings had no choice. They all had a choice: they could become doctors, lawyers, or CPAs. I wonder if my grandmother was a Jewish Puerto Rican? Anyway, I'll be getting enough to cover all three years of law school and living expenses without the loans. How awesome is that?"

"That is really terrific." Tim realized the sugar daddy angle was no longer an option in attracting the fabulous Izzy Ramirez. "So the way I figure, you're in New York for about another nine months. Just long enough for you to write a play, get it produced, star in it, win a Tony, and put off law school."

"You really think it will take that long?" she answered, deadpan.

"Nah. I just wonder how long some of the people I see in that Starbucks with their laptops open have been there writing the Great American Novel."

"Or maybe just some trashy screenplay for a movie that will never be made. It probably gives them the artistic angst that they value as much as rappers need some sort of criminal street cred. But on the other hand, J.K. Rowling wrote her first *Harry Potter* in a coffee shop."

"You know what? If you're going to be that dedicated, I have a small apartment, a pied-à-terre, in the West Village you're welcome to use. And there are plenty of coffee pods for the Nespresso, so you'll save a fortune on that and never stand on line for the bathroom."

Izzy was unprepared for what she guessed was more than an innocent gesture of generosity. It didn't take long for her response. "Let me try to understand this. You live in Gramercy Park and have an apartment like twenty blocks away? Did you say pied affair?"

Tim was now playing defense. "I've had it for a long time, and I won't deny that it comes in handy for romantic interludes. I'd be lying if I said I wasn't interested in you, but that was not my intention. If you're offended, then I am sorry." He believed that the truth was never a last resort.

"You know what? I'm actually flattered. I appreciate the offer and will consider it, as long as l am not obligated for anything other than replacing the coffee pods and rinsing out the coffee cups. And making sure to leave the toilet seat up when I depart."

Tim took a sip of coffee, put the cup down, and said, "Pied affair. That's hilarious. Like I said, it's available if you'd like to use it."

CHAPTER
18

DEBBIE ROSEN WOKE at the crack of nine and put together a breakfast of toast and coffee. She wished she was a smoker. It would have gone well with the coffee, maybe make her appear younger and more hip. Maybe just the type of woman that would appeal to Matt Bernstein, super stud lawyer.

She got right to work with a box of plastic garbage bags and Harry's closet. If nothing else, he had expensive tastes when it came to clothes. There were probably a dozen designer suits, all of which were newly dry cleaned, that went into the first bag. She methodically went through the rest of the closet and did the same for his sport jackets, slacks, shirts, and ties.

Next, she went to work on his dresser. Another few bags filled with underwear, socks, tee-shirts, and shorts. When she picked up the last pile in the drawer, she gasped. There lay a small revolver and a box of ammo. She quickly closed the drawer and wished it could have been unseen.

It was time to move on to another task, but she thought it best to pour another coffee. Before taking the first sip, she added more than a dash of Kahlúa. The liqueur sweetened the coffee and calmed her nerves. She need not do anything with the pistol now but did think about her options. The first was to put it in one of the garbage bags, but then she wondered if the better decision would be to call Matt and ask his advice. Maybe he'd want to come over and see it for himself? In which case she'd make a quick trip to Victoria's Secret. *Hey, you never know.*

Debbie finished the coffee with more sober thoughts about her chances with Matt. She turned on her computer and found her way to a popular dating website. By the time she was about halfway through the essay questions, it reminded her of an SAT exam. Everybody knocked the bar scene, but since she hadn't tried it, she wouldn't. Besides, as soon as her girlfriends heard the news of her divorce, she was sure she would hear "have I got a guy for you" dozens of times.

Her mind wandered back to the gun. *Why does Harry need one? Was he planning to use it on me? If doesn't get it back, will he get another? Does he have another? Maybe I should keep quiet about it and have it for my own protection?* She went back to retrieve the weapon and laid it down carefully next to the computer. If she was going to keep it, she should know how to use it. There were self-help videos online for everything else. Why not for how to use a gun?

Her search determined that what she had was .38 special that held five rounds. With the help of a short video, Debbie was now capable of loading the gun and ejecting the spent cartridges. There was no safety on it, so she was extra careful. She raised the gun, aimed it at the window, and pulled the trigger. She heard the click and thought, *Nothing to it.* Then she imagined Harry charging through the front door. She raised the gun, aimed at the door, and pulled the trigger. *Click.* "Just let him try coming at me," she said. Debbie loaded the gun and placed it in the bottom of her handbag.

She heard her phone ring and glanced at the incoming number. It was one she didn't recognize, so she figured it was just another robocall. Either she won a cruise or was going to get a fantastic offer to pay off her credit cards. She answered anyway and in a sour voice said, "Who's this?"

"Hello, is this Debbie Rosen? It's Matt Bernstein from the Cassidy law firm."

Debbie's voice went from sour to sweet faster than a race car driver could downshift. "Oh, hello, Matt. Sorry I sounded so I rude. I thought someone else was calling."

"Not a problem. I'm glad to get a hold of you. We have to submit a financial disclosure to the court. It essentially details your income and expenses, and your assets and liabilities. I can make myself available to help you with that, if you'd like."

Oh, I'd like that all right, she thought. She managed a less enthusiastic tone and told him, "That would be helpful." Matt told her what she would need, and they agreed she'd bring it to his office the next afternoon.

She called the garage and asked that her car be ready in an hour. There was no way Debbie was going to that meeting unless she looked spectacular. A call to the salon for hair and makeup in the morning and a trip to the mall for a new outfit were on the bill for today. She rummaged through her closet, which was all hers now, and picked out a long skirt, matching top, and a vest. After looking in the mirror, she couldn't decide if she looked like Annie Hall or that cowgirl from an old TV western, Dale Evans. Her personality had turned her humorless over the years, so she decided on the cowgirl look and put on a pair of boots.

Harry, that prick. She thought back to the gun and decided that if it was for personal protection, it would be with him or in in his office. If it was for protection against a home invasion, which was as likely as snow in July, especially with the doorman, then the gun would have been in a handier place than the bottom of a dresser drawer. Her conclusion was that it was meant for her. *There is no telling what he might do now,* she thought. She grabbed her bag, and as she started to leave she stopped in mid stride. All these people getting shot during routine traffic stops. Suppose she got pulled over, opened her bag to get her license, and the cop saw the gun? *Do I become a casualty and a headline?* She envisioned Harry telling the story over a steak dinner, laughing the whole time, about how the cops killed his almost ex-wife. That fucking prick. Debbie took the gun out of her bag and tucked it inside the top of her boot.

CHAPTER
19

H ARRY PARKED THE rental car in front of the building he used to live in. He was there to pick up the Hefty bags containing his belongings. Yesterday, he lived on the Upper East Side and drove a Mercedes. Today, he was driving a rented wreck of a car, looking for a place to live. The irony never struck him that he was at that moment a homeless realtor, like a barefoot shoemaker.

Of course, this situation was only temporary, since Nikita and Boris, or whatever the fuck their names were, were going to solve his problem. Harry remembered what Tim said about how the police were going look for him first. He decided that he'd better hire a divorce lawyer and do it quickly. If he didn't, maybe the cops would figure the reason he didn't hire one was because he didn't think he would need one, and he didn't need one because he knew Debbie was going to turn up dead.

Whenever he sold a house and the buyer asked if Harry knew a lawyer who could help with the contract, he would recommend Dan White. Dan would show his gratitude by giving Harry tickets to a ball game, always for the Mets but never in decent seats. Harry figured that if he went to any of the games, which he never did, it would have cost him more to ride the subway than what Dan paid for the tickets. Ice in the winter, that's what it was like getting from Dan. An admirable quality, because Dan had you believe otherwise. "Harry, my boy," Dan would say with a slight bit of an Irish brogue, "you're not going to believe the good fortune that has come my way, and how much I'd like to experience this, but I'm passing along to you two of the hottest tickets in town. The amazing Mets are hosting the mighty Marlins of Miami, and I'd like you to have them."

Dan White was tall and stout. He could break the tension almost at will with a self-deprecating comment or regale the room with an entertaining story about a person or event in his life. Any of these stories may or may not have been true, but they managed to get many a contentious negotiation to a successful conclusion.

Harry figured Dan could handle his divorce and would do it on the cheap, given all the business Harry threw his way. After telling Siri to dial his future divorce lawyer, he heard Dan's voice on the other end.

"Harry, me lad, how goes the real estatin' business?"

Harry doubted whether Dan had ever set foot in Ireland but couldn't care less. Like everyone else, he was bowled over by the man's charm.

"Hi, Dan, business is fine, but I'm calling you with a personal matter."

"And just how can the law office of Daniel White, Esquire, be of service to an old, esteemed friend?"

"My wife is divorcing me."

"Should I be sorry to hear this?"

"Only if you think being without a home or a car or a wife is something to be sorry for."

"Well, Harry, two out of three isn't so bad."

Even Harry chuckled a bit at this and asked, "Would you be willing to handle this for me?"

"I'm a real estate lawyer. Matrimonial work is beyond the scope of my expertise."

"Come on, Dan, a negotiation is a negotiation. What's the difference?"

"Donald Trump convinced the American people of that, and how did that turn out?"

"Your point is well taken. Who would you suggest?"

"Well, that depends. Is this going to mediation or to court?"

"I believe she declared war."

"Do you know who her lawyer is?"

"Yeah, Karen Cassidy."

"If that's who I think it is, you're going to need Clarence Darrow."

"Is he expensive?"

"Harry, he would give anything to be in a courtroom again."

"That's fantastic. Do you have his contact info?"

"He's dead, Harry. Since 1938."

Once again Harry had to laugh, even though he was the butt of the joke. "So I guess he doesn't have a cell phone?"

He parked the poor excuse for a car in front of a fire hydrant near his office and hung the counterfeit handicapped parking permit from the rearview mirror. Not that it mattered, but maybe one of those cold-hearted traffic cops would give him a break if they happened to come by. Who was he kidding? There was no mercy from the parking cops that gave out tickets. Whether a meter expired, the car's inspection was over-due, it was blocking a driveway, or any other infraction, these folks would leave that orange notice on your windshield like they were getting paid a commission.

A few trips up and down the stairs schlepping the garbage bags from the car to his office tired him out. Harry was back downstairs breathing heavily and sweating like he was in a sauna. "Son of a bitch. I was gone like five minutes. Cockroaches." He grabbed the parking ticket off the wind-shield and tucked it under the windshield wiper of the car parked in front of him. So the other guy pays the ticket, or the car rental place gets stuck for it and they chase him down to collect. "They got a better chance of winning the lottery," Harry muttered to himself. Seated behind the wheel and with his chest still heaving, he continued, "Maybe I'm having a heart attack? I should be so lucky?"

Harry still had to find a lawyer. If he was having a heart attack, it would have to wait. He wouldn't want to find out the two commies bungled the job and ratted him out. "Better I should drop dead than go to jail and she's still alive. I won't give her that satisfaction." When the thought entered his mind, he felt stunned by his own brilliance. Suppose he could turn the tables on the Russians? Then he wouldn't have to pay them off. *Maybe they've already put an end to Debbie, may she rest in peace, and they'll end up in jail.*

His second trip around the block, he was able to find a legal parking spot. Breathing almost normally, he walked up the avenue and stopped just before he saw the sign on the awning. The only word on the sign in English was "Attorney." The rest was in Spanish but easily translatable: "immigracion" and "matrimonio." Harry needed the matrimonio repre-sentation.

He pulled the door open to see a well-dressed middle-aged woman sit-ting at a desk behind a wall with a sliding glass window between them.

"Good morning. May I help you?" she asked.

"I'm Harry Rosen. I have the real estate office down the street. I need a lawyer to handle a divorce."

"Please have a seat, and I will check to see if Mr. Ramos has time to see you."

Have time to see me? What is she, kidding? Harry thought. *Of course he'll see me. Who wouldn't want my business? He probably deals with guys that don't have two nickels to rub together. She's going to tell me to come back some other time? I don't think so.*

There were several uncomfortable-looking chairs and a small table with magazines that were current three months ago. Harry sat in one of the chairs, and it was more uncomfortable than it looked, made of hard plastic, without arms, and just wide enough to accommodate most but not all of Harry's butt. He admitted to himself that maybe he could shed a few pounds, but maybe this was designed by some skinny-assed guy in China who never saw an average-sized American.

The woman returned and told Harry that Mr. Ramos would make time for him. She pressed the buzzer that allowed Harry to open the door. She led him to an office that had a vanity wall behind the desk. It had various diplomas, proclamations, certificates, and photos with people he did not know but assumed were important. There was a small, round conference table at the other end of the room. The wall behind that was filled with baseball memorabilia, mostly dedicated to the New York Yankees.

"Hello, Mr. Rosen, I'm Bill Ramos."

Ramos was just on the other side of six feet tall, with dark hair, almost jet-black, combed straight back. Stocky, with a little paunch and in his late thirties, he looked like the type of guy your wife would leave you for.

Harry would have bet anything he introduced himself as Guillermo to the Hispanic clients. "Hello, Bill, call me Harry. Thanks for seeing me without notice." The little charm that he could muster was coming out.

"How can I help you?"

"My wife wants a divorce. I can't believe that after all these years she decides she's unhappy."

"It happens. I've seen it many times before." Moving the conversation from therapy back to business, the lawyer added, "Has she retained counsel, or does she have an interest in mediation?"

"She's got a lawyer, and I hear she's a pretty good one."

Ramos shrugged. "Not that it matters, but what's her name?"

"Karen Cassidy. Ever hear of her? She's supposed to be one scary bitch."

"No. But maybe she should be scared of me. My parents brought me to this country from Cuba when I was seven, and I grew up in this neighborhood. I'm not going to tell you what that was like. So unless she keeps a knife in her belt or a gun in her purse, she's not going to scare me, and even then I may not back down. And for what it's worth, unless there's something egregious, the court is going to pretty much divide the property in half. I'd suggest mediating this and saving both of you some legal fees."

Harry liked what he heard and said, "Tell me what the legal fees would be for this."

Ramos looked him straight in the eye and said, "If I can hammer out something without going to court, it will run you about twenty-five hundred. Should we to go to court, expect to spend about ten thousand."

Harry thought about this and figured it best to go the cheaper route. Assuming that Debbie was done, this was going to be the easiest negotiation Ramos ever had. "Bill, I am going to heed your judgment, so let's get this thing wrapped up. Please start this immediately."

"I'll need some personal information from you and a check for my retainer."

"Of course. How much is the retainer?"

"Twenty-five hundred," the lawyer answered, again looking straight into Harry's face.

"Isn't that the total fee?"

"Yes, it is. If you don't have the money, I can refer you to Legal Aid." Ramos picked up his phone and started to dial. "People have the wrong impression about their lawyers. Most of them are quite capable." Ramos picked up the phone and dialed. Harry heard the lawyer say into the phone, "Hola amiga, como esta?"

He signaled Ramos to hang up. "I think you may have misunderstood. In my business I don't get paid until the deal is closed, nor do the real estate lawyers. I just thought you worked the same way. Your fee is not a problem. I just don't have a check with me."

"I'm glad to hear that, Harry. Make an appointment with my receptionist, and we can get this going."

Harry stood up to leave, and they shook hands.

As Harry got to the door, he heard Ramos yell, "Hey, Harry. About that check: get it certified."

CHAPTER
20

I zzy stopped in front of the building and looked to check the address. What was to be a dry run for Tim's proposition was getting off on the right foot. The brownstone had a stoop that led up to an outer wooden door with a glossy finish that practically lit up under the bright sun. She walked up the steps and pressed the button for 2A, which was labeled "Cassidy." The door buzzed, and she pressed it open. As she walked toward the staircase, another tall, slender man of about her own age was tapdancing down the stairs.

"That was amazing," she said as he reached the floor.

He took an exaggerated bow and said, "Thank you. Thank you."

"I mean that was like really great. You could probably do that professionally."

He smiled as he walked past her and said, "I'm working on it."

With that, she walked up the one flight and down the short hallway and knocked. Tim answered the door and was greeted with an air kiss. Izzy was still in awe over the dancer and recounted this to Tim.

In a blasé manner, Tim said, "Oh him. Yeah, he's on Broadway in *42nd Street*. I think he lives on the third floor." Beneath that, like everyone else, there was that excitement of having a celebrity in one's midst. You shrugged it off as though he were just another guy in the building when someone asked you, but you couldn't wait to broadcast it to anyone who would listen.

"Come in and I'll give you a tour. It's a small apartment, so it won't take long." Tim proceeded to show her the bedroom in the back, which had a queen-sized bed, night stand, dresser, and a flat-screen television mounted on the wall. He walked her past the bathroom, which had only a shower stall, commode, and sink. He said, "Make sure you leave the seat up when you're done." Izzy snickered as they continued on to the galley kitchen, which was fully stocked. She noticed a collection of liquor bottles on the breakfast bar that separated the kitchen from the living room. "Drinks are on the house," Tim said as he gestured in that direction. There was a small table in the front of the apartment looking out onto the street. On it was a vase with fresh flowers. Izzy was sold.

"Okay, Tim. I'll take it if you pay the electric bill, too. It's within my budget, and I'll make sure you get the rent by the first of every month," she joked.

Tim smiled and said, "You drive a hard bargain, but I like you, Isabella Ramirez, so the place is yours." She threw her arms around his neck and hugged him in a manner that was more like a teenager that got a car for a birthday present. All of his romantic intentions departed, and he suddenly felt more like a favorite uncle. Yet he was not disappointed in this new role.

He handed her the keys, and as he left he said he would stay in touch and that they should get together soon.

Izzy put her bag down by the table and made herself a coffee. First she took a few pictures of the apartment and posted them on Instagram with the caption "my new writing studio." She took her laptop out and took a seat at the table. Gazing out the window was distracting, and she couldn't stop thinking about the dancer. *I'll bet he didn't have to go to law school,* she thought.

Hours passed, and she hadn't written a page or even devised a plotline. At least writing on a laptop kept her from wadding up sheets of paper and tossing them into a waste basket. All she did was keep deleting word after word. *Write about what you know* kept coming back to her, and it made her think that she didn't know anything.

Izzy poured another coffee and wondered about the dancer. Was he in a relationship? Was he gay? When would he be coming back? She turned her attention back to the laptop and decided her plotline would be "boy meets girl." She would be Juliet. Was the dancer going to be Romeo? "Enough for one day," she announced to herself. She opened Instagram. "Wow. Sixty-eight likes already." Izzy then realized why it took so long to write a play. How long did it take Neil Simon to write a play? How long would it have taken him if he had to keep up with social media?

CHAPTER
21

WHEN DEBBIE GOT to the garage, her car was waiting. Just like the closet, what was once theirs was now hers. She reminded the garage attendant of that and told him about the pending divorce. "Under no circumstance is anyone else allowed to drive this car."

The garage man nodded and answered, "Sí, yo comprendo."

Besides, she thought as she got into the car, *maybe he says something to someone else who lives in the building, and maybe they're single, and who knows?* She hit the gas and headed for the mall.

The two Russians were sitting in the van as Debbie passed them. Andrei and Yuri were close friends as children, as were their parents. Both families made their way out of Russia into the Ukraine, and then to Israel. Andrei and Yuri left together for the USA. They settled in the Brighton Beach section of Brooklyn, which was more like Moscow than Manhattan. The food, culture, and language was Russian. As children, they grew up speaking Russian and learned Hebrew and English going through school in Israel as young teens.

As children, neither made friends very easily, and they found themselves almost isolated. To avoid the bullies and teasing that came with being different during the mean years of middle and high school, they became gym rats. There was a subculture at the gym that drew them in, and they found themselves in a comfort zone. No one really cared about much except muscle groups, bis and tris (biceps and triceps), traps and lats (back muscles), and the like. It became a support group for them, with encouragement and advice limited mostly to bodybuilding, which was at least something for them to get lost in. They worked out relentlessly and became behemoths.

In New York, they found construction work and learned how contractors would do work without building permits and hire people who were illegally in the country and would work for lower wages.

One day they were approached by the owner of the building where they were working. The owner was having a problem with a tenant that was reluctant to move, even though he had made a generous offer for the tenant to leave.

"Maybe you can talk to him and convince him to leave," the landlord said.

Andrei said, "Maybe you should raise your offer."

"In this country, you know money talks," Yuri chimed in.

"Well, if you can convince him to leave, I'll make it worth your while. How does five thousand sound?"

Andrei and Yuri looked at each other and then back at the landlord. "You know what sounds better? Five thousand each, and another five thousand cash for the guy you want evicted," Yuri said.

"When can you get this done?"

"When can you bring us the cash?" Andrei quickly replied.

"Tomorrow."

"Then we go to work tomorrow," Yuri told him.

The following day, the landlord showed up with a paper bag that could have been carrying his lunch. He handed it to Yuri, said, "The guy lives in apartment 3B," and walked away. Yuri opened the bag and was surprised that fifteen thousand dollars took up so little space. Three bundles of hundred-dollar bills. He looked up and said to Andrei, "Let's count it first."

They walked up to the apartment and knocked. The man who answered the door was obviously intimidated. "What can I do for you?" he stammered. The Russians looked at him and then into the apartment. The place was a mess, with paint peeling everywhere and the sound of water dripping.

Andrei said, "Why do you want to live here?"

"I've been here over twenty years, and the rent is cheap."

Yuri stood there and glared at the tenant. "You get a good offer to leave?"

"Yeah."

"Okay, deal just got better. Here's one thousand dollars. After we leave, you call landlord and tell him you accept his offer."

Yuri then added, "Otherwise we come back and you give us two thousand dollars."

Andrei shrugged. "One way or another, you don't live here anymore. Make the call."

The two turned and left the tenant standing there with ten hundred-dollar bills in one hand and a cell phone pressed to his ear in the other.

The newfound wealth provided them with the seed capital to start their own business, namely the down payment for a van. The story of their strongarm exploits spread and would eventually provide startup funding for their real estate empire, a two-family home in Staten Island.

Andrei was sipping his coffee when he saw the car they were waiting for leave the garage. Yuri was sitting in the driver's seat, looking at his phone. "Andrei, look. She's leaving. Let's go." With that he put the van in gear and pulled out into traffic.

Debbie was oblivious to the outside world sitting inside her car. She cycled through four stations on her satellite radio before settling on a station that played showtunes. Singing along with the lyrics she knew and humming through those she didn't, she was completely unaware of the white van that was following her from the time she left the garage until she pulled into a parking garage at the mall.

It was a great time to shop, a weekday before lunch, so the garage was practically deserted. After she parked and started walking toward the entrance, she saw a white van barreling toward her. Debbie jumped out of the way as the van stopped short. She was dumbstruck as a man about the size of her car got out, grabbed her, and threw her inside the van. Yuri, who moved from the driver's seat to the cargo area, pinned Debbie to the floor as Andrei covered her mouth with a strip of duct tape. He then pulled her wrists together and wrapped them with duct tape as well. "Don't worry. Nothing bad going to happen. Your husband owe us money. He pay and we take you home."

This was not reassuring to Debbie. Her hands were taped in front of her, and she easily raised them and ripped off the tape covering her mouth. Though fearful, she managed to tell them that she was divorcing Harry and that the last thing he would do was pay a ransom for her.

"You get his money, then you pay us. Don't care who pays. Money is money."

Andrei then took her pocketbook and fished around until he found her car keys.

Yuri asked, "What are you doing?"

"Why leave the car? We'll take car and sell it. Get good money. Down payment."

"Good idea. You know where we're going. I'll follow you."

The kidnapping took less than a minute. Debbie was shocked and terrified in the back of the cargo van as it pulled out of the parking garage behind the Mercedes.

"You make noise. I stop car, come back there and stop you. Understand?"

"Yes. How much does he owe you?"

"Hundred fifty thousand. You have?"

"I will get it." Under duress, people will say anything, and she was no different.

They headed south on the parkway that would take them to the beach. The weather was helpful to the two Russians. There was a long stretch of a barrier beach that would be deserted due to the strong winds and overcast skies. It was along this stretch, in a salt marsh that was preserved for fish and wildlife, where the dead body of Debbie Rosen would not ever be found.

CHAPTER
22

H ARRY GOT OUT of bed, or rather what used to be the sofa in his office. It hadn't functioned as a place to sit for years. Like every other flat surface, it was just another place to pile up stuff. He wanted everything where he could see it, thinking it would be easier to locate when needed. His filing cabinets were empty.

He rooted through the garbage bags for his bathroom essentials and over to the closet, carefully stepping over the mounds of papers that were previously on the sofa, to pick out a suit for today's closing.

With the suit bag slung over one shoulder and a backpack on the other, he strolled over to the neighborhood health club.

Harry saw the perky young lady with her perky little smile and heard her say a perky, "Good morning."

"I'd like to sign up for a membership."

"Wonderful. We have variety of plans to choose from and..."

Harry cut her off. "Look, sweetheart, this is going to be the fastest and easiest sale you've ever made. Do you have lockers? I'll need one of those too."

"We have an annual plan where the monthly payment is only..."

Once again, he cut her off. "Fine, I'll take that one. Just give me an agreement to sign so we can move this along."

Her mood just slightly changing, she responded, "I'll need your driver's license and a credit card."

He reached into his wallet and gave her what he hoped would be a credit card that still had enough credit. "Hey, miss, if you don't mind, I'll give you a check for the first month, and you can keep that on file for the rest of the payments."

"That will be fine. Are you interested in our personal training program? It's only another..."

Once again he interrupted. "Do I look like I give a rat's ass at all about personal training, or that I ever did? So stop already and let me know how much to make the check out for. And I'll need a lock too."

She was beaten down almost to the point of tears when Harry told her, "It's going to be fine. Things will work out for you. You'll meet a nice boy, get married, have children, and move to the suburbs. You won't have to deal with schmucks like me anymore. And if you're smart, you'll marry for money. It lasts longer than love and good looks."

He signed the agreement and picked up his things.

Harry was sure the check he was writing wasn't any good, but they wouldn't find that out for a few days. A credit card they would know about immediately.

"Where are the lockers?"

"Downstairs and to the left."

"Thank you, sweetheart. You have a snappy day."

As he walked downtown, Harry thought that maybe he'd just solved his housing problem. He could sleep in the office and use the locker room showers. "It's genius. Who needs a big expense for rent? Maybe those millionaires and billionaires. Not me," said the man wearing a two-thousand-dollar suit.

CHAPTER
23

TODAY WAS THE day. He was finally going to have a few bucks in his pocket. Tim was going to close on the deal to buy the Ramirez property. By the time Harry got to his closing, the conference room was once again full. This time there was a completely different mood. The Ramirez family was all smiles, and Tim was already signing the documents that would convey to him ownership of what he felt was a sure bet. There was no such thing when it came to gambling, but real estate at the right price was a winner. The attorneys were all chatty, especially the one representing Tim.

Holy crap, where did he find her? Harry thought to himself. *Maybe at the Playboy mansion. If they had attorneys for hire, that's where she'd be working. And maybe not practicing law either.*

He was warmly welcomed by all there and thanked by Rafael Ramirez for bringing them such a fine buyer. Their attorney apologized for having him make a second appearance in order to complete the sale and asked if he had an invoice so that they could write a check for his fee. Even Tim was cordial when he said, "Hey, Harry, you look good. Nice suit."

"Thanks. I stopped by the gym this morning."

"Funny, you never seemed the type to me."

"I'm pretty sure that I'll be going there every day from now on."

The attorney for the seller passed over an attendance sheet and asked Harry to sign in. As he reached into his jacket pocket for a pen (Harry always carried a Montblanc), he scanned the sheet. He turned pale when he saw the name Karen Cassidy. That was the name of the hot-shit attorney Dan White mentioned. His skin went from ashen to bright red when he saw the name Timothy Cassidy on the line above.

At that moment, Tim looked up and asked, "Harry, are you okay?"

"I'm fine. Why?"

"You seriously look like you have a blood pressure issue."

"I didn't know you were a doctor. All these years I thought you were a..."

Tim cut him off in mid-sentence. "What's important is whether you're having a stroke or something."

"Let me ask you a question. Does your lawyer happen to be your wife?"

"Yes, she is."

"So, Mrs. Cassidy," Harry said as he started to explode, "I believe we may have a mutual acquaintance."

"Who might that be?" she coolly replied.

"It might be some giant rat from the sewer. It also might be my wife. I can never tell them apart." He continued, "And I say this with all due respect: good fucking luck with her and good fucking luck getting a fucking dime out of me by the time my lawyer is through with you and her both."

"Mr. Rosen, it is inappropriate for me to speak with you directly. Please have your attorney contact me, and at a more proper time." She smiled and continued, "Besides, we are working very quickly here so that you may collect your hard-earned commission. Please be careful how you use the money. It's hard to hang on to a dollar these days." *Especially if I'm representing your wife,* she left unsaid.

The other lawyer in the room diplomatically suggested that there was another conference room where Harry "could catch up on some calls or other business that he may wish to pursue privately." He then picked up a phone and asked someone to come in and "please show Mr. Rosen to another conference room and provide him with any refreshments he may want." And then to Harry: "We should be finished here shortly, and I'll bring your check over when we're finished.

On his way out, he heard one of the Ramirez brothers call out, "Good luck, and thanks again for getting this done for us. My daughter especially is going to appreciate it. I'm going to use the money to pay for law school."

Tim put a few puzzle pieces together, and almost all the color drained from his face.

Casey noticed and asked if he was okay.

Tim joked, "No, just the thought of another lawyer in the world scares me."

A small giggle came from most of the people in the room. Except Casey. *Bullshit,* she thought.

He quickly recovered after realizing the only thing he was guilty of was thinking about a romantic relationship with Izzy.

"Does she happen to work at P.J. Clarke's?" he asked.

"Yes, she does," her father answered.

"Crazy but true. I had lunch there recently, and she was the server. She seemed extraordinarily happy. I asked her why, and she told me about this. Go figure. In some way I'm a party to that. Small world."

Casey smiled at him and once again thought, *Bullshit.*

Ramirez answered, "Yeah, small world." Thinking, *Bullshit.*

In another, much larger conference room, Harry sat alone and wondered aloud if this was where the UN convened. "Sweetheart," he yelled to the woman that had led him there, "are we still in New York? Because I want to use your phone to make a call. I need to know if I have to dial an area code first."

She laughed and assured him that they were indeed still in the same area code.

"Good, now if it's not too much trouble, maybe I could get a coffee?"

"Regular or decaf?"

"It's like 10:00 a.m. Who drinks decaf this time of day?"

"Well, you could probably use some."

"Okay, Joan Rivers, enough with the jokes. I'll have a regular coffee, and if you don't mind, maybe a bagel with cream cheese if you have one. If not, I'll take a muffin or a couple of donuts."

"You do know that this is a law office and not a deli, right?"

"Again with the comedy. There should be a cover charge for your act."

She told Harry that she'd see what she could do as she left the room.

Harry used the phone on the conference table to call Bill Ramos. He figured the lawyer might not pick up if he saw who was calling.

He was right. Ramos picked up the phone and answered on the second ring with a crisp, "Hello, this is Guillermo Ramos speaking."

"And this is your newest client, Harry Rosen."

"Hello, Harry. I gather by this that you'd like to move forward. And that you have my retainer?"

"Why else would I call you, to buy a Pontiac?"

"Pretty funny. You do know they haven't made those for years."

"Like I care. I gave up on American cars when I got over the fact that World War Two was over, and it was time to let bygones be bygones."

"When was that?"

"As soon as I could afford a Mercedes-Benz."

"I'm glad things are going well for you, except perhaps for your current marital issues. I am glad to be on your side."

Bullshit, Harry thought. This guy was happy to be on anyone's side as long as he was getting paid. "Well, I'm glad to hear that, especially because of the huge monetary investment I'm going to make in you. I expect you to earn that hefty fee many times over."

"Come by my office later, and we can discuss your expectations and explore various strategies to meet or exceed them."

Harry's rants rattled around inside his head. *Jesus, this guy sounds like he should be selling self-help books on late-night television. Maybe this is what I need after seeing and hearing those snooty asshole lawyers in the closing room.*

"Look, Guillermo," Harry said in a slightly mocking tone, "I just happened to meet the insulting bitch lawyer that's representing my wife, and nothing would make me happier than you squishing her like a cucaracha. That's the various strategy I want. I'll see you later."

Harry hung up the phone and wondered how long it was going to take to get the coffee and a bagel.

He looked up from his cell phone when the door opened. "Hello, Joan Rivers. What? No coffee?"

"I hope you're not disappointed, Mr. Rosen, but all I have for you is your check. It's for forty thousand dollars. You don't mind signing for it, do you?"

"For a check like that, I'd kiss your ass in a Macy's window."

"Fortunately, I just need your signature."

Harry opened the envelope that contained his check, stared at it briefly, then put the check back in the envelope and slid it into his jacket pocket. He got up and headed back to the room from which he had been banished.

Tim was shaking hands with all of the members of the Ramirez family, as was Casey. There were smiles all around, so when Harry reentered the room, he boomed, "Just what I like to see at my closings. Everybody happy." And to the Ramirez family: "I hope I've served you well and thank you for your trust in me." Always the salesman, he continued, "If you ever want to buy or sell another property, I'm your man. Buena suerte, mis amigos."

He hoped his Spanish was correct for "good luck, my friends." They in turn thanked him, and one of the Ramirez sisters said, "Thank you, Harry, but we probably only speak as much Spanish as you. Growing up, we were only allowed to speak English in our house. Whatever we learned was on the street." She then added, "My brother does, however, speak fluent Russian."

Harry froze and thought, *The Russians. Holy shit.*

CHAPTER
24

Y URI FOLLOWED DEBBIE'S car south on the Meadowbrook parkway for about twenty minutes. The Meadowbrook is essentially anchored by a mall at the northern end and the Atlantic Ocean to the south. The Ocean Parkway runs along the ocean and is a colossal traffic jam in the summer and just as deserted when it's not a beach day. This was not a beach day.

The Mercedes pulled off onto a gravel road used primarily by fishermen with four-wheel-drive vehicles. He stopped where the gravel ended and sand began. It was bordered by tall marsh grass and dunes, which made the road invisible except to any on the same path, and no one was on this path.

The van stopped behind the Benz and Yuri walked between the front seats headed toward the back of the van. There was no reason to leave any traces of blood in the van. It was a simple plan they had concocted. Yuri carries Debbie out of the van and drops her into the tall grass. Andrei fires a few rounds into her, they drive away on the Ocean Parkway, wipe the fingerprints off the gun, and throw the gun into the Great South Bay.

Debbie remembered an incident from eighth grade. One of the girls in her class had thought Debbie was moving in on her boyfriend, which she was, but in a way that she thought wasn't obvious. The offended girl confronted Debbie and got in her face, threatening to "kick her ass up and down the street." Without thinking, she had reached down and flashed a box cutter.

"Let's see how much he's gonna like you with a few scars on your face."

As the girl backed away, Debbie heard, "Hey, if that cheating shithead ran around on me, he ain't worth it. I'm outta here."

Debbie felt relieved that she didn't have to use the blade and wondered if she really would have. She definitely knew they weren't going to hug it out but was glad they didn't have to slug it out. There was also a gnawing sense that maybe this wasn't the end of it, and she'd have to watch her back.

Yuri could only muster shock as he inhaled his last breath. Debbie had reached into her boot and pulled out the gun as he got within arm's length of her. It was as if the first shot only stunned him, so as she did the first time she pulled the trigger, Debbie pointed the gun at the monster, closed her eyes, clenched her jaw, and fired a second time. In the slow motion of her mind, the few seconds seemed to take hours. The three hundred pounds or so of now-dead Russian fell forward with a thud that rocked the van, his head within an a few inches of Debbie and eyes open with a piercing stare.

Hearing the gunshots, Andrei ran to the van and opened the sliding door on its side. He saw his friend lying there bleeding profusely, trying to process what had happened. While he was doing that, Debbie aimed squarely at the large Russian's head and fired again, this time with her eyes open. He was no longer moving toward her. He was now piled on top of his lifelong friend.

With more blood spewing from her second victim, she broke down in tears. It took several minutes for her to process what had happened. She then noticed the pool of blood had inched underneath and onto her skirt. With a head that cleared like a hangover after another drink, she spat out a string of curses at the dead that also contained the phrases "I only wore this once," "You know how much I paid for this?" and "This was my new favorite look."

She put the police special back in her boot, rolled onto to her knees, and even though her hands were still taped together, she managed to open and exit the rear door of the van. The doors to her car were open, and on the front passenger seat was her pocketbook, which contained her phone and key fob. Further digging yielded a nail file, and with some dexterity her hands were freed. "First things first," she said to herself as she pressed a button on the key fob and heard the trunk open. A neatly folded towel was under an umbrella — god forbid that a wet umbrella would land on the carpet in the trunk. She unfolded it and spread it evenly on the driver's seat. There was no chance for a stain on her upholstery. Not on her watch.

As she maneuvered the car past the van, a wave of panic came over her, followed by a cloud of indecision. Call the police? She murdered two people, and yes, it was self-defense, but maybe she'd be arrested anyway. Maybe she wouldn't? What if she did nothing? Would it be worse for her if she got caught? *Would* she get caught? Would the police show up and even care, assuming that the two men were probably criminals anyway? Why would the cops even be looking for her anyway?

Maybe she should toss the gun off the bridge? Maybe someone would see her doing that? Or maybe, just maybe, she could figure out how to get the gun back to Harry.

Harry owed them money, so they said. He would hold a lot more interest to the cops, for sure. Maybe the cops think he was the one that was kidnapped. He fears for his life and shoots them both. He gets arrested, convicted, and spends the rest of his miserable life in prison. The thought of that scenario parted the clouds like Moses parting the Red Sea. The sun was beginning to shine in her world.

As she drove the car over the bridge that spanned the bay, she brought the Benz to a complete stop. There was no traffic in either direction, and if she was going to get rid of the murder weapon, this was her chance. Again, there was more indecision. What if someone found the gun? Would they be able to trace it back to her? What if this wasn't because Harry owed these guys money? What if he got someone else to try to kill her? Maybe she would need it again? Maybe she should use it to take out Harry?

Debbie got out of the car, leaned over the railing, and puked.

CHAPTER
25

H ARRY STOPPED IN the lobby to open the envelope that contained his check. The adrenaline rush was euphoric. The amount was secondary to the result. He had closed the deal. He won, and nothing was better than that. The check could have been for ten times that amount, and the feeling would not have been any different. Harry would only gamble more and shop more. He could use another watch, he thought.

He came out of the fog when he felt the arm on his shoulder. It was Tim, who was all smiles too.

"We had a great day in there, Tim. You're gonna make a small fortune on that deal."

"That's the plan. But you know what else is making me smile? You have my money, and we can settle up right now."

"It's not that simple. I'll have to open a new bank account so my wife can't get her money-grubbing paws on the money. And I say that with no disrespect to any animals that may have paws. Your wife knows about it, and she represents my wife, so maybe she says something and all of a sudden, my current financial situation takes a downturn."

"Simple solution. We go to the same bank that the check is drawn on, and you open an account there."

"That's a great idea, but I'm supposed to be at my lawyer's office like ten minutes ago, and you can blame that on your wife."

"Harry, you can blame that on *your* wife. We'll go to the bank and settle up, and after that you can go about your business."

"Speaking of which, is it fair to assume that you'll start taking my action again?"

"Sure thing." Tim knew one thing was a sure thing: people didn't change. Alcoholics always wanted to drink, and gamblers always wanted to gamble. Harry wasn't going to stop, and Tim wasn't going to stop him. It was only a matter of time until Tim would have Harry's bankroll.

Unless his or Harry's wife got it first. He added, "And since I know you're good for it, you can go to two g's a game." At two thousand a game, Harry could tap out before the Super Bowl.

"Hey, Tim, how big is your biggest briefcase?"

"Why do you ask that?"

"Because you're going to need it next week to pay me off. I've got a great feeling about the Eagles."

"That feeling is probably drug-induced. Rooting for the Eagles in this town has nasty side effects, and even collecting a winning bet won't make up for the loss of friends or blot out the memory you'll leave behind. It'll go on your tombstone, Harry: 'This Motherfucker Bet on the Eagles.' You could build a hospital or cure cancer, and what you'll be remembered for is rooting for Philadelphia."

Harry waved as he started to walk away and said, "We'll talk tomorrow. I'll call you for the spreads. I gotta go uptown to see my lawyer." He almost got away with a great escape until he was reminded of the trip they were going to make to the bank.

Conveniently for Tim, and inconveniently for Harry, the bank was on the corner.

Half an hour later, Tim had his cash.

Harry had a listing agreement for the property Tim just closed on, which, with a ten percent commission, was going to be worth about a hundred fifty thousand to him. He also had an ATM card, a checkbook, enough cash to pay his lawyer, and enough money to pay for incidentals. Maybe a steak and a massage after he sat down with Ramos the abogado.

A cab ride later, he once again walked into the office of Guillermo Ramos. He was greeted cheerily by the receptionist, who gave him a retainer agreement to review. She told him that Mr. Ramos was on a call and would see him shortly. A bullshit story, but he nonetheless took a seat and started reading the retainer. After three sentences, he was bored and in a voice loud enough to be heard a block away asked where should he sign this. It had the desired effect of getting the lawyer out of his office and off the phone, if he ever was in the first place.

With a big smile, Ramos gave a firm handshake and with his other hand grabbed Harry's left shoulder as though they were the best of long-lost friends.

"Good to see you, Harry."

"And you too. I'm glad you could see me on short notice, but I really want to put this behind me and move on with my life without that hundred-fifty-pound tumor." Harry had no idea how much his wife weighed, but what the hell, he never worked in a carnival, guessing ages and weights, so who cared?

Ramos had an instinct he referred to as a "bullshit detector." Right now the needle on the dial was deep into the red. Last meeting he wanted everything, and now he wanted to settle quickly. Whatever it was that happened was not his business, and he was going to make sure that it didn't become his business.

"That's my job. I'll try to make this quick and painless," the lawyer lied.

Sure, that was his job, but in between there was the opportunity for additional work that meant additional fees. The problems he saw were that Harry might not have the money, and if he did, he might not pay. Ramos was practical. It wasn't what you billed, but rather what you collected, and he didn't think it would be good for business if he were suing his clients for payment. Better to smile grudgingly and let the client know that he was going to eat the unpaid balance, because he didn't want money to get in the way of the relationship they had developed over the course of this devastating event in their life. Some of the women he represented bought the spiel, and he would invariably end up with a home-cooked meal and a blowjob.

"Quick and painless. You should be my dentist," Harry said.

"I actually thought about going to dental school, but I thought the money wasn't as good."

"For the money, you should have gone to plumbing school."

The lawyer chuckled a bit and asked, "Did you hear about the plumber who used to be a gastroenterologist? He still dealt with a lot of crap, but the money was better."

Like many speakers, a bit of humor came before the serious discussion. So it was with Ramos. At that time, he proceeded to ask if Harry had any questions about the retainer agreement, and did he understand that if more time and attention were required for his case that he would be responsible for additional fees and expenses? "But I'm going to do my best, and am very confident that that is not likely to happen."

Harry pushed the agreement he'd signed earlier across the desk. The lawyer looked at the retainer for any changes that Harry may have made (there were none), and for the signature.

"Okay, the only item keeping me from representing you is the deposit described in the agreement."

"About that..."

Ramos tensed up but contained himself to hear the tale that was about to be told.

"I wasn't able to get you a bank check."

"We spoke about that, and I made it very clear that..."

Harry cut him off, reached into his suit jacket breast pocket, and pulled out an envelope, then went on. "So I brought cash instead." Harry momentarily thought he might try to work around the payment but realized this guy wasn't going to buy a story. Besides, he had a different, more important one to sell.

"Good one, Harry. For a moment I really did think you were going to try to sidestep this and that I was going to have to send you over to Legal Aid."

"Just breaking balls. Are we okay? Because I'm relying on you to get this thing finished."

Finished. The lawyer thought that even for a character as shallow as he thought Harry was, this was curious. Finished? As if the last however many years they'd been married were like a bad meal. Awful experience, until you ate again the next day. Finished. Last time they met, Harry was homicidal, and now he was anxious to pay his way out. *This was a guy who didn't want to part with a dollar to pay me, and now all of a sudden his wallet is wide open.* Two and two always makes four, but this wasn't adding up.

Ramos had spent four grueling years going to law school in Brooklyn at night, driving a bus during the day, and struggling to find a twenty-fifth and twenty-sixth hour each and every one of those days to try and keep up. It wasn't as if he could read, write, and study while he was working his day job. He wasn't going to see those efforts go to waste by jeopardizing his license to practice law, even though there were days he thought he maybe should have resigned himself to the life of a driving a bus for the city. Do this for twenty-five years, collect a pension, and move to Miami.

Twenty-five years was a sentence you could get for second-degree murder. Sometimes he thought that a convicted murderer should be sentenced to driving a bus. Let them sit behind the wheel in crosstown traffic during a rush hour with honking horns, pissed-off passengers, and trucks that would block an intersection so no others could travel up or down an avenue. Not to mention the pedestrians who thought it was okay to cross whenever traffic was momentarily stopped. The jails would be empty, since he was sure no one would ever commit a crime if they knew the punishment was going to be driving a bus.

All in all, it was as if there were no vehicle and traffic laws in this city, only guidelines and suggestions. God forbid any member of the NYPD should write a ticket for any of these. It would have made his life better then and his law practice better now.

He bluntly asked Harry about the sudden change of heart. "Tell me, why such a hurry?" He didn't bother to add that the first to make an offer was a sign of weakness. Although he didn't particularly care — his fee was fixed unless this went to court — Ramos wanted to make sure he would not be subject to disbarment or a malpractice lawsuit.

Harry told him about how he was threatened by the two goons but just closed on the sale of the property and that the sellers were going to return their deposit. That problem was solved, and the relief he felt was enormous.

From there he went on to say, "It felt so good to be rid of that problem. How good is it going to feel to get rid of my wife? And I don't mean like with concrete blocks tied to her ankles over the side of a boat. Just the thought of not listening to her carp all day, every day, about everything is going to be worth a few bucks. Hell, the way this real estate market is going, I'll probably make it all back in less than a year."

Harry felt like he sold the story, which was essentially true, except for the few nagging omitted details.

The lawyer thought about Harry's response and asked if he had been served with a summons.

"Summons? No. Instead of that, I got all my stuff packed in Hefty bags and a key to the apartment that doesn't work anymore. I think her intentions were pretty clear."

"Not to pry, but when was the last time you had sex with her?"

"What kind of question is that?"

"If you haven't in the last twelve months, it would be grounds for divorce on the basis of abandonment."

"I remember we went to see the movie *La La Land* when it first came out. It was sometime in 2016."

"And that, my friend, is our case."

Harry now knew that his best strategy was to buy time. Let things play out with the divorce, with Igor and Boris, and start a negotiation that could drag on until, well, until there was nobody to negotiate with.

"You know, I remember when we first talked, you thought a settlement was the way to go. Maybe I got a little emotional, when rationally I should listen to you." Harry reached in his pocket and pulled out a stack of business cards. While he was looking through them, he continued, "I was at a closing this morning. Whenever I go to one, I always make it a point to get a business card from everyone there." Harry found the one for Karen Cassidy and passed it across the desk, saying, "Here's the one for that slut lawyer."

Ramos let the comment pass and told Harry he thought that was the smart play. The lawyer got up and reached across the desk to shake Harry's hand. This was the way Ramos let Harry know the meeting was over.

"I've got something that has priority but will reach out to her no later than tomorrow to get this rolling."

CHAPTER

26

THE WORDS WERE spoken by rote: "911, what is your emergency?" The operator sounded almost bored as she spoke them, while the caller was beside himself. "I'm down by the ocean at the four-wheel drive entrance to the beach at Democrat Point. There's a van blocking the entrance, and it looks like there are two dead bodies inside."

The operator did her best to calm the caller down and obtain the requisite information. "Your name?"

"Peter Hicks."

"A description of the vehicle?"

"It's a white van."

"Please stay where you are, a car is on the way."

Within a matter of minutes, although it felt like hours, the New York State Park Police had arrived.

"Are you Mr. Hicks?" the officer asked in a somewhat nervous manner. He was more accustomed to treating sunburns and ticketing nude beachgoers than being the first to arrive at a murder scene.

"Yes, I am."

"There will be investigators here shortly, but I need to know if you touched anything in, on, or near the vehicle."

"No. I came down here to do some kitesurfing, and the van was blocking my path. After a few minutes, it still hadn't moved, so I got out to see if maybe they needed some help. That's when I saw the bodies and called."

Much to the relief of the park policeman, a caravan of cars was barreling through the parking lot heading toward them. There were various makes and models of cars displaying the markings of the particular units they were assigned (crime scene and emergency services, to name just two) and the lettering on those from the myriad law enforcement agencies responding. In addition to the Park Police, there were the State Police and Suffolk County Police, some in marked cars and others unmarked.

Add to that the number of news vans from televised media, printed media, and radio stations sending reporters, the seasonally, virtually empty parking lot was anything but. Added to that was the additional layer of chaos beyond the yellow crime scene tape created by the industrious owner of a food truck who amazingly did not raise any of his menu prices. Business was so brisk that he even sold out of decaf coffee.

After sorting the hierarchy of who was who on the scene, the county police were going to lead the investigation. The commissioner was there to face the cameras and send the message that this case "was the highest priority, and all available resources will be devoted to seeing that the guilty party or parties are brought to justice." He must have liked this statement, because he used it whenever he was at a crime scene and there was a video camera pointed at him.

Walking away from the scrum of reporters, he waded into a smaller group that included the chief of detectives. "Who caught this one?"

He got his answer and could not have been more pleased.

"Laurel and Hardy."

They were Jack McGuire and Mike Sorrentino. Both were in their late forties and with enough time in to pull the plug. They loved the work and were good at it. Never mind that retirement gig. At 5'10, McGuire denied that at 200 pounds he was overweight. He contended that he was short for his weight. McGuire also insisted that his "three p's diet," pizza, pasta, and pale ale, was healthy and of no consequence to his physique. By contrast, his partner, Sorrentino, was four inches taller and forty pounds lighter. Their comical physical appearance gave them the nicknames.

But there was nothing funny about the way they did their work. It was all business and by the book. They never sought the spotlight. That was why the commissioner was pleased. Never mind that they closed a higher percentage of their cases than everyone else on the homicide squad.

They had already spoken with the poor bastard surfer kid who had the bad luck to find the bodies. The interview was brief and would have even been more so had McGuire not asked what kitesurfing was, how one could travel into the wind, and by the way, "Would you mind if we swabbed your hands for gunpowder residue?"

Peter Hicks explained that going upwind was not done any different than you would on a sailboat, "by tacking," going at angle somewhat upwind and then turning back in the opposite direction against an angled upwind.

The conversation relaxed Peter, and he had no objection to getting swabbed. He giggled and said he thought the term sounded kinky and that he was going tell his girlfriend that he was really horny and wanted to get swabbed. Sorrentino laughed along and asked if they lived together. Did he come here directly from there? Would he mind if they called her just to confirm that he was not even a person of interest? By the way, they wouldn't ask if he was swabbing her this morning. Peter was totally cooperative and laughed again when heard the comment about swabbing. While they were laughing, McGuire asked for her name and number and gave her a call to confirm what they already knew — that he was not the perp. Right by the book. No loose ends.

They walked back to the van while the crime scene unit was still at work. One of the investigators asked humorously, "Well, was that our guy?"

McGuire answered, "I'd bet we could've got him for possession, but surfer boy is not our guy." Before he turned away, McGuire told him that he wanted cell phones and IDs from the victims.

"I'm way ahead of you, Detective. Here are the phones and wallets." The detective dropped the phones into his pocket and then looked through each wallet until he found a driver's license, which he photographed with his smartphone. There was $45 in one wallet and $380 in the other. Robbery was not a motive. McGuire returned the wallets with the contents to the investigator and advised him to note the amount of cash. Translation: keep your hands off the money.

Sorrentino was looking in the van and couldn't believe what he was seeing. "Holy shit. Look at the size of these guys."

His partner was just as amazed. "I think you would have needed an elephant gun to stop either one of them."

"So what did stop them?"

"The guy at the bottom of the pile took two, both in the torso. The guy on the top of the pile took one in the forehead."

The two detectives started thinking out loud. McGuire started. "So they were facing the shooter, which puts the shooter in the back of the van."

Now Sorrentino, "And the first guy is in the driver's seat, gets up, turns around, catches two pills, and falls forward, while the second guy exits from the passenger door, slides open the side door, and gets his in the coconut as soon as he pokes it inside."

"Not quite," his partner corrected him. "The second guy leaves first, and as he's coming to open the passenger door, the driver turns around and buys it. Just then, the door slides open and Godzilla here catches one."

"So how does our guy get away? On foot? Boost a car?" Sorrentino added.

"Why were there three of them in a two-seat van? How long were they in there? Where did they come from?"

"There's a second car, likely the shooters, and they're meeting here for what? A drug deal? It goes bad and bam!"

McGuire thought for a moment. "I don't know. The shooter gets out of the second car to get into the back of the van?"

"Maybe to make sure whatever he was there to pick up was what he was supposed to pick up."

"Or sex? Gilgo Beach ring a bell? The gorillas convince a pro to meet here and she shows up prepared."

At that point, the two abruptly stopped. Years ago, fifteen bodies were found throughout the barrier island from Gilgo Beach, a little farther to the west, and Oak Beach, a little farther to the east. Some of the victims were identified and determined to be sex workers that solicited clients via the Internet. The crimes remained unsolved, and the mass murderer was still at large.

Sorrentino's eyes narrowed, and he spoke barely above a whisper. "We never had this discussion. No one knows this, and for now this stays between us, otherwise this could go nuclear. If it gets out, they'll be strutting around high-fiving at HQ, and then if it goes south, the shit will rain down on us."

"Side bet the registration is in the glove box?" asked McGuire.

"No bet. You get it, and I'll try to put names on these two."

Sorrentino asked the nearest CSI to get their wallets and cell phones. He took photos of the driver's licenses and credit cards and returned them to the investigator but kept the phones.

The two gathered the information and compared notes. McGuire chimed in first. "Registered to a construction company in Staten Island."

Sorrentino continued, "And Staten Island has now lost two of its citizens. I'm going to be shocked if they come up empty when we run the names."

"Well, partner, let's saddle up and head on yonder to Staten Island," McGuire said, doing his best to sound like John Wayne.

"If John Wayne was from Brooklyn and had a raspy voice, he'd sound just like that. You were trying for John Wayne, weren't you?"

"That was a great John Wayne. Speaking of superstars, let's try to sneak past the commish on the way out of here."

"Egotistical son of a bitch. Fastest way to fuck this up is to let him get involved."

They continued on and almost made it to their car before they were intercepted by one of the commissioner's henchmen, who told them, "The boss wants to see you."

As they approached the commissioner, he broke away from the circle surrounding him and asked the detectives, "What do you think? Is this related to the Gilgo Beach murders?"

Sorrentino answered, "Sir, we don't know what to think yet. The two stiffs in the van, God rest their souls, are from Staten Island, and we're taking a road trip there now."

"I know you guys don't need me to micromanage this, but I do want updates daily, or sooner if something significant comes up."

With a "yes sir," they continued to their car. Despite the height difference, McGuire used the Spanish translation for little Mike and said to his partner, "Good work there, Miguelito. God rest their souls, nice touch. Did you mean you felt sorry that they were dead or that they lived in Staten Island?"

CHAPTER
27

HARRY DID NOT want to keep Tim waiting. He checked to make sure he had properly completed the listing agreement, needing only a signature from Tim. A big payday was on the way, and he could use one. "My end, six figures. Touchdown!" he thought out loud.

By the time Harry got to the property, Tim was already inside but had left the door open. "Anybody home?" Harry bellowed.

"Come on in, Harry." There was the sound of footsteps on the staircase as Tim excitedly bounded down the steps. "It needs some work, but I believe this is going to be a bigger winner than I initially thought."

"Better for both of us. I want to start pitching this right away. That's why I brought a listing agreement with me." Harry was going for a fast close and lied, "There are a few people I have in mind for this." He took an envelope out of his jacket pocket and unfolded the document before he passed it over to Tim. "It's everything we discussed. It needs only your John Hancock. I'm thinking we were a little too conservative when we thought about the pricing. Maybe we should put this up for a million nine?"

Tim was a bigger fish than Harry thought. "You really think that?"

"Hey, you never know. It's easier to come down than go up, and why leave money on the table?" Harry was in full realtor mode, and Tim bought it hook, line, and sinker. He practically snatched the agreement out of Harry's hand and asked if he had a pen.

"That's like asking the hot dog guy if he has mustard," Harry answered as he passed a fake Mont Blanc pen from his shirt pocket to Tim's out-stretched arm.

Giving it a quick read, really only looking at the handwritten entries Harry made, he pressed the paper against the wall and scrawled his name where the sticky yellow tab with an arrow told him to sign.

"Here you go. Let's make some money." He turned from a sceptic into a believer. Yes, he was a convert to the religion of real estate. Hallelujah. Harry folded up the agreement and put it back in his jacket.

"I think I want to take out the carpets and redo the floors, maybe bring this up to date and turn it into a smart house."

Whatever the hell that is, Harry thought. The words came out differently, though: "Mint condition will bring you a mint."

"New kitchen, bathrooms, fresh coat of paint. It's going to be a showcase.

"Have you got an architect? If not, I know a guy."

"Why do I need an architect?"

"Why, because it's the city of New York, that's why. You can't put a light bulb in without a permit."

"So I'll find an architect. How hard can that be?"

"Make sure he has a good expediter."

"Expediter? What's that?"

"That's the guy who's going take the architect's approved plans and get you a building permit."

"Can't I just do that myself?"

"Sure you can, if you're also the type of guy who wants to be on the phone for three hours with some guy from Bangalore that you can barely understand trying to help you fix your computer. You get a good expediter, and you get your permits without having to wait for February 31st."

"There is no February 31st."

"That's what I'm trying to tell you. There's no permit either."

"So then I get started on this?"

"Sure, if you're a licensed plumber, electrician, and home improvement contractor."

"Harry, you're killing me."

"Better to do it the right way. You get these guys, they try to take a shortcut, and then they find a buyer but can't close, because they never got a C of O."

"C of O?"

"'Certificate of Occupancy.' After the work is done, an inspector comes out to make sure the work was done properly, and you get your C of O. So then you get to closing, and no problems."

"Harry, you are real buzzkill."

"Not me. It's the city of New York. I'm just telling you like it is. I want to tell you something else, too: this city makes more money for more people than you can imagine. And almost all of it is on Wall Street or in real estate. I got a client who came here from somewhere in South America, probably illegal at the time too. Got a job in a pizzeria in Brooklyn, worked like eighteen hours a day. Saved enough to buy the business a few years later, and the building a few years after that. Fast forward, and now he owns six brownstones probably worth about thirty million. And you know what? He's still making pies."

"The American Dream."

"And he's got four kids. All doctors."

"Give me the number of your architect. I want to get this party started."

CHAPTER
28

D EBBIE PULLED INTO a mall parking lot. It wasn't one she knew of or would ordinarily care about. The only stores in there were ones that she could afford, which was why they were precisely the ones where she didn't shop.

She grew up with a mother who did most of her shopping for the year on two days: Black Friday, when the Christmas sales traditionally started, and the day after Christmas, when there were the biggest markdowns. Since then, Debbie compensated for what she felt were those demeaning experiences and committed the worst sin her mother could imagine: paying retail, and at upscale stores to boot.

The store was virtually empty of customers, the sales floor almost devoid of help as well. All of which was fine with her, as she imagined she looked as bad as she felt. The smell of vomit and gunpowder permeated her and her clothing. A new wardrobe, shower, and massage would help her physical being, but she still had to sort out her emotions and the path forward.

There were racks and racks of clothes, many of which she considered unflattering. Her mother would have had her trying on all of them. She flashed back to her mother: "Look at this one! Very nice, and it's sixty percent off, with another fifteen percent too. Try this on. It'll make you look gorgeous."

"Thanks, Mom, so unless I wear that, I'm not gorgeous?"

"That's not what I'm saying. You're putting words in my mouth. I'm only saying it will look good on you."

The memory propelled Debbie to buy a pair of mom jeans as well as every other garment she'd need so she could discard what she was wearing, except for the boots. She would drop dead before she gave those up.

The Lucchese boots were a birthday present from herself because her cheap ass husband remembered at the last minute and gave her a box of chocolates he'd bought at the drug store. A month later, he got a bill from Neiman Marcus for two thousand and went nuclear, but Debbie couldn't have cared less.

"They look great and make me feel great. Next year, remember my birthday like it's a national holiday. Buy me something nice, take me to dinner, romance me a little."

Weighing his response and still steaming, Harry thought it was worth two grand not to do any of the above but brought his emotions to a slow simmer and said, "You know, you're absolutely right. Just wait until next year. I am going to treat you like a queen." He would treat her like a queen, all right: Marie Antoinette. If he could only find a guillotine.

After picking out the new outfit, including bra, panties, a pair of socks, jeans, and a top, she found a cashier halfway across the store. The cashier pitched the benefits of applying for a store credit card, including an additional discount on her purchase. Debbie knew her credit was probably shot by now and such an application would likely be turned down, and besides, the card she already had was in Harry's name, so let him fucking deal with it.

"No, thanks, I'll use this card. We need the miles." Debbie hoped the card was still good. If not, there had to be one in her wallet that was. Magically, the purchase went through.

"Is there a dressing room I could use to change? I'd like to wear these home."

"Of course. It's against the wall behind you." The sales clerk smiled and pointed, then quickly added, "That outfit will look great with those shoes." She had to wonder why someone with a platinum card and boots that cost more than she made in a month would be shopping here.

Debbie's body convulsed when she sat on the bench and removed her boots. The gun slid onto the floor as she pulled her leg out and made what she imagined was a loud clank. No one else, if there was anyone else around, heard the noise, or if they did, they pretended not to notice. When Debbie emerged from the dressing room, the clothes that she had meticulously chosen that morning were in a shopping bag. She had jammed the pistol back in her boot and felt a bit less uneasy handling it.

The Benz was just a short walk away in the largely deserted parking lot. A press of a button set off a flash of the tail lights and unlocked the doors. Feeling a bit less overwhelmed, Debbie drove around the parking lot until she found a large pink donation box letting everyone know that the donations made here would be of great benefit to those in need. It read like it was a scam, but it served her purpose, and she emptied the contents of the shopping bag into the box.

She had to talk to someone about what happened. Her impulse was to do nothing until the police knocked on her door, if they ever did. But could she live with herself? Her lawyer, that's who she would call, her lawyer. Could she tell her, though? Would Casey turn her in? Would she have to if she knew a crime was committed? What was that attorney-client privilege she always heard about on all the cop shows?

Debbie pulled into a mall parking lot.

Should she go to the police? Maybe later. "First I'll get a massage." Debbie knew how to prioritize.

Debbie was struck with the delightful smell of vanilla as she entered the dimly lit entranceway. The reception area consisted of two small loveseats facing a counter manned by young woman wearing a tee-shirt that covered one shoulder and a pair of skinny jeans that she barely fit into. Her makeup was perfect, with the reddest of red lipstick that Debbie had ever seen. A fire engine would be proud to be this red.

There was incense burning in a porcelain holder shaped like a flower, with the stick placed vertically in the center of the flower. Large candles gave off just enough light to make the room and everything in it visible. She saw another woman wearing a white terrycloth robe slouched in an oversized stuffed chair. Her head was slouched back, with earbuds in, looking as relaxed as humanly possible, almost dead to the world, in a most blissful state, with a slight smile on her face.

"Hi, I'm Sharon. What can I help you with today?"

"I'd like to get a massage."

"Sure, did you have an appointment?"

"No, I was driving by and..."

Sharon cut her off. "No matter, we can get you in. Did you want a facial, mani-pedi, or makeup today?"

"No, thanks. Just a massage."

She heard a voice, presumably the woman in the chair, announce, "Moe. You definitely want Moe."

Sharon told her that Moe, Maureen actually, was available for the next hour. Seeing the condition of who was presumably her last client, Debbie agreed. She was led to a small, dimly lit room. Soft jazz was playing at a barely audible level. It was equipped with a massage table in the center, a small table with an assortment of tubes and jars, and a dresser. There was a robe hanging on hook behind the door. Sharon told her to change into the robe and to put her things into the dresser drawer. "I'll let Moe know you're here. She'll be in shortly."

Debbie's stress level had dropped several levels since walking into the spa and several more since entering the room. As she had just finished putting on the robe, a woman walked in and introduced herself. "Hi, I'm Maureen. Mostly known as Moe."

Moe was wearing a pair of black yoga pants that complimented every curve of her calves, thighs, hips, and butt. She had the body of a person that the pants were meant for. Her black tee-shirt came within a few inches of the waist band and exposed a firm, flab-free stomach. There was a muscular definition to her arms. She had short, dark, spiked hair with blonde highlights and a friendly smile.

"Is there any part of your body that is sore, aching, needs special attention, or needs to be avoided?"

"Um, not really." Debbie could hardly get the words out, but it diverted her mind from her dilemma.

"Okay. Let's get started. Turn around so I can take off your robe, and then lie face down on the table." Moe looked her up and down and found her client quite attractive. Pretty decent body from the back, and a glance in the mirror showed her pretty face and a pair of delightful-looking boobs. She hung up the robe and grabbed a towel from the table. Moe then covered her rear end with the towel and said, "I'm doing that so I don't have be jealous of your gorgeous ass."

The joke relaxed Debbie, who could not believe she even responded, let alone say, "Yeah, right. As if you should be ashamed of yours."

Moe laughed and told her it was time to get to work. She poured some massage oil into her palms and started gently kneading her neck and shoulders. "Now, if I do anything that hurts or makes you uncomfortable, just speak up."

"You're doing great." Debbie was unwinding faster than she'd thought she would.

"Your neck muscles are as taut as violin strings. Is that from an injury or just everyday stress?"

"Stress, but not everyday stress. I'm in the midst of a divorce." Debbie continued on about her miserable life with Harry. There was nothing more attractive to Moe than a woman going through a divorce, and since Moe was not currently in a relationship, Debbie just might fit the bill. She passed the once-over test, just below "wow," and at an age where she wouldn't be too needy, but needy enough that Moe could take care of her. Moe liked the old-world standard where the men provided for the family, and she was just the woman to do that for her little lady. As she continued working on Debbie, her massage took on a more sensuous tone.

Playing to her captive audience, Moe said, "It must be just awful. Seriously, I would probably just kill the bastard."

"I dream about that all the time."

"Why dream about it? Just do it. Seriously. I'd bet most murders are unsolved. All you'd need is an alibi. You could always say you were at the spa when it happened."

"I wouldn't want to go to prison," Debbie lamented, even though she had committed two murders within the last few hours. This thought crystallized her thinking about going to the police. Here she was on a massage table, thinking not about contrition for her misdeeds or acting like the victim of a kidnapping. The awful truth was that Debbie discovered she could live with herself. Not to mention the fact that she was going to have an alibi. With that, much of her stress disappeared.

She assessed the situation. Her masseuse was attractive, compassionate, and cared about her. She had experimented with another woman, girl actually, in her youth, and perhaps the inexperience of both had dimmed their interest in any future encounters. Debbie said, "I can't believe you would do that. No one ever cared that much about me. But I am going to kill him, just with a lawyer who's going to take him for every dime he has. That will hurt him more than I ever could with a knife or a gun."

Moe's bravado subsided. She said, "Probably more torturous, and for much longer." By this time, she was rubbing her hands down Debbie's back, along her spine, exerting enough pressure to make her exhale a delightful sigh. "Not to change the subject, but for someone in their thirties, you have a terrific body."

Debbie was flattered. She told herself those days were behind her, but she did appreciate the compliment, especially from someone who was in really great shape.

As Moe worked her way down to her back, she asked Debbie for some feedback. "How am I doing?"

The words came out of Debbie's mouth as if she were in a hypnotic state: "Unbelievable. Probably the best massage I've ever had."

"Just what I wanted to hear. I want you to keep coming back."

Debbie was starting to regain some of her composure and said, "I'm sorry for my bitchy rant. Thanks for being so supportive."

"It's fine. I mean it. I think you're really special and would love to get a cup of coffee with you and just chat. Get to know you a little better. No strings."

With a giggle, Debbie said, "I'll bet you say that to all the girls."

"I don't. Seriously." Moe added, "I have a good feeling about you."

They both laughed. Moe said, "Maybe that didn't come out the way it was supposed to."

Moe brought the robe over and held it open for Debbie to put on. They hugged, and Moe asked for her number so that she could text Debbie hers. "And I'm serious about the coffee."

"I'll get in touch. There are a lot of things going on in my life right now, but I will get in touch."

They both laughed. This time Debbie said, "Maybe that didn't come out the way it was supposed to."

Moe busied herself straightening up the room while Debbie got dressed. Looking over her shoulder to make sure Moe was not watching her, Debbie slipped the pistol into her boot. She then got up, gave Moe a hug, and told her, "Thanks for making this a much better day." Debbie waved and blew a kiss as she walked out the door smiling from ear to ear. The massage was great, but securing an alibi witness was even better. *What the hell, what's wrong with meeting her for a coffee? I will give her a call.*

When she was out of hearing range, Moe mumbled, "No tip. Fuck her. Glad I gave her a bullshit phone number."

CHAPTER
29

CASEY CASSIDY HAD a light calendar the morning that her phone rang. The receptionist told her that there was an attorney named Guillermo Ramos representing Harry Rosen calling for her. The receptionist was a luxury in the age of automation, but Casey was willing to spend the extra money for the human interaction that left callers feeling warm and fuzzy.

Ramos always liked starting off with his given name when dealing with other lawyers. He thought they would underestimate him and consequently give him an edge. His modus operandi was to tune in and not broadcast. Ramos believed that Mark Twain was right when he said, "It's better to keep your mouth shut and appear stupid than to open it and remove all doubt."

Casey got on the line. "Good morning, this is Casey Cassidy."

"Good morning, Ms. Cassidy, my name is Guillermo Ramos, and I represent Harry Rosen. I believe you represent his wife."

"I do, Guillermo, but isn't this a little premature? We haven't served him yet."

"Yes, I know. This is really more of a courtesy call to let you know that Harry will be filing, and even though they are at each other's throats, there's no reason we can't be civil."

"That's very interesting, Mr. Ramos." Casey didn't think he was looking to start a legal battle, otherwise why telegraph his intention? No, this guy was as dumb as bag of rocks or looking to start a negotiation. Either way, he just gave her leverage. His opening, she decided, was a bluff to entice her into a less generous settlement.

She was going to call the bluff but wanted to hear him out. "I'm not sure what to make of that. Of course, you're aware of our ability to counterfile. During that time, and until we get to trial, we will get to exchange several Christmas cards. Is that what you had in mind?"

Ramos wanted to do this quick. He knew he wouldn't get a penny more from his client, so the thought of spending an extra minute, let alone years, had no interest to him. On the other hand, since his client was going to bitch about whatever the settlement was, why not take her first offer? Because he wasn't wired that way. She wanted a fight, and he was going to go toe-to-toe with her. Nobody pushed him around, ever.

"I'll email you my contact info so you know where to send those cards. I'm not much of a Hallmark guy. Send me one from the humor section." He added, "And by the way, my client wants his car back, pronto, and sixty percent of the market value of the apartment. He figures he's entitled to even more, since he made all of the payments on it, but I was able to bring him to a reasonable level. Wouldn't you agree?"

Casey loved this. *He's playing this exactly how I would,* she thought. *Make me believe he's a bumpkin that's going to reach for his wallet, pulling out a hammer instead. Banging it over my head.*

"Mr. Ramos, I've met your client, and in the interest of his health, my client is going to keep the car. He needs the exercise, and the walking will be good for him."

Even Ramos could not contain his laughter. "Be that as it may, I'm his lawyer, not his personal trainer."

"If anyone could use one, it's your client."

"What can I say? The guy is a real piece of work, but he does have a grievance. As does yours, I'm sure. We can break balls and issue empty threats, or we can get this done, earn our fees, and move on."

"Ramos, ordinarily I would break your balls, but I get the feeling we can work this out over a Scotch and a Cohiba."

"My grandfather used to hand-roll cigars back in Cuba." Surprised to hear that she smoked them, he followed with, "You enjoy a good cigar?"

"Only a good Cuban," she answered in a somewhat husky voice.

Ramos was caught off guard by the seductive double entendre. After a pause to refocus the conversation, he told her, "Reach out to your client to create a framework for a settlement. I like the way you conference."

"I'll get back to you. And please, call me Casey."

"And me, Bill. Adios, Casey."

"Adios, amigo."

After Casey hung up, she summoned Matt Bernstein to her office. "Find out all you can about the opposing counsel in the Rosen matter. His name is Guillermo Ramos. I want to carve him and his goddamn client up like a Thanksgiving turkey. Little prick thinks he's going to dictate terms to me. That'll be one cold fucking day in hell."

Matt had seen her this mad before and knew the best thing to do was to say, "Yes, ma'am. I'm on it." He race-walked out of her office.

CHAPTER
30

S ORRENTINO WON THE toss and chose to drive the outbound leg to
Staten Island. The westbound journey was about sixty miles and with
rush hour approaching might take anywhere from an hour to forever. As
the car approached the vicinity of JFK, he started to regret the decision.
"I can't believe this fucking traffic. If I had to commute to work in this
every day, I'd be a homicidal maniac. We've gone like a hundred yards in
the last five minutes."

"Sorry, partner. It's moving in the other direction. I just hope it keeps
up when we turn downwind. Speaking of homicidal maniacs, you think
either or both of these guys are good for the Gilgo Beach murders?"

"I don't know, but from what I hear there are plenty places to dump
bodies on Staten Island or just over the bridge in New Jersey. Why would
you put up with driving in this mess if you didn't have to? And last I
heard, sex workers weren't exclusive to Long Island."

"Both excellent points, Miguelito."

The traffic started moving again. They were now traveling at the break-
neck speed of twenty miles an hour. McGuire said, "Maybe Magilla
Gorilla and the Great Grape Ape were tied in to the Russian mob?
Enforcers?"

"Maybe, but this wasn't staged like an organized hit. The hitter alone
in the back waiting for them to make a move. Nah. Maybe they were
gonna hit the guy in the back, and surprise! Pop. Pop. Pop."

Mac swatted away that scenario. "Why doesn't our guy, who's sitting in
the back, move up and put a couple of slugs into the back of their heads?"
He offered his own rationale. "The second car. Magilla is driving the van,
the shooter is in the back, and the Great Grape Ape is driving the second
car."

Miguelito picked it up from there. "And the shooter waits for the van to stop because he's got to get both of them at pretty much the same time..."

From there Mac continued his partner's thoughts. "Because a gunshot scares off the second guy."

They looked at each briefly without speaking. This signified their agreement on the way the murders went down.

Miguelito picked it up. "So why do they want to grab the guy and put him away?" Then, in a singing voice that could only be described as terrible, "And so faraway, doesn't anybody..."

"Enough with the Carly Simon, and everyone else for that matter. I don't know what you did with the money your mother gave you for singing lessons, but I'd almost be willing to pay you not to sing. Please, please, for like the one thousandth time, if am within the sound of your voice, please don't sing."

Miguelito was irritated but not surprised. Despite the almost universal condemnation of his singing, he persisted. The world was wrong. "Sorry, partner. Was the hitter sitting in the back, or did he move to the back? Why a second car? Why not the three of them in one car?"

"Had to be a meeting. The two of them, going out there for whatever reason, got ambushed. And maybe there's the hitter and a getaway driver?"

"Hmm," Miguelito said. "Could be we have a hooker with a driver. Like some of the other murders, she gets in the van and things get out of hand, so to speak, in more ways than one."

"Ha! Good one. Problem with that is why do they come all the way out here? Like you said before, there's no shortage of hookers where they're from. No, this is a straight up drug deal or a hit gone bad. You still have their cell phones and photos of their driver's licenses, right?"

Miguelito answered, "Yup. They're in my jacket pocket. Just for fun, try using the date of birth or year they were born for the password. Maybe we'll get lucky and see who these guys like to talk or text with."

Reaching into the back seat to retrieve his partner's jacket, Mac said, "I'm going to call the shop and see if I can get someone to run the licenses and plates. My guess is these guys are on someone's radar."

He made the call and was on hold only briefly when the shocking news came back that these guys had never been arrested.

"That can't be right. Did you input the names correctly?"

The voice on the other end replied, "Here's what I put in: V-O-L-K-O-V, first name B-O-R-I-S." He then repeated the spelling for Igor Kilimchuk.

Except for a few parking tickets, the van was clean as well. Before he hung up, Sorrentino heard his partner say, "Humor me. See if any car thefts were reported in the vicinity of the crime scene." When the answer was negative, he disconnected. "Boost a car. Like it was 4th of July weekend and the lot was full. So our perp would have had a choice. Fucking ridiculous thought there, amigo."

Sorrentino cruised at the speed limit now. He shot him a quick glance and said, "Maybe there was another one of those kite surfers out there?"

"Good point, but our two victims lure the perp out there on whatever pretense and have the tables turned. It's the only thing that makes sense." Switching gears, Mac continued, "Let's see if these guys had any tech wizardry beyond four consecutive digits for a password."

"I'd be willing to bet on 0-0-0-0."

McGuire looked at the date of birth and tried that first. First the two digits for the month and the last two for the year. Nope. Then just the four digits for the year he was born. No dice.

"Those two goons weren't smart enough to complicate the passwords."

"How do you know that?" Mac asked.

"Because they were stupid enough to get knocked off by the guy they were going to hit."

"I hear you." He tried the other phone with the first combination of numbers that had failed on the other phone. "Bingo. Right numbers, wrong phone."

They were now nearing the Verrazano Bridge that would take them to Staten Island and to the home previously occupied by Boris and Igor. Sorrentino suddenly laughed and told his partner, "Quick. Check out the sign." On the side of the road, prior to the exit, a sign was posted that said, "Leaving Brooklyn. Fuhgeddaboutit."

"I thought the 'fuhgeddaboutit' crowd left a while ago, replaced by craft brewers and five dollar cups of coffee."

"And lots of beards."

McGuire scrolled quickly through the photos and found nothing meaningful. Same with the texts. He decided to work the phone log later.

It was nearly two hours since they'd left the crime scene. Miguelito could do it during the return trip.

They pulled into the empty driveway and double-checked the licenses and registrations taken from the deceased just to make sure. No need to incite anyone by entering the wrong house and having some hothead call the media about an abuse of power by the police.

Both detectives put on gloves before they left the car and walked to the door. They looked at each other and nodded. Sorrentino knocked while his partner stood off to the side, hand on his gun. No answer.

"You want to look under the doormat for a key?"

"A beer says you're wrong."

"It's a bet."

With that, Sorrentino lifted the mat. "Looks like I owe you a beer." He picked up the key and put it into the lock, knocked again, and announced loudly, "Police. Anybody home?" Still no answer. Turning the doorknob, he again yelled, "Police. Anybody home?"

Opening the door, they entered slowly, scanning the interior. "Let's make sure we're clear," said McGuire, his hand still on his holstered weapon. One went left, the other to the right. They opened all the doors and the closets before they relaxed and declared the premises unoccupied. McGuire removed his hand from his gun. They both clipped their badges to their shirts.

Sorrentino went into the kitchen. Nothing on the stove. There were two laptops on the table. His partner went into a bedroom on the left. Empty closet. Empty dresser. Down the hall and into a second bedroom. Much larger. Two dressers, both filled with clothes. Two closets, both organized. Sorrentino entered the room, asking, "Anything here?"

"Nada. How about any computers or laptops?"

"I saw two on the kitchen table and figured we could grab them on the way out."

"Only what I believe is a his and his bedroom."

"Not to be judgmental, but I think that clears them for the serial murders."

"Agreed. Not at all likely we have two gay guys from Staten Island killing hookers on Long Island."

Sorrentino said, "Yeah, but now we have to consider a lovers' triangle motive."

"Let's finish this before NYPD shows up and breaks our stones."

"Too late. We're already here," came a voice from the doorway.

"Jesus. Doesn't anybody knock? No manners," Sorrentino joked before introducing himself. "I'm Detective Sorrentino, that's my partner, Detective McGuire. We're Suffolk County PD. Homicide."

"You here because of the Jones Beach murders?"

"Yeah. We caught it." Not bothering to correct the geography.

"Looking for the perp or the vic?"

"The vics. Two of them. Both formerly of this address," McGuire said.

"You guys almost done here? I don't want to call this in and turn this into a clusterfuck for you."

"Thanks. I think we got it. Are we good?"

"Yeah. You're covered. You left before we got here. But if you do come back, bring a warrant."

With that, the four of them left. Sorrentino kept the key.

CHAPTER
31

G YM MEMBERSHIP HAD its advantages, but Harry's current living conditions were wearing on him. *Why should I have to live like this?* He decided that an apartment might be a better alternative. Vacancy rates were at an all-time low, and investors were scooping up those apartments and using them as short term rentals through Airbnb.

The idea was so brilliant, it stunned him. Harry grabbed his phone and dialed Tim, who picked up on the second ring.

"What's going on, Harry? Everything okay?"

"Couldn't be better. I'm getting a lot of interest in your property and wouldn't be surprised if we got a deal on it before it's even done. What do you figure, maybe another three months or so?"

"More like the 'or so.' I'm putting quite a bit more time into this than I thought I would. It's not as easy as it looks."

"Ever think about a tenant for the upstairs while you're working on the lower level?"

"Who'd want to rent an unfurnished place for such a short time?"

"To tell you the truth, I could use a place. I could be like a house sitter, you know, keep an eye on the place. Make sure no one steals the appliances or the copper pipes or something."

"Yeah, right. And I could get a little sign made up in the shape of a shield that says, 'Protected by Harry Rosen.' I'm sure even Seal Team Six wouldn't fuck with my property then."

"Listen to me. I had a client who used to travel on business a lot, so he asks me if I can watch the place and take care of his dog. He'll pay two hundred a day. Just make sure the place looks occupied and walk and feed the dog. I tell him no problem. Then he goes, by the way, you'll have to cook for the dog, but it's easy, just grill up a steak. I'll leave some in the fridge."

"What kind of dog was it?"

"How the hell do I know? It was one of those kinds of dogs that the only place you see them is on TV, when they broadcast one of those dog shows. It was a hairy little mutt."

"I doubt it was a mutt if the guy was feeding him steaks."

"Not what he ate the three days I was there. I ate the steaks. He got a can of Alpo."

Tim couldn't contain his laughter.

Harry continued, "But wait, the guy calls me after he gets back and tells me, 'I can't understand it, my dog won't eat steak anymore.'"

"So what did you tell him?"

"What did I tell him? I told him my cooking and romance have the same effect: she's ruined for everyone else."

Tim laughed uncontrollably. "I'm sorry, but the thought of you romantically entangled is one I'd wish never entered my mind."

"Laugh if you want, but if I ever made a sex tape with a woman and it got on the Internet, it would get thousands of hits."

"So do car wrecks."

Harry continued, "Anyway, I'd be willing to spend a few bucks on some furniture and toss you a grand a month while I'm there. After you finish the downstairs, I'll move there so you can work on the upstairs."

"I don't mind helping you out, and I like the thousand a month part, but not the 'while I'm there' part. You'd have no incentive to sell the place."

"Are you kidding? At two million, my end is two hundred large. I'm like a partner."

"Tell you what Harry, you can have it for sixty days. You furnish it however you want and move it out with you. Four thousand. Cash up front."

"Tim, you merciless son of a bitch, I'm going to take you up on that offer."

"Sixty days. And the clock starts when I get the cash."

Harry could not have been happier. There was nothing like a few bucks in the bank to make life a little better. He'd bought some time, and if he was right about Debbie's fate, may she rest in peace, he would be back in the apartment shortly. The best course of action was to appear as if he was taking a permanent step out of her life. A lease on a new apartment would show that. *Why would I sign a lease if I thought my wife would turn up dead? Who would move out of a rent-controlled apartment?*

Harry got off the couch, currently doubling as his bed, and sidled over and into the chair behind his desk. Opening the computer and staring at the home page, with its latest news headlines, drained the color from his face. "Holy shit. Holy fucking shit." He read past the headline and learned about the shooting deaths of the two Russians and how the killer was on the loose. *Could it be? What are the chances?*

His impulse was to call Debbie. *Under what pretense, though?* Bad idea. Did she have anything to do with it? *Impossible. She'd need a gun. No way she had a gun. If she did have one, she'd have killed me.* Harry's mind was racing, his pulse quickening. *My gun. What did I do with it?*

Years ago, crime had been rampant in the city, the kind that was almost as rare as the measles now: murder. Harry had bought a gun from a crack dealer. He gave the guy a hundred and asked if it included the bullets. The dealer pointed the gun at him and said, "Let's find out." Harry threw his arms in the air. The gun was lowered, and the dealer opened the cylinder, showing Harry the empty chambers. "You need bullets, you go to a sporting goods store. Now get the fuck out of here before I point a loaded one at you."

Carrying the gun had given Harry a sense of security. Over time, it found a home in a dresser drawer.

What if she had the gun? What if she did kill those guys? What if she comes after me? In full panic mode, Harry started tearing through the plastic garbage bags that contained his possessions. No luck. *Shit fuck.* Where the hell was it? Did he misplace it? Maybe it was somewhere in his office? And then the worst, most likely explanation: *Debbie found the gun.*

Trying to sort out his thoughts, he concluded that the fate of the two goons had to be a coincidence. These were two dangerous guys who'd met their match. No, Debbie didn't do this. He'd bet on it.

He turned his office inside out searching for the misplaced weapon.

Several hours of fruitless looking left him with the unsettling conclusion that he wasn't wrong. Debbie had the gun and the ammunition.

Maybe he should go to the cops? What would he tell them? That he hired a couple of hitmen to kill his wife? That she found the handgun that he illegally possessed and used it to kill the two guys?

He imagined a police interview: These guys thought I owed them money, and they threatened to hurt my family. *How much money did you owe them?* I didn't owe them anything. They thought I did. It's a long story. They reneged on a real estate purchase and the sellers owe them the money, but the two palookas were pressuring me to pay them. *Did you call the police?* No. I told them the property was once again in contract and scheduled to close, and they would get the money in a few days. *What do you mean by pressuring you, Harry?* Like I said, they threatened my family. *Harry, if they threatened my family, I'd have called the police. And I own a gun. And know how to use it. Do you own a gun, Harry?* I do or I used to. I couldn't tell you where it is. *Why is that, Harry?* I haven't seen it in years. It used to be on a shelf in my bedroom closet, but my wife threw me out with my clothes dumped into a few garbage bags. *Where were you yesterday?* I was at a closing. In fact, on the same property those two reneged on. So stupid. They would have made a barrel of money. By the way, I come across some great deals if either of you are ever interested.

In his imaginary conversation, Harry pushed his wife into the role of suspect. Let her deal with the fallout.

Harry was convinced nothing would tie him to the murders. He had to find out if the goons got to Debbie before whoever it was got to them. The idea struck him like a brick to the side of his head. Just walk over to the garage on the pretense of wanting the car and then ask a few questions. The guys that worked there would answer all his questions for a ten-dollar bill, which was about ten more than he ever tipped them. Ever. Even around the holidays, when most of the monthly renters would fork over twenty or a fifty, Harry was good for a handshake and a "Feliz Navidad."

When he arrived, he greeted them with a hearty "Hola, amigos!"

Their muted response prompted Harry to speak up. "I'd like my car."

One of the workers answered in unaccented English, "Mrs. Rosen told us that we were not to release the car to you."

"I pay for the garage space, and I pay for the car, and I want it now."

"Unless I hear from Mrs. Rosen, I can't do that."

Harry was going to get exactly what he wanted. "Then get her on the phone. I want to hear it from her."

The attendant walked to the small enclosure that served as an office to find her number and make the call. Harry looked through the window into the office. Unable to hear them, he did see the man nodding and attempting to put the phone down several times. *Yeah, that's her on the phone,* Harry thought.

After finally disconnecting, Harry heard the bad news and the worse news. She wasn't giving up the car, and that meant she was still alive.

CHAPTER
32

AFTER SHE HUNG up on the guy from the garage, Debbie started to realistically assess her options. The first was to go to the police, but a long time ago her father told her, "Even if you stab someone and the bloody knife is in your hand, deny it."

She could tell the truth and even add a story about a sexual assault. The risk was that it might not matter except to get her a reduced sentence, and if the jury didn't buy into it, she might end up with a lengthy sentence.

Another option was to do nothing. Why would the police suspect her? She remembered the bastards that did this saying how Harry owed them money. Was it possible Harry had nothing to do with it and that they thought kidnapping her was a way to get whatever it was he owed them? Maybe they were debt collectors looking for Harry to make good on gambling losses? It gave her a momentary pause. *No way in hell. He was in on this.*

If he was in on it, Harry could easily deny it by claiming to the police that unless he paid up, they would kill her. And if he went to the cops, they'd kill her. Harry could claim that he was trying to raise the money to free her.

Why would anyone believe that? I started a divorce, for Christ's sake. Debbie started to think she would have the upper hand. She was going to the police. Her story was that she killed two men, went shopping, and stopped for a massage. Then called the police.

Even if she omitted the last few details, it wasn't likely the cops were going to say "thanks for coming forward." No, she'd likely be arrested. If she did turn herself in, she should go with a lawyer. Casey would know how to handle this. Debbie would call her.

"Ms. Cassidy's office, may I help you?"

"This is Debbie Rosen. It's urgent that I speak to Casey."

"One moment, Mrs. Rosen." Casey told her assistant to give the call to Matt.

"Hi, Debbie, this is Matt. What's going on?"

"Matt. I don't think I'm in trouble, but I might be."

"Why is that?"

"Have you heard the news about what happened on Long Island?"

"No, I haven't, give me a minute." Matt clicked his mouse to view the headline news on his computer and said, "Jesus. Don't say another word. Get over here immediately, and when you get here make sure you start your conversation with the word 'hypothetically.' Got it?"

Matt hung up and ran to Casey's office, knocked, but didn't bother to wait for his boss to say "come in." He pushed the door open and announced, "Debbie Rosen is going to be here in little while, and you're going to need to put on your criminal law hat."

"What do you mean?"

"I mean, hypothetically she may have committed a double homicide."

"You're joking. Please tell me you're joking."

"Ma'am, I am serious as a tequila hangover."

"Ouch."

The ten minutes that it took Debbie to arrive were excruciatingly long. The receptionist had been told to immediately notify Casey when she arrived. When the phone on Casey's desk finally rang, she picked it up and said, "Bring her into the boardroom immediately." Casey then dialed Matt and ordered him into the boardroom and punctuated it with "now."

Both Matt and Casey were in a conference room that contained an enormous table surrounded by sixteen chairs. There was a silver tray on the table, upon which were several bottles of water. The two lawyers were seated next to each other facing the door when Debbie was escorted in by the receptionist.

Casey walked around the table, gave Debbie a hug, and spoke first. "Good to see you again. Matt told me you were coming in, and I wanted to make sure I'd see you."

Matt did not wait for Debbie to speak. "Debbie is here to discuss her divorce and also had some hypothetical situations she wanted to ask about."

Casey pulled a chair away from the table and asked her to have seat.

"Would you care for some water? We have a coffee bar or other assorted beverages if you prefer."

Debbie thought it best to act natural. "A cappuccino would be wonderful. Thanks."

Matt picked up the phone, tapped a few digits, and placed Debbie's request. "It'll be here shortly," he said as he hung up. "We received a call from Mr. Rosen's attorney. He wanted to negotiate a settlement before your husband had been served."

Casey took it from there. "To me that's a sign that they know they have a weak hand. I have every intention to get you everything you deserve."

Debbie blurted out, "What if he's trying to kill me?"

"Harry? Is he trying to kill you? What makes you say that?" Casey countered.

A knock on the door preceded the cart that brought in Debbie's coffee order. Her cappuccino was served, and the cart disappeared quickly and quietly.

"This is all hypothetical, correct? I did hear you say 'if.' Am I right?" Matt wanted to make sure there was nothing that would obligate him to report a crime, as was his duty as an officer of the court.

Casey said, "If Harry committed or attempted to commit such a crime, then we would report it to the police, who would investigate, and if proven to have probable cause, they would arrest Harry."

"What would happen after that?" Debbie said.

Matt responded, "After the arrest, he would be brought in front of a judge for arraignment. The judge would determine if Harry would remain in jail or get released on bail."

"This sounds like every *Law and Order* episode I've seen."

"It's not much different," Matt said.

"So he could get out on bail?"

"If he or his lawyer made arrangements for a bail bondsman in advance, he'd likely be out in a matter of hours."

"How much would that cost? The bail, I mean."

"It's ten percent of whatever the judge decides."

"So how much would that be?"

"I'd only be guessing, but attempted murder would definitely be at least six figures."

"What if he did murder me? And a friend that was with me?" She was projecting onto Harry her own double murder.

Casey, who had become silent as Matt fielded Debbie's questions, spoke up. "Do not say another word. Please enjoy your coffee for a moment while Matt and I excuse ourselves."

Casey and Matt got up and left the room. They walked a few paces down a hallway lined with offices and found one that was empty.

"No notes," Casey said.

"No notes," Matt said.

"We are totally off the record. Understood?"

"Yes ma'am. Totally."

"Holy fucking shit. She did it." Casey had only experienced a few moments in her life where she'd been shaken. This was one of them. With a few deep, cleansing breaths to regain her composure, she told Matt, "I got this. Let's get back inside."

They went back into the conference room. "I'm sorry if we kept you waiting. Matt and I determined what the likely effect may be if Harry were to have done anything like you imagined. First, he would need enough money to post bail, most likely in the fifty to one hundred thousand dollar range. Then there is the cost of a criminal legal defense. I can't speak for other firms, but here it would cost at least another hundred thousand, and possibly more with a lengthy trial. Beyond that, expect news reporters and TV cameras will stake out your, I mean Harry's apartment building and follow his every move."

Debbie was bowled over. *Where would I get all that money? I was just protecting myself. Why should I have to endure all of that? This is totally unfair.*

Casey continued, "This will help our divorce case if Harry were convicted and jailed. You might end up with everything he doesn't spend on his legal defense." She kept up the projection of guilt on Harry. "Do you understand everything I am saying?" She wanted to confirm that Debbie knew who the real subject of this conversation was.

Debbie only nodded.

Matt piped in, "It wouldn't be all doom and gloom for Harry. Many times, there are movie and book deals made after a headline-grabbing crime."

Casey did all she could to contain herself. Matt was going to close this deal. From a small divorce case, there would be a murder trial with publicity galore. The attendant fees the firm would generate from the criminal work and the book deals, the TV and movie rights. *Maybe I could get Netflix and Amazon in a bidding war for this?*

Debbie didn't take the bait, but she did nibble. "You really think there would be a movie? With Harry in it?"

Matt answered, "There's no assurance of anything, but people still remember O.J. Simpson."

"How much do you think he'd get for the movie rights? We would be able to get some of that in our divorce, right?"

"It's like I said, there's no assurance of anything, but I would be surprised if it was less than half a million." The fish was circling the bait, so Matt threw some chum in the water.

Chum is ground-up fish. It's oily and smelly and attracts fish, but if it gets on you, every cat in the neighborhood will follow you. It was what cable news did to their audience. Keep throwing chum out over the airwaves until the viewers stank enough to repel all who weren't covered in the same oily slime.

Casey admired the way Matt was working this. Her law firm consisted of finders, minders, and grinders. The finders brought in the clients, the minders took care of the relationship with the clients, and the grinders were at the bottom of the totem pole, the ones who did the legal work. Matt just climbed up a notch. Winning cases was one thing, but generating fees was the name of the game at the Cassidy Law Firm.

Debbie was starting to weigh her options. She did the easy math. *Let's say I get $500,000 for the movie rights, and it costs $200,000 for the defense. I would make $300,000. What about the divorce? What would Harry get? If he ended up with everything, the whole thing would be worthless.* Debbie would rather not get a penny out of this if Harry got anything. Besides, she could up in jail. Unless she could put it on Harry. *Does he have an alibi? Did he hire those guys? Were they working on their own, trying to get the money they said Harry owed them?* There were enough loose ends that Debbie didn't see any upside to turning herself in, at least not right now.

"So what would your strategy be with Harry's divorce lawyer?"

Casey took the question. "I think we should always play hardball. I believe in the old theory of negotiating that the first person to speak loses. They spoke first, so we are not going to settle unless it's on our terms.

We will keep looking for any undisclosed assets Harry may have. We will search corporate records, bank records, and property records. If he owns anything more valuable than a pair of underwear, we will find it. And he'll be lucky if we let him keep that." Casey was going full throttle to reassure Debbie that she was on her side, even if it didn't yet entail a criminal matter,. "By the way, were you aware that Harry owned the building his office is in? And that you are on the deed as a co-owner?"

"It's been so long, I'd forgotten about that."

"You're going to have several million fond memories of that building when this is over."

Debbie smiled. She walked in as an indecisive, trembling wreck, and was going to walk out a multimillionaire. "One question, if you don't mind. How long will it take to get the money?" Debbie was cut off from her, Harry's actually, credit cards, and her bank balance wasn't going to last very long.

"There's no easy answer to that. First, I have to negotiate with his lawyer, and then his lawyer is going to have to convince Harry, who is not going to be easily persuaded. Can you imagine Harry saying, 'Okay, here's two million dollars. Sorry I forgot about this.' Then, assuming he doesn't have that kind of cash, Harry will have to mortgage the property to raise the money, which will take a few months. I expect it will take at least six months until we can wrap this up."

"That long? To be honest, I'm not sure I have enough money to keep going for six months." She had enough money to last six weeks, provided she didn't eat anything for five of them.

"Keep in mind Harry may not be able to get a mortgage and may have to sell the property, which could take even longer."

Debbie was now completely out of her euphoric state. Casey saw that and decided to throw more chum in the water. "Another option would be for you to hold a mortgage on the property for the amount he owes you, collect monthly payments at an above-market interest rate, and when and if he misses a payment and is in default, you could foreclose. You'd get the building, and Harry walks away with just the lint in his pockets."

That was just the thing Debbie needed to hear. *Hello, Boca Raton. Maybe I'll get a place on the ocean? I wouldn't even have to schvitz in the summer. I could get a summer rental in the Hamptons.*

She looked up at her lawyers and said, "Such good news. I can't get enough of it. Maybe I'll call my landlord and tell him I'm ready to give up the apartment."

"Under the right circumstances, you mean," Matt corrected her.

"In our preparation for settlement talks, Matt has done some market research as to the value of your lease to the owner of the building. Would you like us to represent you in that matter as well?" Casey offered.

Debbie was glad they were on her side. If they could do to the landlord what they were going to do to Harry, maybe she could buy instead of rent for the summer. "Sure, that would be great."

The two lawyers stood up. Matt reached out to shake Debbie's hand. Casey walked around the table to give Debbie, who was all smiles, a hug. *Why couldn't Matt be the one to give me a hug? It wasn't like I was going to stick my tongue in his ear. But then again, maybe I would have.* "I can't thank you enough."

"Matt will call to arrange an interior inspection of the apartment. We will need that for our negotiations."

"The sooner, the better." *Oh, he's going to get an interior inspection all right.* "I'm ready to move on with my life."

CHAPTER
33

DETECTIVE McGUIRE WAS behind the wheel for the ride back to Long Island. His partner asked if they were still being followed by the city cops that interrupted their search. Sorrentino answered, "Nah. They dropped off after a few blocks."

"You're sure?"

Sorrentino checked the mirrors then turned his head around to check the blind spots as well. "Nothing in sight."

"Good. Let's go." McGuire made a right turn. No one followed. He made another turn a few blocks later. Again, no one was behind them. Another right turn and they were headed back to the former residence of Volkov and his partner, Kilimchuk.

He glanced at the other detective, and before he could say a word, he heard Sorrentino say, "Yes, I do have the key."

"I'll sit in the car. You go inside and grab the laptops."

"Call my phone if anyone shows up so I can get out the back door."

"I'm sure as shit not going to call 911."

They pulled into the driveway, and as soon as the car came to a complete stop, Sorrentino hopped out and was at the front door with the key in the lock in seconds. Daylight savings time worked in their favor. Even though it was barely into happy hour, a dark, cloudy sky helped hide the detective from view. In less than two minutes, Sorrentino was in the car with two laptops and on the way home.

"Nice work, partner. You put the key back?"

"Nah. Who's gonna look for it?"

The traffic getting to the Verrazano Bridge, which would take them off Staten Island, was bumper-to-bumper. Neither detective had had anything to eat since breakfast. The events of the day had distracted them from their regular routine, which included lunch and an afternoon cappuccino. Homicide investigations were stressful but nothing like rush-hour traffic in New York City.

McGuire asked, "You hungry? I know where we can get some good pizza in Brooklyn right over the bridge." It was either hunger or stress that was causing a spike in his appetite, and it didn't matter which. He was going to stop anyway and knew his partner would not object.

"Better than sitting in traffic. Let's do it."

The two of them ended up at a pizza joint in Bay Ridge on a busy street with tables on a concrete patio surrounded by a chain-link fence. There was a walk-up window to place orders and pick up your food, provided your food was pizza. It gave off the impression of what a cafeteria at a minimum-security prison might be like. "The food must be pretty damn good. Look at this line."

"Not food: pizza. That's the only thing you want to order. Unless you want spumoni. But we're gonna have the pizza, and only the Sicilian slices. There are none better anywhere."

"It's that good, huh?"

"I'll give you a money-back guarantee."

The two cops from Long Island waited their turn on line. Each had the same order: two slices of Sicilian pizza and a canned soda. They found a table and went to work on their dinners. After several bites and an uncharacteristic silence, Sorrentino said, "I am seriously pissed at you."

"Why? You don't like the pizza?"

"All the time we've been partners, and you never told me about this. I didn't think we had any secrets. You talk about intimacy issues with your wife but keep this to yourself. You selfish bastard, this is the best thing I ever put in my mouth."

Back in the car, it was time to get back to work. Sorrentino gained access to the victims' phones and checked the photos. There was nothing interesting to him or important to the case. No porn or violent scenes. Nothing with guns or other weapons. Only the typical stuff that other people would show you — food they were going to eat and places they'd been. Things people would show you all the time and you'd say, "Oh, wow. That's amazing," when what you really meant was "bor-ing."

He pressed the message icon, hoping that the texts were in a language he understood, which was exclusively English except for a bit of Spanish that he just picked up along the way. Good news and bad news. The texts were in English, but nothing that gave him an indication of who they were or what made them tick. The incoming texts were mostly of a business nature. *When can you start this job? How long will it take you to finish? I need an estimate. When can you come by?*

He shared this with McGuire. "I make the vics for construction guys, based on some texts."

"We should check with whoever it is that issues licenses. See what they know."

"Yeah, maybe the Better Business Bureau too."

"Ha. You'd need a big set to confront those guys to their face."

"Well, someone did."

Sorrentino snorted as he continued searching the cell phone. He tapped the phone icon, and then the one for recent calls. *This has to be the motherlode,* he thought. "No phone calls the morning of," he told his partner. "I will give him credit for organization. There's a name for every call, which means he has them all in a contact list."

"Gonna call them? Starting with the most recent? That'll be a fucking riot. Someone's phone is gonna ring, and if they saw the news, they'll shit a brick wondering if they're getting a call from the boneyard. Make sure you put it on speakerphone. I gotta hear that."

Sorrentino loved the idea and couldn't wait. Why bother calling from his phone when a call from the dead might do? He clicked on the first name in the call log and introduced himself. "This is Detective Sorrentino from the homicide division of the Suffolk County Police Department. We're investigating the murders of Boris Volkov and Igor Kilimchuk. You're on a speakerphone with my partner Detective McGuire as well."

"Hi. This is Detective McGuire. You'll excuse me if you hear any cursing. I'm driving in rush-hour traffic, so it wouldn't be directed at you." He wanted to take the edge off. Maybe loosen them up a little so they dropped their guard, if they were playing defense. A few minutes with the first caller told them what they already knew. The victims were construction workers that took work as subcontractors from larger companies and did smaller jobs on bigger projects.

After making six calls and hearing similar stories, they concluded one thing: a piece was missing. Why would a couple of contractors get popped? The seventh call gave them a little more. That caller told the cops how the pair were "very intimidating" and many landlords, "Not me, of course, I only used them for construction work, but others would hire them with problem tenants. You know, to collect rents or get them to vacate a rent-controlled apartment."

Sorrentino and McGuire looked at each other after the call disconnected. McGuire spoke first. "Sounds like a motive. They're leg-breakers and tried to intimidate the wrong guy."

His partner offered, "Okay, so someone is behind in their rent. Why do they bring him out on Oak Beach? Why not flex some muscle right in his face? Why a second car? What are they going to tell the guy, 'Take your car and follow us out to Long Island, we have a surprise for you'? Sorry, Miguelito, I am not buying that."

"How about this: a landlord lives out there and owns a property in the city, they do some work for the landlord, and on payday they meet him out there to collect."

McGuire finished the story. "And there's a dispute over the payment, or nonpayment, and the landlord or whoever the hell it was comes locked and loaded."

"I like that. They meet, and he shorts them on the payment, they throw him in the back of the van to take him for a ride, and things go sideways."

"We got a possible 'why.' We need a definite 'who.'"

Sorrentino dialed another recent caller from the phone log. "Hello, is this Mr. Harry Rosen?"

"That's me. If you're trying to sell me solar panels or something else, I already got it or don't want it. Anything else?"

Sorrentino, who had pushed the speakerphone button before dialing, cracked up laughing, as did McGuire, who said, "I'm sorry to bother you, Mr. Rosen," and then introduced himself, adding, "We're investigating a double homicide and want to know what you can tell us about Volkov and Kilimchuk?"

Harry held the phone at arm's length away from his body and took a deep breath before he answered. He was as nervous as a teenager going on a first date.

"What can I tell you?" he repeated before saying, "I can tell you they're dead, but you know that, along with anybody else who has a TV, radio, newspaper, or Internet connection. I can also tell you it will be easier to find the killer than anyone would mourn them."

"Bad guys, huh?"

"Bad guys? These guys were like fingernails scratching a blackboard. Good riddance."

"Why do you say that, Harry? I hope you don't mind if I call you Harry?"

"Mind? Why would I mind? That's my name. I say that because they reneged on a purchase where they could have pocketed about half a million."

Sorrentino took over from there. "And probably cost you a few bucks too."

"Cost me a few bucks? No, I lined up another buyer almost immediately, and without another broker, so I didn't have to split the commission. Very profitable for me, and I got the listing to resell the property too. You guys ever want to get in the game, I'm sure I can find you something." Maybe he could push the conversation in a different direction.

No dice with that. "Our job is to find out who committed these murders, not to buy and sell real estate." Sorrentino pressed him. "Why did they walk away from such a big payday?"

"Walk away? Because they got greedy and tried to renegotiate a lower price, and the sellers had principles, which is something you rarely see in this racket."

"What do you mean tried to renegotiate?"

"Tried to renegotiate? They told the sellers they weren't going to pay the contract price and threatened them if they didn't accept the offer."

The two cops became keenly interested in Harry's story at this point and wished they were in the same room with him, but this was starting to go somewhere. McGuire nodded. It was a signal to Sorrentino to keep going. "How did they threaten them?"

Harry then figured, brilliantly by his estimation, how to get the bloodhounds off the scent. "They said something like bad things could happen to the property, and then one of the sellers, it was an estate sale so there were five heirs, was a cop and pulls out a gun and tells him in effect if there was any trouble he'd come after them."

This was like an earthquake to the detectives, and as Harry thought, they were going to buy it.

McGuire couldn't contain himself. "Are you telling me that a cop drew his weapon at the closing? Are you sure he was a cop? Where did he work? What's his name?"

Harry, a bit more confident, answered, "He did pull out a gun, and he was cop. A big deal inspector or something in the NYPD named Ramirez."

"I need you to stand by for a moment." Sorrentino pressed the mute button and saw the amazed look on his partner's face. Making sure that the technology behind the mute button was working, he yelled, "Harry, are you there?" When there was only silence for a few moments, he looked at his partner and asked, "Well, what do you think?"

"No way."

"He would have had a motive."

"No way in hell."

"And a weapon and the expertise."

"No fucking way in hell. I want no part in looking at any cop in the NYPD, let alone an inspector. I can't believe I'm saying this, but I'd rather let this go cold case than bring that guy in. There is no upside. Guilty, you're a rat. Not guilty, you're a stone-cold loser. You gotta retire or wear a uniform at a school crossing after that."

"If he's guilty, I want to bring him in. Let's do a little digging around the edges. I'll run with it if you want to get the flu for a week or so."

It was like a marital spat that was going to end with no one happy at the end.

"You fucking prick. I can't believe you want to go down that path."

"I have to see where this takes us."

"You know where it's going to take us. Early retirement to a double wide in Lake Okeechobee. Motherfucking prick bastard. Get him back on the phone."

Sorrentino pressed the mute button once again and asked, "Harry, still there?"

"I'm here."

"When and where was this closing? I want the names of everyone else who was there."

"Hold on. I got some business cards from the lawyers. I always pick up a business card. You never know when you might end up with a deal. Maybe you get a referral. You never know."

"I've got an uncle that collects stamps. I'm not interested in your business card collection. I want the name of that lawyer that was in that room when you saw the weapon and heard the threat."

Ordinarily, Harry would have been shaken to his core, but he was happily sorting through the stack of cards piled on his desk. His filing system was simple: the most recent ones went on top, which brought him to the card he was searching for in seconds. *Fancy and Schmancy. Here it is.* Harry read the information from the card to the detectives.

"One last thing: where were you on Wednesday morning, the day of the murder?"

"I was at a closing. You can call the same lawyers."

"Quite a coincidence that it was the same lawyer, isn't it Harry?"

"No, it's not. It was the same property." He regretted saying that as soon as the words left his lips. This was not going to misdirect the investigators.

"Were all the same people there? Including the inspector you earlier referred to?"

"Yes. Definitely." Harry knew better than to try to cover up his miscue with a lie.

Somewhat dejectedly, Sorrentino wrapped up the call. "Thank you for answering our questions. We may call again for some follow-up."

"Sure, any time, and remember, if you're ever interested in making a real estate investment, give me a call."

McGuire was smiling like he just won the lottery. There was a dead silence in the car until he broke the ice. "Well, Miguelito, at least I don't have to go shopping for a double-wide."

"Very funny, asshole."

CHAPTER
34

TIM WAS LOOKING over the work in progress at his new venture when Harry knocked on the door. Tim didn't answer, and Harry didn't wait. He walked in.

"Hiya, Tim. Is this almost ready for me to show? I've got some buyers lined up," Harry lied.

"It will all fall into place soon. You'll be the first to know."

Harry handed Tim an envelope stuffed with hundred-dollar bills. "Here you go. Four thousand, cash. I'll be moving in enough things so that I can sleep here tonight."

"Just remember, sixty days. That's it. Whatever you bring in goes with you or out to the curb."

"Hey, no problem, but do you mind if unpack the stuff before I move out? Or maybe I should leave it packed so it's easier for me to move out."

"How come everything with you is no problem? You're like Lou Gehrig. The luckiest man on the face of the earth."

"I don't have any problems? Between my wife, her attorney, who happens to be your wife, and my attorney, who thinks I don't know that he's going to be a money pit, worrying about packing up a rental in two months is nothing. I should have Lou Gehrig's problems."

"Are sure about that? He died at thirty-seven of ALS, a horrible muscular disease. Named it after him."

"On top of that, that the cops called me yesterday."

"About?"

"Remember I told you about the two guys who walked away from the deal on this house? They were murdered."

"Why are they interested in you?"

"They were interested in them. My number was in one of their phones, so they called me like I had some inside information that was going to help them solve the case. Like I could be a suspect. Could you imagine me trying to take on those guys? I think someone would literally have to pull my head out of my ass."

"I book your action, and I have to say that sometimes the way you bet, I think it's already there."

"A real comedian. One day I may clean you out. We'll see how funny you are."

"Harry, I hope to see that day, and also hope that it's very far in the future. It's in my interests to see you stay alive until we both see that day. Maybe you should join a gym. Lose some weight."

"I already belong to a gym."

"Do you ever go?"

"Every day, Tim. Every day."

"Here's the key to the apartment upstairs. Sixty days, Harry. No stories. Start looking for another place."

Harry walked up a flight of stairs to get into his new living quarters. As always, after a trip up any flight of steps, it took him a few minutes to catch his breath. He started to think Tim had a point. *Maybe I should get some exercise.* It was then that Harry made a life-changing decision: he was going to buy a pair of sneakers.

He sat on the steps waiting for his furniture delivery, which was already an hour late. His life was a hot, stinking mess, but maybe changing for the better. He'd be rid of Debbie, and without violence. He was somewhat regretful that he tried to have her killed in the first place. Maybe it was the phone call from the cops that shook him up. If Debbie was alive and the two Russians were dead, then no one would know about his deal. Harry was probably better off the way it worked out, otherwise they might have blackmailed him forever.

The divorce was going to cost him a place to live, but that was the worst of it. It wasn't like he had a bank account or any savings to speak of, so all in all, he figured this would cost him the difference between what he currently paid in rent and what he was going to have to pay, which was going to be — *ouch!* The Benz was leased with less than a year left on the contract. *Let her have it. It'll be worth paying just to watch Mercedes try to take it back from her.*

Emotionally and financially, Harry came to the conclusion that he was better off without Debbie, regardless of how that came about.

When the delivery truck arrived, Harry walked in with the driver and showed him where the bed should go. It was the only piece of furniture he'd bought. Mattress, box spring, frame. Less than thirty minutes later, Harry had something to sleep on. When UPS arrived later, he would also have sheets, pillowcases, and pillows. At least that was what the email message said about the delivery status. A bar of soap, shampoo, and a towel would complete the necessities for his immediate use. Since he had these things in his gym locker, there was no purchase necessary.

He walked through the rest of the apartment. *Three bedrooms? What do I need three bedrooms for?* He thought about all the money he'd just paid for this. It was a waste of space, unless he could sublet the other two bedrooms. If Tim found out, he'd be out in no time.

Harry would not want to let an opportunity to make a few bucks pass him by. It came to him in a flash. Why not cater to his passion? A craps table. He became animated with thought and in his mind got as far as stocking a bar. Reality set in with a thud. Too many chances for Tim to discover the scheme. There would be no way to explain a craps table if Tim walked upstairs and in the door. That would really land Harry at the curb.

On the way to the gym, after an intermediate stop to buy sneakers and a pair of sweatpants, Harry looked skyward, as if for divine intervention, and smiled. The idea was brilliant. It met Harry's main criteria of very little investment and would likely meet Tim's approval, and maybe even his participation. Life without Debbie was becoming better already.

There was a row of treadmills facing the front window. Harry checked in at the front desk and surprised the receptionist when he walked to the treadmills instead of going directly to the locker room, as had been a daily habit since he joined.

Getting started was not as easy as Harry thought. There were sets of arrows, indicators, and readouts. Not to mention a video screen with various controls. There was a woman wiping down the machine next to Harry, He interrupted. "Excuse me, are you an astronaut?"

"No, why would you ask that?"

"I thought you'd have to be to operate one of these."

"Can I ask you a question?"

"Sure," Harry answered. "Go ahead."

"Are you a moron? Or just illiterate?"

Harry was taken aback. "Why would you ask me that?"

The woman answered, "Because the instructions are posted under the section that says 'instructions.'"

For the first time in his life, Harry found himself opposite someone as obnoxious as himself.

"Who can read that? The print is so small. I can't squint that hard, and I haven't joined AARP yet, so I don't have the free magnifier you get for joining."

"All right. Pay attention. First power on the TV. Let me guess, you want ESPN, right?"

"Unless there's another station that doesn't talk about politics, real estate, or food."

"There are no stations like that, but I'm surprised to hear you say you don't have any interest in the food channels."

"Very funny. I happen to have an eating disorder."

"Yes, I can tell. Order dis, order dat. Okay, so you select the TV station here. Now input your age."

Harry shaved ten years off and entered forty-one.

"That's incredible, because you don't look a day over seventy. Now, your weight?"

Harry hesitated before blurting out, "Two-ten."

She looked at him, tilted her head downward to take in the enormity of Harry, and then looked him straight in the eye and pointed her index fingers at her boobs and said, "Right, and these are thirty-eight double D's."

Harry could not contain his laughter. "Are you sure you're not confusing those tits with a college transcript? Sound like your grades."

"Touché. Seriously, I used to have a weight issue too. I learned that for me, food was a substitute for love. The more I ate, the less attractive I became, which drove me to eat more. Chocolate ice cream is not judgmental, so it became my constant loving companion to the exclusion of men."

Harry paused for few moments, trying to interpret his own thoughts. Here was a woman who he'd never met and with no interest in anything other than to help him. In his world, everyone was either a sharpshooter or a sucker. People were not like this, especially not his wife, ever, so he was quite confused.

"Nice of you to offer all of this help, although I could use less of the editorial comments. I'm Harry, Harry Rosen," he said as he held out his hand to shake hers.

She wiped her hand on the towel that was hanging around her neck, grabbed his outstretched hand, and introduced herself. "I'm Susan, Susan Stone. I'm a personal trainer here. This is my passion. My past experience is what drives me to encourage others to lose weight and maintain a workout regimen so they become and stay fit." She then added, "In my other world, and in order to pay the bills, I'm a real estate broker, so if you ever want to put a few bucks into real estate, I've got some terrific deals I'm working on."

Harry's head nearly exploded. "You've got to be kidding. It's a joke, right?"

"Well, you got me there. My real name is Susan Stein. It used to be you could give someone a fake phone number to get rid of them. Now you get Googled."

"Not that part. The real estate part. I'm a broker myself."

"No kidding. Where?"

Harry immediately went into full-on hustle mode. He told her about his office that really wasn't on the Upper East Side and continued the charade by telling her how he worked by himself and catered to wealthy investors. "You know, I happen to have an exclusive on a property that I am not going to put on MLS for a while. If you found a buyer for this, I'd work you in for 2.5 percent."

Susan was slightly taller than Harry and half his weight at a svelte 130 pounds. She had shoulder-length blonde hair tied into a ponytail that stuck out through the back of a blue baseball cap with the logo of the New York Giants on the front. Susan was curvy and pretty. She was also every bit as smart as she was attractive. "So, Harry, tell me about the property and why I should work with you."

Harry told her of all the grandeur of the property and the enormous potential of the rent roll. He continued on about the gentrification possibility of the neighborhood and how banks were bending over backward to lend money, so almost anybody with decent credit and even a small down payment could land this great deal. Harry concluded with, "And the reason you want to work with me is that this is going to go for a million eight, and at 2.5 percent that means forty-five thousand for you."

Not one to be bashful, Susan told Harry, "Even though I majored in in English Lit at Colgate, I know that 3 percent would come to 54 thousand. And by the way, on my college transcript it's all A's and B's." Then, pointing to her chest, "And these girls are C's."

"You should come by and take a look. I can do 3 percent for you." Considering his fee from Tim was an enormous 10 percent, he would still net some big money.

"Give me a card. I'll call. Meanwhile, let's get you going on this treadmill. I'm going to sign you up for twelve sessions, that's three times a week for the next four weeks. Plan to be here Monday, Wednesday, and Friday. Call ahead for times. It's going to run you fifteen hundred. The appointments with me will be for an hour. I also expect you to come the days we are not training."

"You're kidding. That much?"

"That much? It's a cheap price to pay, Harry. You're going to spend a lot more on a new wardrobe in six months after we get about fifty pounds off you. The next fifty will take another year after that."

The gym was lined with mirrors that served two purposes, firstly as positive reinforcement for those that were diligent, successful, and proud of their accomplishments in toning their bodies, and secondly, to play on the insecurities of the others.

Harry looked into one of the impossible-to-avoid mirrors and for the first time in his adult life did not delude himself. He told Susan Stein or Stone or whatever her name really was that he'd be there on Monday for his first session.

"We're going to get started on the treadmill today. After you leave here, you're going to make one small change to your diet. No more potatoes."

"No more potatoes, easy enough."

Susan showed Harry how to set the distance to half a mile, with an easy pace, and told Harry not to get off until the treadmill stopped. "When you come tomorrow, same settings. The day after that, set the distance to .7 miles."

"That's like what? A marathon distance?"

"No. A marathon is just over twenty-six miles. That's going to take us eighteen months. You're going to run in a half marathon in a year. No more bullshit, Harry. Press the start button and get moving. Monday you're going to do a mile, and then we're going to start working out."

Harry was enthused about his prospects and was looking forward to his next workout and to seeing Susan as well. He pressed the start button and began his journey.

CHAPTER
35

M ANY PEOPLE USE the same passwords for all of their electronic devices and websites. Volkov and Kilimchuk were no different. The two detectives were able to gain access to the laptops and started searching for anything relevant to the investigation. They sat at their desks, each with their fingers tapping away and with their eyes glued to the screen. Intermittently, you would hear one of them emit a "hmm" or a "huh" and an occasional "oy vey," which meant something outrageous was in view. When that happened, one of them would typically utter the phrase "You're not going to believe this," followed by the laptop turned around so it was in view of the other detective, since their desks faced each other. Most often it was a tasteless photo or inappropriate joke.

Just as they did on the phones, they were methodically searching messages, photos, emails, and browser history. McGuire was searching the Volkov laptop. He named it 'The Volkov Laptop" in advance and told his partner that it was going to be as valuable as the Hope Diamond because "I'm not figuring these guys for the likes of Einstein."

When Sorrentino heard, "Oh baby," he knew something good was coming. "What have you got?" he asked.

"Remember the name of that real estate guy?"

"Yeah, really nervous. Tried to put us on to the Deputy Inspector in the NYPD."

"Yeah, that guy. Harry Rosen. Guess whose name pops up in the search history."

"Double or nothing on the cerveza fria I owe you that it's Harry Rosen."

"No bet. It's one and the same." In a mocking infomercial tone, he continued, "But wait. There's more. A special bonus courtesy of the Volkov Laptop. The browser history points to a site that provides his address, and a search of his map history shows that very same address."

"They wanted to pay Harry a visit, and I don't think it's because they were interested in buying any property."

"We should pay him a visit ourselves."

Sorrentino said, "Let's find his office and look for him there. I'd rather make the drive and not find him than give him the opportunity to come up with some cockamamie story."

"Or a lawyer."

"Especially a lawyer."

They both stood up, put on their jackets, and headed out the door.

In less than ninety minutes, they parked at fire hydrant in front on Harry's office. Sorrentino stayed in the car. McGuire got out, walked up to the door, and gave it a tug. It was locked. There was a doorbell with a handwritten note housed inside a case above the bell that read, "Real Estate." McGuire rang the bell and waited. No answer. He went back to the car and cursed the bad luck. "Son of a bitch. He'd better show up soon, otherwise we'll have to deal with that fucking traffic getting home."

"Want to grab some lunch while we wait?" Sorrentino asked.

"What? From this chicken joint? Are you out of your mind? I saw a poster in the window with a phone number for Poison Control."

Sorrentino was hungry. He'd skipped breakfast, thinking he'd grab a bagel later on that morning, so the chicken didn't look that bad. Better to wait. They came here to interview Harry, and he wasn't going to jeopardize that over a drumstick.

A short, fat man wearing a blue running suit and a pair of matching running shoes was walking toward the car.

"Get a load of this guy. Looks like someone did put Humpty Dumpty back together," Sorrentino commented.

"Yeah, I saw him. I hope that's our guy, because if he tried to run I wouldn't have to break a sweat to grab him."

They watched as Harry approached and then turned into the doorway that led to his office. It was an improvement that had come quickly after such a short time at the gym. He was able to climb up the steps with only a little effort.

Harry settled in behind his desk only moments before he heard the knock on his office door.

"If you're looking for the bathroom, it's across the hall."

"Police, Harry. Can we come in?"

"Can you come in? Why can't you come in? The door is open."

The two cops held up their badges and introduced themselves. Without asking, they sat down opposite Harry in the two chairs on the other side of his desk. "I'm Detective Sorrentino and this is Detective Mcguire. We're with the Suffolk County Homicide Division. You may remember we spoke over the phone."

Harry hoped his nervousness wasn't apparent. "Remember? Of course I remember. I'd offer you coffee, but I broke the pot and haven't replaced it yet. I've been pretty busy lately."

McGuire spoke for the cops. "Not a problem, Harry, but we appreciate the hospitality." This wasn't going to be "good cop, bad cop" scenario. They sensed there was something Harry was hiding. He was not a suspect. His alibi was checked and confirmed. Whatever he was hiding, they were going to uncover it. No small room with bright lights and uncomfortable conditions. They were going to question him relentlessly, giving Harry time only to answer and not think about what his answer should be.

Sorrentino asked, "When was the last time you saw Volkov and Kilimchuk?" Typically, they knew the answers and would ask a string of questions that all required a "yes," until they got to the last question, which was "Did you kill ——?" With that answer, it was over. Game, set, match. They knew Harry didn't pull the trigger, but he was hiding something. That was what they were going to find out.

"The last time I saw them?"

Before Harry could answer, Sorrentino raised his voice. "I know the question. I asked it. That's how this works. I ask the questions, and you answer them. Not with any bullshit, either. We're not like those rubes that you peddle your fucking dollar-and-a-dream real estate investment story to. Okay, you got me? So when did you see them last?"

Harry was shaken, almost to the point of coughing up the truth, but not quite. "I saw them when they walked away from the closing."

"And never again after that?"

"Never."

"Then why did they have your address in the GPS in their vehicle?"

"How would I know that? They met me once at the property they wanted to buy. Then at the scheduled closing." Harry was going to return the hostile attitude but then thought better of it.

"They had your address in their GPS, your home address, because they were looking for you. So what happened when they found you at home?"

Harry was now elated the suspicion was going to turn away from him, and not even by his doing. "They wouldn't find me there. My wife is divorcing me and threw me out a few days earlier."

"Where were you living, Harry?"

"Right here."

"And how could we confirm that?"

"Check with the doorman who gave me a few Hefty bags with my clothes. Check with the gym I joined so I could have a place to shower. Check with my attorney."

Partly inquisitive and partly to annoy Harry, McGuire finally asked a question. "Was it a boyfriend? Was it one of the two victims maybe? After all, if your home address is in the GPS, maybe one of them was entertaining your ex-wife?"

Sorrentino jumped in. "Maybe someone is jealous. Maybe you. Or maybe he doesn't want the competition from you."

Harry answered, "I don't know too much about the women in Suffolk County, but unless you're worth a lot of money, fifty-year-old women here in the city don't find men like me more attractive than younger men who have muscles on top of their muscles. Maybe you should ask her those questions."

The cops got up and walked toward the door. McGuire turned and with a smile on his face said in a very soft voice, "Harry, nobody closes more homicide cases than we do. And the reason we drove here is because we know you're in this up to your neck. Maybe you're a coconspirator, maybe you know who pulled the trigger and you're more scared of them than you are of us. We will be back, don't doubt it for a minute, and when we come back you'll be leaving with us in handcuffs. Sleep tight, Harry."

Adding to their frustration, there was a parking ticket on the detectives' car. "No fucking courtesy," Sorrentino said. His partner opened the driver's door and told him to calm down. "It's not like we have to pay it. Get in so we can get out of here. I'll take you for an even better pizza." He knew how to dial down his partner's anger.

As soon as Harry heard the footsteps going down the stairs, his body went cold and he couldn't stop shivering.

CHAPTER
36

D EBBIE WAS HAVING trouble picking out an outfit. The weather was starting to turn colder, but she didn't think about spending much time outside. Although another trip to Long Island for a massage with Moe was on her mind. Matt Bernstein was coming over, and maybe he knew something about how to give a woman a massage. She turned her attention back to her wardrobe and decided to go with something black and lacy from Victoria's Secret underneath a pair of denim jeans and a black V-neck shirt.

There was a carton of orange juice and a bottle of champagne in the refrigerator. It was too early for wine or cocktails, but the perfect time to offer Matt a mimosa.

The apartment was clean, even by her standards, and the bed was made. *Let's see how long that lasts.* She turned on the stereo. *I wonder what kind of music he likes?* She settled on a station that played soft jazz. Another look around the living room and she was as ready as she could be. Debbie had a second cup of coffee and tried to read the paper but couldn't concentrate. She waited as impatiently as an expectant father in a hospital. Finally, the intercom buzzed and she heard the words she'd been waiting to hear since they had arranged the visit: "Mr. Bernstein is here to see you." Debbie's excitement level went to defcon one, but she was able to internalize that while telling the doorman to send him up. *Send him up. I'm going to send him up, all right.*

Moments later, the doorbell rang. This was it. Showtime. She looked in the mirror and was satisfied with her hair and makeup. Debbie turned slightly to the left for a glance, and then did the same to the right. She faced the mirror once again and undid one more button on her blouse.

It was a moment that seemed like forever. Debbie opened the door to welcome the totally adorable Matt and found him there with another man, somewhat older, with a clipboard in hand. Goodbye, romance.

Matt introduced the man, whose name she instantly forgot. He was going to appraise the apartment. He apologized for the inconvenience and told Debbie that they shouldn't be that long. He was all business, and not monkey business either.

The appraiser walked through the apartment room by room, measuring and taking notes. Matt told Debbie that the best way to negotiate was with hard facts. The appraiser was going to assign a value to the unit based on the market value, less the cost of improvements.

He added, "That will be our asking price. Seems odd, doesn't it? That you as the tenant are essentially selling the apartment to the owner."

Debbie came out of her funk and returned to form. "How much do you think I'll get, and when will I get it?"

"We will have a better idea when Mick is finished with his work."

She guessed that Mick was the forgotten name of the uninvited appraiser and was about to ask how much longer he would be there when Mick came out the bedroom.

"Sorry to be so long," Mick said.

"No problem at all," Debbie said. "How much do you think we will get?"

"I can't answer that, but I can tell you that when updated, it will bring about 1.7 million. Subtract a hundred thousand for the improvements and the net market value would be 1.6." He left off the million. "Of course I'll need to sharpen up the figures, but the range may vary by a hundred thousand or so, one way or the other."

Debbie turned to Matt. "So when do you think I'll get the money?"

"First we will reach out to the owner to see if he is interested in buying you out, which I'm sure he will be. After that comes the negotiation, which won't take long if we make a reasonable offer. Keep in mind that he will want to earn a profit, so your expectation should be the market value less..."

Debbie became impatient and cut him off. She started to sound much like her soon-to-be-ex-husband. "I'm doing him a favor by leaving. It's the only place I've ever lived, and I'll be glad to die here too. Let him know that when you speak with him."

Matt assured her that he would, and, doing some quick math, told her, "When this is done, I suspect you're going to have about a million dollars in your pocket."

Angered by the change in her plans more so than anything else, she said sarcastically, "That's great, but it seems like it's going to take a long time to get it, and there's a big gap between a million and a million seven. He can take less, and you should make it happen. And soon. I have plans."

"I represent you and will do the best I can, and as quickly as I can."

Mick the appraiser seemed to be silently wondering how he could get out of the apartment during this outbreak and was called on by Matt to get that appraisal report ASAP.

Understanding the situation, Mick answered, "It will be hand-delivered to you no later than tomorrow morning." The rest of his workload was going to be pushed back. Mick was going to get this done like his dry cleaning, in by ten, out by five.

The two men said their goodbyes and left the apartment.

Debbie picked up the phone and called the spa on Long Island. She really needed an appointment for a massage with Moe.

CHAPTER
37

A S HAD BECOME his custom while the house was under construction, Tim was sitting in a folding wooden chair that had a canvas
seat and back. It was placed behind a table with legs that could also be
folded beneath. This was his temporary office furniture. Tim would show
up every day and set up the office wherever the construction workers
weren't. He would pile the desk with newspapers, his cell phone, iPad, and
a clipboard with a pad of lined yellow notepaper.

He needed a new place to operate his business, and in his line of work
he could not operate out of a coffee shop. Maybe he could do a bar like in
the old days, but there would be more intrusions than he cared for. This
house was more than adequate. Tim didn't have a heavy workload, maybe
a dozen calls a day and twice that on weekends, and usually concentrated
for a few hours before game times.

He was on the phone when Harry burst in. Without any regard for
that, Harry barked out, "I have a brilliant idea that will make us a fortune."
Tim had the phone pressed to his ear. He looked directly at Harry and
held up his other hand with the index finger pointed straight up. Afterward, he thought he should have given him the middle finger.

"Is it possible for you to be any more rude? You couldn't see I was on
the phone?"

"Sorry, Tim, but this is such a great idea, I couldn't contain myself."

"What's your great idea that it couldn't wait ten seconds until I ended
my phone call?"

"Thanks for renting me the space upstairs, and it's a great apartment
with plenty of room and..."

"Stop right there, Harry. No roommates, sublets, or Airbnb."

"Of course not. I myself am keeping this on the down-low. Who needs
the aggravation of some building inspector giving us a stop work order?"
Harry said this as if he had an ownership interest in the property.

To a small degree Tim was offended by that and responded, "What do you mean 'we'? I'm on the hook here and doing you a favor by letting you have the place."

"No. No. No. Listen, I do have an interest. I want you to get this place sold, and quickly, so we are on the same side here. But you gotta hear this..."

Once again Tim cut him off. "I don't have to hear anything, Harry."

"Tim, I'm begging you, please just give me a minute. I've got an idea that will make us thousands a day."

"Okay," Tim answered like a patient parent listening to a child who was going to explain why pizza was a vegetable. "Tell me your great idea."

"You're going to love this. It's so simple, it's brilliant. And we can do this with almost no up-front money and almost no expense." Harry was never short of enthusiasm or exaggeration. "Like I was saying, there's plenty of extra room upstairs. We could run an after-hours poker game."

"This is your great idea? How do you come up with this stuff?"

"I've been going to the gym every day, and I'm on the treadmill an hour a day. It gives me plenty of time to think."

"You're actually doing that?"

"That, and three other machines that are supposed to strengthen my upper body. Don't ask me what the machines are or what muscles they strengthen. I have no idea, but my trainer has got me on this program where I'm going to lose a hundred pounds."

"I don't mean the working out part. I mean the thinking part."

"She showed me how to turn on the TV like three times, and she gave up. If I can't watch *Let's Make a Deal,* I might as well do some serious thinking."

"No serious thinking required for a game show?"

"Not that one. *The Price Is Right* is another story."

"Really?"

"Let me ask you something. What's the list price for a one-pound box of spaghetti?"

"How would I know?"

"See what I mean? You have to think about it."

"Harry, I could think about that all day, and I still wouldn't know."

"That's what I mean. Instead of wasting time thinking about something I'd never figure out, I try to think of brilliant ways to make money."

"Kind of like Ralph Kramden."

"I don't know the guy, but if he had an idea this good, he'd be rich."

"He was a bus driver, Harry." Tim didn't mention that he was a fictional character on a TV show in the 1950s.

"Well, he obviously never had an idea this good, or he'd be driving a Bentley instead of a bus."

Maybe it was the distraction, or maybe the annoyance, but Tim knew he was going to have to hear Harry out if he wanted to put an end to the madness. "I can't wait to hear about this one."

"Follow me: we buy a table big enough to seat eight players and a dealer. A buffet table with some food and drinks, and a server. And we hire a bouncer, just in case. Then all we need are a few decks of cards and chips." Harry was excited and stopped just long enough to take a breath. He then continued. "We start the game early, around 7:00 p.m., this way guys can go do their day job, and the game ends at midnight. We take a five percent rake, and after all is said and done, our end will be about two grand. Not bad. A thousand each for a few hours' work. Which isn't even work, if you think about it."

Not being a card player, Tim had to ask, "What's a five percent rake?"

"The house takes five percent from every pot."

Tim got very interested and followed Harry down the path. "Where do you get the players?"

"Where do *I* get the players? *You* get the players. Your customers are gamblers. Gamblers gamble. Football. Basketball. Poker. Who cares? Trust me, I know. If they're betting on sporting events, they'll be interested in a poker game."

Tim had to admit the idea had merit, especially if you could set up more than one game a week, and maybe two tables a night. If Harry's math was right, two tables twice a week would bring in a total of eight thousand.

"Just so I understand, Harry: I'm finding the players, and the game is going to be in my house. What exactly are you doing to take half the money?"

Once again, Harry had hooked a fish. "What am I doing? You think Steve Jobs makes all these iPhones by himself? It was his idea. It's the intellectual property that's valuable."

Tim didn't bother to tell him that Steve Jobs was dead, but he instead offered, "Coming up with the idea of running a poker game is not intellectual property. And by the way, I say this with all due respect, but I never would think of you as an intellectual."

"I appreciate that, because you know it's not so popular to be an intellectual. Remember Barack Obama? A lot of people didn't like him because he was an intellectual."

"Don't worry, Harry, you're no Barack Obama."

"Okay, thanks. Look, I see your point about the split. Why don't we do this: 60/40 your way. And we can take the expenses off the top."

Tim revealed his plan for multiple nights and multiple games. "Since the dollars for your end will be much larger, 75/25 is going to be the split that makes this a go, Harry."

Harry stuck out his hand, indicating that they had a deal. "Let me know when you've got the players lined up and when they'll be there. I'll make sure everything else is taken care of." Knowing better than to talk himself out of a deal, Harry did the thing that was most difficult for him: he shut up.

While he would soon have to move out of Tim's place, Harry had thoughts of grandeur. *I could get a nice place to live in and run the game out of there. I wouldn't need Tim. I could keep all the money for myself. Pay my rent and make a few bucks beyond that.*

Tim shook Harry's hand, knowing he made a sweet deal. Time wasn't on his side, as he had to sell the house in order to cash out his wife. He knew that she wasn't going to jeopardize her lucrative legal practice by her association with an illegal poker game. Harry's lease was going to run out soon, and Tim was thinking about where he could move the game. Also, would it be worth it to keep Harry on as the operator and a twenty-five percent partner?

The place on Perry Street would be perfect except for one thing: Izzy. He couldn't throw her out. If he did, she would think he was just a lecherous old man who was doing that because they weren't romantically involved. But he wasn't romantically involved, and by his estimation the games would bring in sixteen thousand a month at a minimum.

He was very fond of her, but business was business.

CHAPTER
38

I ZZY SMELLED THE coffee. The mug was on top of the nightstand next to her side of the bed. *How did I end up in this situation? He is amazingly normal, and my parents would love him. Maybe I was swept up in the whole show business fantasy?* She smiled and stretched her arms out to offer him a hug.

"One hot delicious coffee for the most amazing, and amazingly beautiful woman in the world."

"Oh, you are such a sweetheart. How lucky am I?"

"Not as lucky as me, that's for sure."

It really had only been a matter of weeks before Izzy had decided that she would move in with Jon Moreland. He was the dancer that lived one flight above Tim's apartment where she had been staying. Prior to moving in, Jon took her backstage at the theater, and she got to hang out with some of the other cast members after the show. Other nights they would end up hanging out with performers in other Broadway productions. These were exciting times for a girl from the suburbs.

After work, the performers would hit the bars. Conversations about people were gossipy and catty. Occasionally, they'd make some truly funny observations about their work, but mostly about other people. Almost all seemed to relish telling tales about how one or another of Broadway's bright lights really weren't that talented but just got lucky.

One particular night, they spoke of jobs they'd had while waiting for acting jobs. For Izzy's benefit, someone told the joke about the aspiring actress who'd had the good fortune to meet a producer in an elevator. When the actress introduced herself as such to the producer, he asked, "Really? Which restaurant?" It was common for aspiring actors to be the ones in restaurants that were telling you about the goat cheese ravioli or serving you your order of tuna poke.

The talk went around the table, and people spoke of restaurant work and temp work and childcare. A particularly buxom young lady said in a southern accent, "I can't say which was my worst job, but I can tell you my best was a boob job."

Raucous laughter ensued, followed by a wisecrack from one of the men: "I heard it was a blowjob."

Not to be outdone, she countered that he'd never find out. "And besides, I'm better at it than you, although I don't get as much practice." Izzy laughed as hard as she ever had.

Jon never had to work at anything other than breaking into the business. He had a trust fund and the support of his doting grandmother, Anne. She had what Jon described as "substantial means." Her husband, Jon's grandfather, had owned a small bank, and upon his death she sold it for a small fortune and moved to New York. Thanks to "Granny Annie," he was able to focus on acting, singing, and dancing lessons. Everyone outwardly liked Jon but slung arrows behind his back. No one doubted his talent, but they felt it was somehow ill-gotten.

The serious talk came when it was time to mention future prospects. Every show always ended, and most actors were always looking for their next job. Who had auditions where, who got a callback, who had potential connections. There was always talk of someone who met someone who knew a somebody. Somebody who could get them from the background to the foreground, a principal role. Maybe not too close to the top of the cast list in *Playbill*, but at least on the list.

Izzy was starting to think in terms of what would happen after she finished writing her play. She'd need actors. Certainly, some of the late-night crowd would participate or at least know people who would know people who might. And with some accomplished actors, even if they had no recognition, it would provide some credibility and hopefully financing. Initially, Izzy thought Tim was the likely source, but since meeting Jon, that scenario was shifting to Grandma Anne.

There were several problems, though. The first was that she hadn't told Tim about her relocation upstairs, which could prove fortunate, because she hadn't broached the subject of backing her play with Jon. Nor had she ever met Grandma Anne. If Jon or Granny Annie didn't want to fund her venture, Izzy could find some other pretense to move back downstairs. As far as Tim was concerned, it would be as if she'd never left.

On the other hand, Tim was aware of her ambitions and liked her well enough to offer her the apartment unconditionally. No blowjob required. She didn't ask him about backing the play, which might mean moving the relationship forward on whatever terms he demanded. A blowjob was one thing, but that was where she would draw the line. He was not going to get a girlfriend experience.

Izzy was going to have to talk to Tim. The timing could be awkward, though, since she had not yet written a single word.

An unmarked police car was parked outside the building on Perry Street. The pair inside were told to be discreet and report back only to Deputy Inspector Ramirez. They had spent parts of several days over the past few weeks observing Izzy and any visitors she may have had.

They drew their conclusions and were ready to convey them to Ramirez. Rather than do this over the phone or in person, they were going to send a text with two photos. One photo showed a tall, young, blonde man sitting on the steps with Izzy. They were smiling and holding hands. In the second photo they were smooching.

In a separate email, they identified the young man as Jon Moreland. He was originally from Chagrin Falls, Ohio. Moreland was a graduate of Yale and currently performing as a dancer in a Broadway production of *42nd Street*. The apartment he occupied was owned by Anne Moreland.

When the deputy inspector received the texts, he smiled broadly. *Young kids in love. My brother will be glad to hear this. That guy Cassidy isn't romantically involved with her. Interesting that he has an apartment in the building, though. He meets her in the restaurant and introduces them?* It wasn't the thought he believed, but the one he wanted to. He was going to share the details from the email and the photos but keep his thoughts to himself.

Sounds like a decent kid. Not sure he'll be happy to hear the "performer" part, but better than a guy at least twice her age.

CHAPTER
39

C ASEY NERVOUSLY PACED the carpeted floor in her stockinged feet. The walls in her office were twenty feet apart, but she felt like she was walking in a closet. She was reading the appraisal report for Debbie's apartment and absorbing none of it. Her mind kept wandering to their last meeting. Casey's usual decisive manner deserted her. She needed to bounce what she thought she knew about her client off of someone she could trust, someone who could provide some guidance.

Tim answered the phone on the first ring. "How's the best matrimonial attorney in the city doing this morning?"

"Pretty damn good in many respects. With one, though, not so much."

Tim was behaving himself, so he knew it had nothing to do with him. "What's the problem?"

"This absolutely cannot go any further."

"Maybe we shouldn't be discussing this over the phone then?" Tim asked.

"Good point. How soon can you meet me?"

"I'm still at home. I can be there in ten minutes."

"Better yet, meet me in the park. Bring a coffee downstairs for me."

The urgency in Casey's voice sent Tim scrambling. He decided to pass up the sounds of construction at his real estate investment for some quiet time at home. There was no time for a shower, or much of anything else. Some deodorant, sweatpants, and a sweater would have to work. He put together a double espresso for his wife and bolted out the door. Tim was a few steps from the elevator when he realized he didn't have his key to the park. He backtracked, grabbed the key, and once again headed out.

Tim reached the entry gate and saw Casey speed-walking about half a block away. He waited and held the gate open, let her pass, and followed her to a nearby bench. The park was deserted except for a matronly woman sitting at the other end of the park with her head buried in a book.

He held out the espresso and said, "For you."

She took the cup and drained half of it in one swig. "Thanks." With another swig, the cup was empty. "This is going to sound so trite, but I really needed that."

Tim had never seen her like this, totally on edge, and that was before the double espresso. He wondered if he should have brought her something stronger. He offered up, "I don't know how bad this is going to be, so I'm go to guess it's somewhere between awful and tragic."

"Oh, it's bad and potentially could put me in a very bad spot."

"Expensive bad? Or going to jail bad?"

"You know that sleazy realtor client you have? I'm representing his wife in a divorce."

"Harry Rosen."

"That's him. She told me Harry was a killer."

"What? No way."

"That's what she said, but I didn't believe her. She inferred it was a double murder. The one on Long Island. It was on the news recently."

"I don't believe it, either. I don't think he could fit his fat fingers onto a trigger."

"I checked it out. He was at the closing when we bought the real estate."

"So why is there a problem?"

"I think she did it."

It took Tim a moment to answer. "You think she did it. Are you sure she did it? The word 'think' implies a degree of doubt."

"Don't be an asshole. I make a living parsing words. Would I be here if there was any doubt?"

"Do you have to go to the police with this?"

"No, because it was a hypothetical conversation and off the record."

"Was anyone else there?"

"Another attorney in my office, Matt Bernstein."

"What is his supposition?"

"Same as mine."

"How likely is she to confess?"

"Not at all."

"What about Bernstein?"

"Never."

"Okay. So hypothetically, maybe she did something that you had no part in or knowledge of, or anyone at your firm either. I don't see a problem here, unless Bernstein folds."

"The problem is if the cops solve this one, I could be up to my ass in trouble I don't want."

"All due respect to the cops, but if it's not a spouse or a business associate, their odds of solving the case go way down. Unless they coerce some poor schmuck into a false confession."

"Or unless they have a shitty lawyer," Casey added.

"I get a client that goes bad, you know, doesn't pay or is a genuine pain in the ass, I stop taking their action and they go elsewhere. Get rid of her. Is she ever going to refer any wealthy clients? I know Harry doesn't have much money, so how much can you get from him, and is it worth it?"

"You make a good point, and I don't see a problem doing that. Right now her bucket list has three items: get rid of Harry, cash out what she can, and move to Florida."

"You might have to sell her out by going easy on Harry in order to expedite her exit from the client roster of the Cassidy Law Firm. She gets to Florida and she's just another New Yorker bitching about the crappy bagels. And the cops up here let it go cold."

Casey was starting to calm down. Tim gave her good advice. Fire the client. On the other hand, maybe he was fighting for Harry's money. *One of us is going to get it. If it's him or me, it's going to be me.*

CHAPTER
40

I N THE LAST two weeks, Harry, as directed by his trainer, reluctantly eliminated potatoes and fried foods from his diet. To satisfy his hunger, he added donuts. He went to the gym and was anxious to weigh in. Harry was sure Susan was going to be impressed with his progress.

They met when Harry arrived, and she led him to the scale. "Get on," she instructed. He started to lean over to see the digital readout when Susan gave him the news. "Congratulations, Harry, you're down another two pounds this week. 259. At this rate you'll be under two hundred by the Fourth of July."

He wasn't sure if she was being sarcastic, but that's what he assumed. "Fourth of July? The one coming up?"

"No. In 2028. Yeah, the one coming up. From now on, no more desserts."

"Nothing? Maybe just a like a sliver of cheesecake, or maybe a cannoli?"

"No sliver of cheesecake. No cannoli. Nothing, Harry. No dessert. You lost four fucking pounds in two weeks. That's like a fly off an elephant's ass. No negotiation on this. You can lie to yourself, but the scale doesn't lie at all."

Susan then took a photo of Harry standing on the scale and one of the readout on the scale. "This is the before. You're going to be the poster boy that's going to build my business. I'll probably be able to get a TV gig when you drop another hundred pounds. So no more candy, either."

"You're killing me."

"No, Harry, I'm saving your life. Let's get started. Hit the treadmill and do two miles." As he started to walk away, Susan yelled over, "By the way, I may have someone for that two-family in East Harlem."

"There's a lot of interest in that. I've had about a dozen people in there already." He was referring to the poker players that were showing up, but why point that out? "Mostly investors. It's really not ready for a public showing yet." It would be difficult to explain the poker tables in the bedrooms and the buffet table and bar in the living room. If someone did buy the house, Harry would have to move. The poker games were going so great that Tim was thinking about adding a third night, and so far each night meant about $500 for Harry.

"Let me ask you something: I don't do any rentals, and I'm looking for a place. You got anything available?"

Susan said, "What are you looking for?"

Harry had to think this through. If the card games remained popular, he could knock out about fifteen hundred a week and maybe convince Tim that free rent should be part of the deal.

On the other hand, if he could run his own game, he could clear four times that. Plenty of money left over after renting something befitting his new enterprise. He needed to entice them to move. A nice space and top-shelf liquor would probably do it. He would add a masseuse as well. Back and shoulder massages during the game. What happened afterward would be between the consenting adults.

"Susan, you know I'm thinking that I should find something equivalent to what I'm leaving. A nice two-bedroom, two-bathroom, living room, dining room. Upper East Side. Maybe a townhouse." Harry didn't want a doorman who might blab about his guests.

"I saw one like that recently on 78th, near York. It was a ground-floor unit and had outdoor space, a nice patio."

A patio? Harry thought about that for a moment. Perfect. Somebody wants to grab a smoke, they can go outside without leaving the building. No complaints about the smoke from the haters. "I'd like to take a look at that." Harry said it with a little too much enthusiasm.

"You didn't hear the rent yet."

"Won't matter if it's not available."

"Good point. You get your ass on the treadmill and I'll make a call."

Instead of watching TV while walking on the treadmill, Harry got lost in his fantasies about what his new life would be like. A nice apartment and money rolling in. He would be working at something he loved, which meant it wasn't really work. Harry ran the game, so he wasn't going to play, since it would look bad if he won, but he could still kibbitz.

Best of all, no Debbie. Though the Russians didn't take care of her, in his euphoric state he decided that he would toss a few bucks her way and get her out of his life. In his mind, Harry paid all the bills over all the years, so it was only right that he get the majority of the proceeds from the sale of the apartment. In order to make her go away quickly, he would agree to an even split.

A ding sounded, and Harry looked down at the display. Time seemed to fly by as he finished his two miles in forty-five minutes. He was going farther and in less time. Just the same as his life. He was going places and was going to get there sooner.

Harry was sweating heavily and breathing heavily. He bent over and placed his hands on his knees. Scared that he was having a heart attack, he yelled for help. Immediately, he was surrounded by a crowd. One of the gym members who was nearby worked his way through the people that were either gaping at Harry or taking photos and videos. Another was live-streaming the event. Death would definitely draw an audience. The man made his way to Harry and told him he was a trained EMT and was going to help.

"What's your name?"

"Harry," he was able to wheeze out through his heavy breathing.

"Harry, are either of your arms numb or tingly?"

"No."

"Are you having any chest pains?"

"No." Harry's breathing came easier, and he was able to stand erect.

"Does anything hurt?"

"No. Maybe I did too much. I was running at a pretty good clip before I went down."

"Try to take a few steps." The EMT led Harry over to chair, told him to sit down, and grabbed his pulse. After a short while, he told Harry that his pulse was in the higher range of normal and asked if someone could get him some water.

As the crowd dissipated, Susan stepped forward with a bottle of water. She twisted the cap off and handed the bottle to Harry.

"How's his pulse?"

"About ninety," the EMT responded. "I think he just needed to cool down."

"It's been a few minutes. Take it again," Susan said, almost demand-ingly.

Another thirty seconds and the EMT announced, "It's down to about eighty."

"Thanks, I think you're right. He should've reduced his pace for a few minutes."

"Harry, I can call an ambulance if you need to go to the hospital."

"No. I'm okay. I shouldn't have pushed myself."

With that, the EMT left Harry, who was sitting in the chair with Susan standing in front of him with her arms folded across her chest. She was pissed.

"Going at a pretty good clip? Did I hear you say those words? I've got an eight-seven-year-old great-aunt who walks faster than that. And she has tennis balls on the bottom of her walker." She was irate. "And *pushing* yourself? You'd better start pushing yourself away from the table. Two things you're going to do: one, you're not going to die, at least until I get my after picture of you weighing 150 pounds. Two, no more bullshit about your diet. I'm giving you an app to install on your phone to track your calories. You eat it. You log it in. You understand me, Harry?"

"Yeah."

"Yeah, what?"

"Yeah, I understand."

"Good. Now follow me. We're going to do some crunches. When you get to 140 pounds, I want to see you with a six-pack."

"I prefer gin and tonic. I'm not much of a beer guy."

"I'm referring to your abs, Harry. Abdominal muscles. By the time I'm done with you, you'll be on a magazine cover posing in Speedos. I'll have a TV show, and you'll be able to look down and see your dick."

CHAPTER
41

I T WAS A dreary, overcast morning. Casey was staring out her office window. Shopping. Christmas was around the corner, and even though the list was short, she wanted to get in front of it. Casey had only Tim, her sister, and her family, a brother-in-law, and three nephews who were still in her childhood home in Elmira, a small city in upstate New York. It would be impossible for that town to be any more different than Manhattan. Restaurants closed mostly by 9:00 p.m. Monthly parking in the city was more than most mortgage payments in Elmira.

Casey couldn't wait to leave, and her sister had helped. She got a job at the prison right after high school and helped support the family. Casey was able to focus on her schoolwork and went off to college with a combination of scholarships, grants, loans, and help from her sister.

Shopping for Tim was easy. He never returned anything and was happy with everything. In fact, she bought him the same gift every year: a cashmere sweater from Saks.

Buying gifts for her family was another matter. They were always appreciative, but she had to balance practicality against what they might consider ostentatious. It was the same sensibility that she was also raised with but had put aside long ago. Casey's accumulation of wealth and the need to project success saw to that. She was what she had. No apologies.

Before she could decide whether or not she should go with Amazon gift cards all around, the ringing telephone jarred her out of her reverie. "It's a Mr. Goldblum calling about a letter you sent him regarding Debbie Rosen." She said to put the call through.

"Good morning, Mr. Goldblum, this is Ms. Cassidy."

"Good morning to you. You know, many people I speak with mispronounce the name. They call me Goldbloom. It's not, it's Goldblum, just the way you said it. It's like they didn't learn anything in school. Maybe they never went. Who knows?"

Casey pulled the phone away from her ear and turned her head to look at it. Was this guy competent enough to enter into an agreement? This was Debbie's landlord. She'd written to Mr. Goldblum on Debbie's behalf in order to sell him Debbie's rent-controlled lease.

"Thanks for calling. As I discussed in my letter, I represent Debbie Rosen. She is seeking a buyout of her lease."

"Who wants what? Tell me again."

Casey was really worried that this guy was non compos mentis, and any agreement they made could be rescinded in court. "Debbie Rosen is seeking a buyout of her lease, as I wrote to you."

"I know. I know. It's just that this is such good news, I can't hear it enough."

Even Casey had to laugh. "She's been there a long time."

"You're telling me? I remember her parents. Very nice people. My father bought the building during the Depression. He lived there and was able to buy it from the bank, so why not? When I was a kid, if I wasn't in school, I had to help keep up the building."

Casey cut in, "Well I believe there's an opportunity..."

Goldblum continued, "You shouldn't interrupt. Do they teach that in law school? So anytime anyone needed something small, I would go to the apartment, maybe change a lightbulb, light a pilot light, you know, little things. Her parents always gave me a quarter."

"How nice of them."

"In those days a candy bar was a nickel and a Spaldeen was a dime. You know what a Spaldeen is?" Not waiting, "It's a pink rubber ball you needed for stoop ball, or stickball, or hit-the-penny. It was a must-have. Anyway, a quarter was a big deal."

Casey was ready to hang herself. "Speaking of big deals, have you given any thought to what her leaving may be worth to you?"

"I'm sure she's a lovely woman, but the apartment is probably a mess. So who knows? Look, I'll refund all the rent she's paid for the last twenty years. Let's round it up to 150 thousand."

"My client will surely appreciate your generosity, but we had the property appraised for 1.6 million."

"Who would think such a small apartment would be worth so much? You'll send me a copy of the appraisal. I have a question: why she should get all the money?"

He was now playing Casey's game. The deck was stacked against him, or so she thought. "You don't have to give her anything. She's a healthy young woman and would be happy to live there another forty years, god willing."

"In forty years, it's not my problem. Maybe not even a problem for my kids. Maybe a problem for my grandkids. You know, I have six. All of them perfect. What they say is true: you should have grandchildren before you have your children."

"Mr. Goldblum, why would you want to leave any of your heirs a problem? Isn't it better to leave them with only the good memories?"

"They'd like it better if I left them more cash. Every summer I take my wife to Tuscany. We went there about twenty years ago, and she fell in love with the region, Florence, Chianti, the whole area. She tells me, 'Let's buy a place here, we can come all the time.' I tell her, 'What's wrong with East Hampton? We have a beautiful house' — it's on the water — 'and we can drive there.' She wants a place there, so I say, 'Okay, maybe something small, only four or five bedrooms.' Well, you know how that goes."

"No, I really don't," Casey finally had a chance to interject.

"Here's what happens: you always want more. So we end up buying something like a, like a manor. And what I had to spend to fix it? Don't ask. Now all my grandchildren go to Italy for the summer, and I never see them."

"You don't go?"

"Nah. My wife got tired of the place."

"Back to where we started. Why not rid yourself of a headache and buy out the lease?"

"You didn't understand. My children and grandchildren will never need for money. Owning the apartment or not doesn't change anyone's life."

"It changes Debbie Rosen's life." Casey went into sympathy mode. "She's divorcing her husband, who has nothing, and has to start a new life in her middle age. It'll be a mitzvah for you to do this."

"A mitzvah. You're Jewish?"

"No, but I know the word. It's a good deed, a blessing. Like you said, it doesn't change your life, but it changes hers. And it doesn't cost you anything. You buy her out, and then you sell the apartment to get your money back."

"Mrs. Cassidy, tell Mrs. Rosen I'm sorry for her troubles, and that I'll give her 1.4 million. She needs to close before year-end for tax considerations, and her husband will have to sign off for legal reasons." He added, "Her parents were always very nice to me."

"Mr. Goldblum, thank you."

Casey hung up the phone less stunned at the outcome than how it came about. Goldblum was a long way from non compos mentis.

Not content to wait for a written agreement to arrive from Goldblum, Casey immediately dialed Debbie. Doing so was against her conservative nature, easily summarized as, "If it ain't in writing, it ain't."

Debbie picked up, giving a terse, "Hello."

"Hi, Debbie, it's Casey. I want to pass along some terrific news."

"Okay." The icy tone reflected her foul mood.

Casey wasn't going to try to shade the conversation as she'd originally planned. Goldblum just made an outstanding offer, and she was going to present it without judgment. "I don't have anything in writing yet, but your current landlord has just verbally conveyed an offer to buy out your lease for 1.4 million dollars."

There was a momentary silence on the line, until Debbie said, "What happened to the 1.6 million?"

"I'm sorry?" Casey said, somewhat confused.

"You said that the appraisal was for 1.6 million."

"It was. That does include selling expenses, like the real estate commission and transfer taxes."

"I was counting on more money."

Casey explained, "You can turn down the offer if you like, but unlike a typical market, there is only one possible buyer. He can always choose to remain the landlord."

"Well, that stinks, if you ask me." After a pause Debbie asked, "If I do say yes, when do I get the money?"

Casey could tell that Debbie was softening. "It would be a very quick deal. For tax purposes, he wants to close before the end of the year and wants Harry to sign the agreement as well to ensure that he makes no claim to stay in the apartment."

"So Harry will know how much money I'm getting?"

"Yes. Do you think that will prevent him from signing?"

"He'll sign it. And I'm not giving him a nickel."

"It may have to be part of the settlement."

"We'll see about that." Without a goodbye, Debbie disconnected.

Casey placed the phone back in its cradle and rewound her thoughts back to before her unpleasant conversation. Her Christmas list, and the inspiring call from Goldblum. Casey was going to find or do something incredible for her sister this year. If it was over-the-top, she'd get over it. A villa in Tuscany, however, was not going to be on the list. Casey thought, *Maybe a new truck? Maybe a new house? They probably cost about the same up there. She was always very good to me.*

CHAPTER
42

EVERYTHING BUT THE donuts. Well, almost everything. That's what Harry logged into the app on his phone. He was making great strides. The report on the app indicated that his daily calorie intake was always between 1,500 and 2,000. Exactly where Eva Braun, or Susan Stein, or Susan Stern, or whatever her real name was, wanted his calorie count to be.

The trouble was that Harry bought a scale, and it needed new batteries. That was the only explanation for why his weight only went down one pound that week. He felt like he was practically starving himself. He dreaded his weigh-in at the gym later that morning. Not so much the reading on the scale, but the negative feedback his trainer would dish out.

Harry had a brilliant idea. He was going to forego the jelly donuts with powdered sugar and switch to cinnamon. And only have one.

Susan was at the front desk chatting with someone who didn't look like she needed a trainer. Harry approached with gym bag in hand and announced his presence: "The H-Train is here and ready to roll." The two women looked at him, very unimpressed.

Harry let them know that his near-death experience a few days ago made him more determined. "By the time we're through with this, maybe I can pose for one of those calendars like the one with the photos of the sexy firemen."

The two women looked at each other. The woman that was unknown to Harry rolled her eyes, grabbed a towel from the stack on the desk, and walked away. Susan answered, "When that happens, not only will pigs be flying, they'll be flying with jet packs." She went on to tell Harry that he was wasting his money and that it would be bad for her business if he dropped dead on her watch. Especially if he did it in the gym. "You're going to have to take this seriously or quit wasting my time. Make a decision. Are you happy with your appearance, your life, your health? I'm not a doctor, but I'd guess you probably have high blood pressure, high cholesterol, and probably diabetes. An actuary would tell you you're not likely to live long enough to collect social security." She looked down at his left hand and saw the wedding ring. "Your wife will be a young widow."

The ring wouldn't come off. The day after his wife tossed him out, Harry tried everything from butter to WD-40, to no avail. He then thought that maybe it was for the better after he made the deal with the Russians. *Those fucking Russians. They can rig a fucking election but can't take out my wife.* If he was still wearing a wedding ring after her untimely demise, he would appear the grieving husband. A man to be pitied, not a man set free from that demeaning, demanding witch of a wife. Debbie was here, the ring was still on, and the Russians were dead.

That was the trigger that sent the message home. Harry was not going to give Debbie the satisfaction of reading his obituary. He pulled a cinnamon donut out of his jacket pocket and tossed it in the trash. He confessed, "I was saving it for later. I swear I only had one this morning."

Susan told him that if he got hungry, he should eat an apple. She described nervous eating and how he should find something else to do instead. Sing a song, tap dance, or take a walk.

"Sing a song. Tap dance. Who am I, Fred Astaire?"

"Whatever. Find anything else to keep yourself occupied. Time for the treadmill. We have a busy day today. Three miles on the treadmill, forty-five minutes of resistance work, and then we're going for lunch. I'm going to show you what a healthy lunch looks like, and you're buying. Then we're off to look at that apartment I mentioned last time."

"Whoa. I'm okay with everything, except for like, all of it. Three miles? And what the hell is 'resistance work'? And forty-five minutes? I'd probably need to pee twice before I got through that. And the lunch? I'm buying? Look, sister, I pay you for aggravation, I mean training, not eating."

"Listen up. Resistance is another word for weights. You're buying lunch because it's the nutritional part of your training regimen. It's not a date, but think of what people will say when then see you sitting with me."

"They'll think I've got a huge bankroll and you're going to be the next ex-wife of Harry Rosen."

"If it helps, I will yell, 'No way I'm signing a prenup.'"

"Not bad. Nothing builds success like people thinking you've got money. They mistake a big bank balance for a big IQ."

"Get started, Harry. It's a busy day. And remember to cool down after you finish."

He programmed the treadmill for three miles and even managed to tune to ESPN on the video screen. None of the scores mattered to him. The poker games consumed his gambling passion, even though he wasn't a player. Much like video gamers were engaged watching others play, so too was Harry with his poker games.

The day was starting out well. With a little more luck, he could have a new place to live and run a card game. His was going to be different and better than the one he currently ran. Tim nixed the idea of having a masseuse. "I'm not a pimp," he'd flatly told Harry. They were going to host a poker game and only that. "I want those guys sitting at the table throwing chips into the pot. That's how we make our money."

Harry had no such reservations about the distraction. An attractive girl or two would bring in the players. He wasn't going to take a cut from their action, so it wouldn't be like he was a pimp. If the girls wanted to make a few extra bucks, that was their business.

A beep came from the treadmill. It had taken him more than an hour to reach the three-mile mark, but with so much on his mind, the time had flown by. Another ten minutes at a slower speed brought his pulse down and made his breathing easier. *I think I've got the hang of this.* Never short of confidence, Harry walked over to Susan, who was waiting at the desk, and let her and everyone else within the sound of his voice hear, "I really crushed it today, and no heart attack either."

The rest of the workout left Harry tired and the slightest bit sore. Susan challenged him with additional weight and more exercises. Harry flexed his arms and said, "Look at those guns. Mr. Universe should worry if I keep at this." She ignored that, as well as all of Harry's other attention-seeking outbursts, and told him they had an appointment to view the apartment. "Take a shower so we can have lunch first." Susan turned her back and walked away.

It was a typical pub with a well-attended bar and a busy dining room. After being seated, Harry picked up the menu and said, "What a workout. I'm so hungry, I could eat a horse."

Conveniently or not, depending on the point of view, the calorie count was listed next to each item on the menu. Susan pointed out, "I don't see horse on the menu, and if it were there'd be too many calories. Look at the calories listed for each item and choose from the lowest. If your goal is 1,500 calories a day, and you have three meals, do the math. You're looking at five hundred calories each meal."

Harry browsed through the menu and saw nothing like that. "I see a nice sandwich here. Chicken with bacon and cheddar. And it's only 890 calories."

A server came by to take the drink orders. Harry went first. "A gin and tonic for me. Bombay gin. And I'll have the chicken sandwich with bacon and cheddar. A side of fries with that." He folded the menu closed and handed it to the server.

Susan did the same and ordered a sparkling water and the same sandwich. Then she added, "By the way, would you make mine without the cheese and the bacon, and without the bread. Also, he'll have his the same way. No fries." Susan smiled, and before she returned her menu added, "Oh, and make his gin and tonic without the gin."

Harry could not believe what just happened. "I hope you don't mind my asking, but what's a sandwich without bread?"

"Healthier."

"And no cheese?"

"Lower in calories and healthier."

"And no gin?"

"Refer to the last answer."

"Not much of a lunch, if you ask me."

"Too much, if you ask me.."

There wasn't much talk during lunch. Nor was it much of a lunch by Harry's estimation. He would grab a bagel after he settled the apartment business with her. He made a few observations about the current real estate climate. Susan couldn't care less. Her goal was to get Harry into the apartment and collect her fee. Lunch was over, and Harry dutifully paid the check. "I hope this apartment is better than this so-called lunch."

A short walk took them what would be Harry's next home, although he did not yet know that. A superintendent was there to greet them and let them in. At once, Harry was all in. The rooms were large, the kitchen and bathroom updated, and a fresh coat of paint was akin to that "new car smell." Its small patio made him feel like "he was in Westchester or Jersey or some place where they have backyards." He always contended that his previous place was a dump, and this proved him correct.

Harry was already thinking about how to set the place up to accommodate a card game, and more importantly, how he could get it moved. "Hey, Susan, did you say you had somebody for my listing uptown?" He said this as if he had many others, when in fact it was his only one.

"Yes. Are you ready to show it? They're cash buyers and in a hurry."

"As long as they have some vision. It's still being built out, but maybe the owner can customize it for them."

"I'll call them later and let you know. How do you like this place, Harry?"

"Not really sure. It's nice enough, but I haven't looked at anything else yet. How much is this gonna run me?"

"It's $3,500 a month."

"Wow. That much for this place? It's so small."

Ignoring the objection, Susan continued. "It's the first, last, and a month's security to move in. That comes to ten-five plus my commission of forty-two hundred. A total of fourteen-seven. You're good for that, right?"

"Of course I'm good for that. But it seems a little high."

"When do you want it? It's move-in ready. I can get a lease for you by tonight. Give me a personal check for the first month now to hold it and a bank check for the balance when you sign the lease tomorrow."

"I have to see the lease first. Suppose there's some crazy prohibition, like pets or something. Maybe I can't have a potbelly pig."

"Do you have a potbelly pig?" Susan laughed, thinking how fitting that would be.

"No. But suppose I want to get one."

"Yeah, right. You want the place or not?"

Harry figured his new venture was going to pay the rent and then some. "All right, it's mine. But maybe we can work something out on your commission. Net it out against your end when you sell my listing."

"We will keep these transactions separate, Harry."

"Maybe a discount for cash?"

"Just bring a bank check for the balance tomorrow."

Harry started to think more about how much he was going to make off this instead of what he was going to pay. A goldmine, he thought. He pulled out his checkbook and made the payment. "I'm a little desperate, and you're catching me at a weak moment, so I'm gonna take it."

"It's a good deal, Harry."

A good deal. How appropriate. There are going to be plenty of good deals in here. "Yeah, I know. Thanks for getting me in here."

The superintendent asked if they were going to be much longer. Susan told him they were on the way and thanked him for letting them in. She nudged Harry and whispered to him, "Give him a fifty."

"What!"

"You heard me. Give him a fifty."

"That is total bullshit."

"Harry, do I have to explain how this whole thing works? You got a maintenance problem, or you need something done, you want this guy in your corner. So go take care of him."

Putting on a happy face, he walked over to the super and pressed the bill into the palm of his hand. "Thanks, man. You'll give me a hand when the movers get here?"

The super looked into his hand and told Harry, "No problem. I going to leave my number on the kitchen counter for you."

Harry left with Susan and let her know that he needed to get his listing into contract and that there might be a little wiggle room on the price.

"Good to know."

"Maybe tomorrow will be a big day for both of us."

Harry Rosen was going to run his own poker game. No more partners. He was going to keep the whole enchilada, and Tim wouldn't even know what hit him.

CHAPTER
43

A GOOD DEAL is typically characterized as when all parties are either happy or unhappy. Casey never settled a good deal. Her settlements were always one-sided and always in her client's favor. One factor in her success was patience, convincing her clients to wait until the other party cracked.

Most people in the midst of a divorce were in a hurry, and in a hurry to see the other party hurt. A good attorney managed the client and their expectations. Clients with demands that reflected personal grievances were setting themselves up for failure.

Debbie Rosen was spinning out of control. It started with her demand for the settlement on her lease, and it wasn't going to get better. *Fire the client.* Tim's words came back to Casey. She was going to make the call to Harry's lawyer.

Whenever another lawyer called her first, she saw that as waving the white flag of surrender. Unless Ramos, Harry's attorney, was the worst student ever to graduate the worst law school, he would see the white flag. Casey was going to fire Debbie by presenting her with the terms of a quick offer, which she wanted, and a settlement below market value, which she didn't.

She was not going to incur the ignominy of defeat. Casey would have Matt Bernstein make the call. He knew he would be showing his cards to Ramos but was going to fight the good fight. "Hello, Bill, this is Matt Bernstein from the Cassidy Law Firm. I wanted to say hello and see when you wanted to stop by our office to discuss the Rosen matter." Matt thought getting Ramos in his office would give him a home field advantage. A sole practitioner, Ramos might see the size and strength of his opposition and feel intimidated.

"Rosen? I'm sorry, who is this again?"

"Matt Bernstein. My firm represents Debbie Rosen, and I believe you represent her husband, Harry."

"Right. I spoke with Mrs. Cassidy about this and still haven't been served yet."

Matt was back on his heels but persisted. "She's been quite busy and asked me to handle this. After reviewing the file, I thought this was better suited to mediation than litigation."

"Mediation, not litigation. I like that. Maybe I'll put a sign up in my window. I can add something like 'save money.' You think it would attract any business? I do. Who doesn't want to save money?"

"Mr. Ramos, feel free to use that any way you wish as far I'm concerned. We don't have it trademarked." Ramos had gotten under his skin. "What would be a convenient time for you to stop by our office?"

"Matt, I'm quite busy myself these days with a ton of immigration work. Would you like to stop by here? We could grab some lunch. There's a place nearby where the mofungos are to die for."

"Maybe we can try to work this out over the phone. You won't upset your workload and I won't upset my stomach."

Ramos had to laugh. "You know how to turn a phrase. Were you an English major? You know, I didn't speak any English when I came to this country."

By this point Matt had had enough. This wasn't going anywhere, and rather than waste any more time talking about mofungos (he'd google that later) or the biography of Bill Ramos, Matt was going to make the first offer. "Our research indicates that Mrs. Rosen is on the deed with Harry for the building on 105th St., and that building has a market value of three million. She is willing to take back a mortgage on the building for one point five, or one point four in cash."

"You're a funny guy, Bernstein. Unfortunately, Harry Rosen doesn't have a sense of humor or a million four in cash. And he's never going to let her hold a note on the building. Her mail doesn't come with a check for the mortgage on the first of the month, she'd be foreclosing on the second. No thanks. Now that you've got that out of the way, tell me something that I can convey to my client with a straight face."

"Sorry, but I'm not authorized to offer anything but that."

"Well, when you're ready to make a realistic offer, I'll be here. Most likely working on these immigration cases that go to the front of the line.

These people have their lives at stake. The Rosen's, it's only about money. They can wait."

"Or I could send a summons," Matt angrily replied.

"Which I'm surprised you haven't done already. So now it's going to be litigation, not mediation? Listen, Bernstein, you want to send a summons, do it, don't talk about it. Or talk to your client and see how reasonable she will be."

Matt was played like a chump. Now he was in an auction and bidding against himself — only the bidding was downward.

CHAPTER

44

THE FURNITURE WAS delivered to Harry's new apartment. He unpacked the Hefty bags that contained his belongings, except for his suits and shirts, which went back in the bag to go off to the dry cleaner. His bedroom, his closet. His new life. He turned on the TV and tuned to ESPN, put the remote on his nightstand, and left the room.

Harry had never lived alone, and the experience was liberating. No mother, no wife, no one dictating what, when, and where he was going or doing. Living with his mother had been a nightmare. She was overprotective and tried to control every aspect of his life. *Where are you going? Who are you going with? Make sure you're home by eleven, otherwise I'm calling the police. God forbid I have to start calling the hospitals to try and find you.* When others his age were testing boundaries and trying to experience all the things, appropriate or not, that teenagers did, Harry sat in his mother's apartment watching *Gunsmoke*. *What's with all the interference? Harold, go move the antenna. You want something from the kitchen? Maybe some chocolate milk and a piece of crumb cake?* Harry always said no, but no matter his protests, his mother always brought the food. *Here, eat something. In Europe the kids are starving.* Harry never turned the food away.

He didn't know at the time that the escape from his mother sent him into another prison, only this time the warden was Debbie. The big difference was that he could go wherever he chose as long as she would go along. Instead of watching television at home, they would go to the movies. And movies meant popcorn and soda instead of his mother's snacks. Now Debbie was almost out of his life. *Free at last. Free at last. Thank God almighty, I'm free at last.*

The second bedroom contained a massage table. His plan was to find an open-minded masseuse, one who had no objection to providing any of his card players with a happy ending, and let her decorate the room.

Harry set up the living room with a dining room table that had three leaves. When extended, it would seat ten. There was enough room left for a buffet table and a seating area that faced a sixty-five-inch TV. Perfect.

He would make more money with the right players at one table than he was bringing in at Tim's. And he was rolling in it. Enough that he bought outdoor furniture for the patio, chairs, table, umbrella, and even one those outdoor heaters. It was a first for Harry. He paid cash. Almost done. He needed only to convince enough of the players to move to his game. He figured that was going to be a piece of cake. He had a plan.

Tim was going to get locked up. That would keep him from retaliating against Harry, and it would leave the entire operation to him. Maybe he could even take over the bookmaking as well.

First things first: get Tim arrested. A complaint from a neighbor might get the police to pay a visit, but a gunshot definitely would. Harry decided he didn't need to fire a gun but only to call 911 and say that he heard one. And he heard it from the building where the poker game was. *I heard a loud pop, maybe a firecracker, but I think it might have been a gunshot. And there were always a lot of people going in and out of there. Men, mostly. God knows what's going on in there. Always noisy, and now a gunshot.*

Harry was going to put his plan into action over the weekend. He would tell Tim he wouldn't be there on Friday night. What he didn't say was that he was going to be at the bodega down the street. Harry would then borrow a cell phone from someone there, make the call to 911, and refuse to leave his name. The police show up, bust in, and bust the game. Probably let the players go and put Tim in the back of a patrol car. Easy-peasy. Just like that, Tim is in the can and the next game is at Harry's new apartment.

CHAPTER
45

TIM WAS SITTING at a makeshift table in what was the living room of what he referred to as the flip house. He was pleased with the progress downstairs and almost ready to work on the apartment above. There were two problems with that. The first was that Harry Rosen was still there, and the second was that he had not yet had the talk with Izzy. His hope was for two evictions in one day. Not one to hope that problems would go away, he picked up his phone and dialed his non-paying tenant. He took a swig from the ever-present coffee cup.

The ring gave way to an answer. "Well, good morning, Tim. Are you always up this early?"

"I'm involved in a real estate project, and the contractors have already been here for almost three hours."

"Remind me never to be a contractor."

"I don't think law school is a career path to becoming a carpenter. Although it sounds like the punch line to a joke, I know an electrician that was also a lawyer."

"You're kidding?"

"No. And it wasn't because of the money. During college he worked as an electrician and decided he liked that work better. You gotta do what makes you happy."

Izzy said, "I'm going to be a writer."

"There are some lawyers that are great writers. Grisham and Turow, just to name two."

She continued the lie. "True, but I'm making great progress on my play and starting to think about the next step."

"And that is?"

"I'm looking for a producer, someone to fund this."

Tim knew bullshit when he heard it but decided to let the story unwind. "Any luck?"

"A few candidates. I was thinking you may want to throw your hat in the ring. After all, you've been such a big supporter so far. Why not get a share of the profits? You know, a return on your investment in me."

Her bullshit was now piled as high as any of the Rocky Mountains. Tim decided to give her a little more rope to see if she would hang herself. It would make his part of the conversation much easier. "Very thoughtful of you. I'm a pretty careful investor and always want to know the risks, rewards, and what exactly I'm investing in. When can we meet?"

"I'm off today. Maybe around three? At our Starbucks?" *Our Starbucks.* Like *our song.* She made it sound as if it were going to be a romantic rendezvous.

Tim swallowed another mouthful of coffee. "Good by me. Bring a copy of what you've written."

"That's not really something I care to do."

The peak of bullshit was now a mountain range. "Why would I invest in a play that I couldn't read first?"

"It just doesn't work like that. I don't have it registered or trademarked yet."

"I'm not asking for a hard copy, or even an electronic copy. I can read it on your laptop."

Izzy said, "I'm not comfortable doing that. I can't believe you have so little faith in me."

"Maybe you're right, Izzy. I'll see you at Starbucks this afternoon."

She immediately switched gears and told him, "I can't wait. You know how much I love hanging out with you."

"So long, Izzy. See you later."

Izzy hung up, looked up at the ceiling, raised her arms, and shouted, "Yes."

Tim hung up and asked the nearest worker if he knew how to change a door lock.

He walked upstairs to find Harry. Tim knocked. "Hey, Harry." No answer. He let himself in and coughed. *New house rule. No smoking.* Kitchen and bathroom, both clean. The door to Harry's bedroom was closed. Another knock. "Hey, Harry." Still no answer. He let himself in. Maybe he was at the gym? Or better yet, looking for a buyer. The closet door was open, the closet empty. The cardboard boxes Harry used in place of a dresser were also gone. Tim checked the bathroom. Empty.

There was no doubt Harry had left the building. *Where did he go? Why?* Tim didn't really care about the where — it was the why. He prepaid the rent, so why move early, and why in secret? *Was it a woman?* Even Tim got a good laugh at that. *Did he reconcile with his wife?* He sent Casey a text.

Her immediate response was "no."

Harry picked up on the first ring. "Big Tim, how the hell are you?"

"Pretty good, Harry. Yourself?"

"Unbelievable. I hope you're sitting down, because when I tell you this, you could fall over."

"Really? That incredible, huh?"

"Better than that. I got someone for the flip."

"That is good news."

"Yeah, so listen. I'm working out with a trainer who sidelines doing real estate. I tell her about your place, and at 1.9 million, and she doesn't flinch. I figure she's just another realtor wannabe, but as fate would have it, she's got someone for it, and they want to come by later today. Tell me that's not hot shit."

"I'm glad I'm sitting down. But to be honest, the place is a mess with all the renovation going on. Not to mention, I haven't started on the upstairs yet. It's probably a mess from the last game. You think it'll be a problem? Should I get a cleaning service in there right away?"

He knows. Harry was hoping to slip away in the dark of night and remain undiscovered until the next game, when his plan went into action. "No, it's clean as a whistle up there. And you're going be as happy as a clam at high tide when I tell you this. I got my own place. Signed a one-year lease. You know how tight the rental market is, right? So my trainer also has a unit in the East 70s that's perfect for me, and a steal no less. I had to jump on it. Maybe she does know real estate, and I got her pegged all wrong. Whaddaya think?"

"I think it's great, Harry. I was a little worried you might never leave." *What's wrong with this picture?* Everything Harry said might have been true, but if it were, why didn't he say anything about it? He would tell you everything about anything, even when you didn't ask. Harry was cooking something up, that much was certain.

"Not only that, I think she's got a thing for me."

"A thing?" Tim asked.

"Yeah. A thing. Hots for the H-Train."

Tim contained his laughter. "Go figure. A trainer, a realtor, and a lover all in one. Sounds like you hit a trifecta."

"A trifecta. I like that. Let me ask you a question: any idea where I can get one of those boner pills? I'm seeing her for dinner on Friday, and who knows what's gonna happen after."

"Do I look like a pharmacist? You're on your own with that."

"You know all those guys that used to sell drugs down in Washington Square? They should move uptown and sell those pills. They'd make a fortune."

"Harry, it's easy enough to see a doctor and get a scrip."

"I don't have time for that. And what if someone is having a drink somewhere and meets someone who's interested? Like he's gonna say, 'Sorry, I gotta see my doctor.' No. There's a guy hanging around selling. And then bingo bango bongo. Anyway, like I said, I won't be around later, so the game is all on you, partner."

Partner. Like he does anything besides hover around the buffet and bite into anything that doesn't bite back. He was going to be an ex-partner soon. Maybe Tim was wrong, and the story about the apartment was true. But getting a date? They say there's an ass for every seat, but Harry? Who would be attracted to him? No, the story was bullshit. *Am I being paranoid?* It didn't matter. If there was any chance Harry was going to torpedo him, Tim was going to be prepared. He was going to bounce Harry out of their deal with the poker game.

It would not jeopardize the sale of the flip. Business was business, and Harry knew that as well as anyone.

"Not to worry. How many billions of real estate have I handled? This is a piece of cake." *Partner, my ass. Your next partner is going to be wearing the same orange jumpsuit as you.*

CHAPTER
46

H E FELT HUMILIATED. Matt was now in Casey's office telling her about the conversation with Ramos. She wasn't as surprised as she was annoyed. "Let me give you some advice: if you want to grab somebody by the balls, you have to be standing in front of him."

Casey opened the file on her desk, then reached for the phone and angrily punched numbers into the dial. In a businesslike voice, she asked for Mr. Ramos.

"Hello, Mrs. Cassidy. Is it Mrs.?"

"It is, Mr. Ramos."

"I'm glad I didn't insult you."

"You didn't insult me, but you did insult my associate."

"My apologies if he took my turning down an insulting offer as an insult to him personally."

Casey did not like the direction this was taking. "I considered it a good lesson for him, and you taught it brilliantly."

"Age and experience will triumph over youth and energy. Teach him that one as well."

"Would you make me the same offer? I mean for lunch. I'm a sucker for good mofungos. How are their tostones?"

"You like tostones?"

"Especially with a good mojo."

"Cassidy? That's not Latina."

"I am not Latina, but that doesn't mean I can't eat like one. Tell me when can we get that lunch. Thinking about it is making me hungry."

Ramos became less formal and suggested, "Any time at all. It's a cozy place nearby, and if you're free this afternoon we can meet there. Some tostones, a Corona or two, and maybe we work this out."

"Send me the address, and I'll meet you there at one. By the way, put me down for a Dos Equis."

Both lawyers hung up their phones feeling good, and for the same reason: they would be rid of troublesome clients.

Casey arrived at the cafe ten minutes late, just late enough not to have to make any excuses, but late enough to make Ramos squirm a little. When she arrived, a hand waved in the air from the booth farthest from the door. Casey assumed it was Ramos, and taken by his good looks, she almost gasped. Her immediate thought was that she should have insisted on meeting at the Waldorf. A nice lunch, polish off the deal, get a room, and polish him off. Back to reality. As she approached the booth, Ramos stood up, stuck out his hand to shake hers, and told her it was nice that she could come on such short notice.

It didn't look like he'd been squirming at all. There was a half-empty bottle of Corona on the table, along with a basket of chips and cup of green salsa.

"I'm Bill Ramos. Nice to meet you in person."

"Likewise. I'm Casey Cassidy. Please call me Casey."

"Casey, I was expecting someone more mature. My impression of you, based on our conversation, was that of someone that had the wisdom of the ages."

"Wisdom does not necessarily come with age," Casey said.

"And age does not always bring wisdom."

"I feel like I might have read something like that in one of Shakespeare's works."

Ramos raised the beer bottle and pointed it toward Casey in acknowledgement before taking a long drink from the bottle. He then called to the server, "A Dos Equis for my guest.

"If he didn't write anything like that, he should have," Ramos continued.

The beer and frosted mug were brought to the table, prompting Casey to comment, "How thoughtful to remember the beer. Do you treat all your guests this way, or only lawyers representing the other side?"

"There's no substitute for courtesy, and good manners cost nothing and maybe gain everything."

"A philosopher lawyer. It's an interesting combination. Most of my clients prefer results to advice. It may start off with 'I need your advice' but always circles back to 'I want that bastard out of my life and to take him for everything he's worth.'"

"My clients beg me to get them a green card so they can stay in this country. When I succeed, they are overwhelmed with joy. When I fail, they are grateful for the effort but scared and saddened for their future."

"Mine are bitter for a long time, regardless of how generous the settlement."

The server appeared and took the lunch orders, which included another round of beers. It was an opportune time, since both lawyers were uncomfortable with the sadness that tinged the conversation, and more beer would provide a temporary salve.

Ramos again drank from the bottle, even though his beer came with the same frosted mug as his drinking partner. He put the bottle down and dipped a chip into the salsa. He bit off half the chip and started telling Casey about his parents spiriting him out of Cuba and resettling in New York after living in Miami for a year. "Pretty ironic, huh? Most New Yorkers can't wait to move to Florida. My parents couldn't leave there fast enough."

"I grew up upstate, in Elmira, and couldn't wait to get out of there. A lot of people wax poetic about their hometowns or home country. Personally, I think it's a load of crap. I'm quite fine where I am, thank you very much."

Ramos said, "Understood. I can promise you that no matter how bad Elmira is, it's a distant second to Havana."

"I know people that leave here, and you know what they complain about? How they can't get a good bagel or slice of pizza."

Lunch arrived. They had ordered the same thing, a Cuban sandwich and tostones on the side. Ramos bit into the twice-fried plantain, about the size of a potato chip. As he was munching on it, he commented, "Maybe people complain they can't get a good bagel. I promise you they couldn't get a tostone at all, good or bad."

Another swig from the bottle and he changed gears. "So, Casey, how are we going to deal with the unhappy couple?"

Casey put her sandwich back on the plate and finished chewing the first bite she had taken. She pointed down at the plate and said, "You know, this sandwich is absolutely fabulous. Even if we can't solve the problems in the world of the Rosens, I'm glad I came here to have this." Then, adding in a voice a little louder than a whisper, "And meeting you, of course."

Whoa. This is definitely a come-on, and she really is smokin' hot, Ramos thought. *I could definitely go for some of that. Forget it. Maybe after this is settled.*

"Very nice of you to say that. Next time you pick the place. And by saying that I am not inferring that we should not try to sharpen our pencils and settle this today. Let's think of that as a victory celebration." With a little luck, Ramos figured he could score twice. Once on the settlement, and once with Casey.

Jesus. What I could do with this guy. A Latin lover, and a fucking Cuban, no less. An afternoon with him in a hotel room, and I'll sharpen his pencil, all right.

"So getting down to brass tacks: most of what they have is real estate. What's wrong with Harry selling the building and splitting the proceeds with Debbie? Fair and square."

Ramos took another bite of his lunch, followed by a big enough drink from the beer bottle to empty it. Casey sat silently, waiting for him to gather his thoughts. Why else would he pick up the sandwich after her offer? He put the empty bottle down and asked Casey if she wanted another beer. She shook her head, and he raised the bottle in the direction of the bar and in voice loud enough for the server called, "Uno mas."

Picking up the conversation about the Rosens, he repeated, "Fair and square. I like that. Is your client going to play fair and square with the apartment? As long as Harry's been living there, he should get half the proceeds from the sale."

"My client has lived there her entire life, and she's on the lease. It's hers. I can promise you that she would never agree to sharing any part of the proceeds whatsoever."

"I could make a similar argument for Harry's building. He bought it and uses it for his business. I'm sure you'd agree that the business by itself without the building is worthless."

"Bill, I will concede the part about the business being worthless, but how do I explain to my client that even though she's on the deed, she has no ownership interest?"

Ramos paused to let that sink in. She brought up "fair and square," and maybe she was serious. He wasn't going to waste any more time if she was peddling a load of crap. It was time to lay it out there. "Fair and square. I believed you when you said that, so what I am going to propose is just that. Let's say his building is worth three million, and the apartment is worth 1.4. Add that up, it comes to 4.4, so each is entitled to 2.2. She wants the apartment at 1.4, she'll be entitled to another $800,000 from Harry."

There wasn't any thought required on Casey's part. What he suggested was simplistic and fair. Not exactly how she was used to settling. This wasn't going to be different. "That's an interesting proposal, but nothing I can sell to my client. I met Harry once and was sick of him in about two minutes. She put up with him for like twenty years. If that were an army assignment, Debbie would be entitled to hazardous duty pay."

Even Ramos had to laugh. He admitted that over the course of two meetings and one phone call, he came to despise Harry as well. "Let's imagine that this goes to court. You think the judge is going to sympathetic to either one? He'd have to adjourn so he could go to chambers and get an air sickness bag."

This guy is hilarious. A sense humor, smart, great looks. If he's got a good-sized shlong and knows how to use it, he could be my next husband.

Casey's mind momentarily wandered. What was wrong with her current husband? Nothing, really. So this guy was younger, big deal. He was a sole practitioner in a poor neighborhood, and probably broke. No way he'd fly first class unless someone else paid. She'd keep him on the side for fun and games.

It was her turn to stall. She took a small bite of her lunch, chewed, swallowed, and picked up a napkin to dab at her mouth. Her thoughts gathered, Casey leaned forward, getting as close to his face as the table between them would allow and asked, "Don't you love the sound of one million? It's really not that different from $900,000. It's like when they advertise crap on TV for $19.95. It doesn't sound like twenty. People feel like it's cheap. So if I can make your offer sound excessive, with a number that starts with a million something, it will be more appealing."

Ramos said, "I have no authority to negotiate for my client. Regardless of how I feel about the fairness of any offer, he's only going rant about how he could have done better. I have to put this in the prospective of how this would be settled in court."

"Typically, I would be glad to take this to court, but my goal is to put this to bed," Casey answered in a throaty voice.

Put this to bed. I'd like to put her to bed. She is just fucking gorgeous.

Those tits! Am I wrong, or did she undo a button on her blouse since she got here? Of course she did. I know she leaned in on purpose. I'd better get a grip, or this could end badly for Harry, but great for me. Would he find out? Would he sue me? Would I be sanctioned or disbarred? Fuck me. I shouldn't have had that last beer.

"Casey, I will run this by Harry and leave the decision to him. Are you confident that your client will be good with that? She gets the apartment and a million dollars."

"And the car. He makes the payments and buys out the lease for her at the end of the term." Casey took a breath, then added, "And $20,000 cash upon signing."

Ramos thought about that, smiled, and thought, *That's probably for the legal fees.* "You know, I really couldn't care any less about this. My goals are to get a deal my client will accept and not get disbarred. Or shot by a jealous spouse."

Why the fuck would he say that? Does he know about Debbie and the murders? That means Harry knows. God knows who else. Shit shit shit. Holy fucking shit! I've got to report this to the police. Holy fucking shit!

Another thought entered Casey's mind: maybe he's trying to intimidate me. That was something she could deal with, and if that was the case, she'd come at him so hard, he'd wish he'd never met her. There was only one way to find out. She looked him in the eye, cocked her head, and asked, "Why would you say that?"

"When we spoke on the phone this morning, I addressed you as Mrs. Cassidy, which you said was correct. Frankly, I'm quite taken by you and would love to spend some, shall we say, 'social time' with you."

A wave of relief washed over every inch of Casey. "As far as I know, my husband does not own a gun." Gaining control of herself, she got back to business. "Let's put this to our respective clients. As for the social time, have you ever had room service at the Carlyle Hotel? I can promise you it's the best lunch you'll ever have. After we get this agreement signed off." Casey then got up and told Ramos, "You get the check. The next one is on me."

He stared at her ass as she walked toward the door. *Harry better approve that deal,* he thought.

CHAPTER
47

WHILE IZZY WAS waiting for Tim at Starbucks, he was at the apartment on Perry Street. It was empty — not even a toothbrush. This was the second eviction that he would not have to make. He walked down the flight of stairs and outside to the van parked illegally at the fire hydrant in front of the building. Tim told the crew to bring up the furniture packed in the van and to change lock on the apartment door.

This was the easiest way to end his partnership with Harry: move the game and limit the players to only his clients. There were people whom he did not know getting into the game, and that made Tim uncomfortable. Who were these guys? Were any of them professionals or cheaters? Somebody loses their temper over a bad loss, makes a stink, and the next thing you know everything spins out of control. Yelling and screaming, kicking and punching, god forbid maybe a weapon or bloodshed, or another chaotic occurrence. Tim didn't mind the unknowns, but chaos was another story. If chaos were a disease, Harry would be a carrier.

Not to mention he didn't buy Harry's explanation about moving out. Harry was up to something, and it wasn't going to benefit Tim. It was better to put some distance between them and to do it pronto. Like taking off a Band-Aid, better to do it quickly. Get it over with. That was what he was doing today. No more Harry, except to sell the house.

And no more Izzy. It was a mistake to get involved when he realized that it was not going to be a romantic relationship. It felt great for about a minute and half when he gave her the use of the apartment without the quid pro quo. After that moment, nothing. He got nothing out of the deal, and that was all it was, a deal. No money, no sex, nothing. The deal between them was over. Funny thing was she ended it before he did. Clearly she had moved out of his apartment and didn't tell him. Maybe that was what was making him angry. Izzy dumped him, but it didn't stop her from asking him to finance her unwritten play. At least she was transparent about that.

Coincidentally, Harry moved out the same way — no notice. What the hell was going on? Alarm bells were ringing in his head. Tim turned his radar on high, and even though he wasn't superstitious, he would make sure not to walk under any ladders or near any black cats.

It was pleasant weather for a walk, but his thoughts spoiled his appreciation for a spring-like day this time of year.

He was going to be about twenty minutes late for his appointment with Izzy. Maybe she'd buy her own cappuccino or whatever the hell it was. *Let her stick her hand in her own pocket.* His anger was building to a level that could fog his judgment. After fuming about Izzy for a few blocks, Tim realized that his head was in a bad space. He had to calm down before he met with her. A few deep breaths, which he held in for several seconds before exhaling, and thoughts of a day at the beach, and then he was ready.

Someone leaving the coffee shop stopped to hold the door open for Tim. *Why is this guy so nice? I can open the door by myself, asshole.* He managed to say "thank you" without a grumble. The act reminded him of what it was like in Elmira. Casey reminded him about going there for Christmas. Another three days of his life he'd never get back. At least two of the three were in the car. Maybe he wouldn't have to explain why he was on the phone so much on Christmas. During one visit, he was about to yell, "Because there are three football games today and I'm a bookmaker. And the reason they put three games on TV is because people like football better than listening to crazy relatives." Fortunately, Casey had spoken up first and distracted them from the inquiry.

An arm was raised with a hand waving at Tim. It was Izzy, and she was already there with a beverage. *Good, another few bucks I can keep for myself.* His anger had not totally subsided. He walked over to the table and accepted the air kiss.

She spoke first. "Wow. You look great. It's really good to see you."

"Sorry I'm late. It's always good to see you. I would have thought my generosity would have resulted in seeing each other more often."

Tim was still angry and looking for an excuse to get rid of her. Actually, he already had what he wanted, and that was her out of his apartment. He decided that his anger stemmed from her trying to play him for a chump. Izzy was lying about her writing and by Tim's estimation looking for a sugar daddy. When they first met, that was his intention. Somewhere along the way it turned into a one-way street. And it went only toward Izzy. Although he no longer cared about pursuing her in any way, Tim wanted her to know that if you want to get something, you've got to give something.

Izzy was flustered and not sure about what Tim meant. Her first reaction was that this was about sex, or rather the lack of it. She had thought that he had no expectations. *Was I wrong?* "I know, and I like hanging out with you. Between work and writing, I've been so busy that I haven't had much time for socializing."

Working was awful, by her account. Demanding customers, and bosses that were even more so. Izzy decided she didn't want to put up with that anymore and figured that as long as she didn't have to pay rent, all she needed was about twenty thousand dollars. That way she could enjoy the remaining months in her gap year. It would be like a continuation of college, without going to class.

"Oh my god. Is this about sex? Is this something that I could hashtag as MeToo?" Izzy tried to sound as indignant and intimidating as she could.

"No, it's not about sex. And the only I hash I know about is corned beef hash, which I don't care for."

"Then why are you harassing me?"

"I would suggest that it's you harassing me for money. You ask me to finance your play, but you're not willing to show me anything. Not a writing sample, nothing."

Ignoring him, Izzy countered, "It sounded to me like you were saying if didn't have sex with you, then I'd have to move out. You were pretty clear when you offered me your place that sex was not part of the deal."

Tired of the banter, Tim said, "It wasn't then and it isn't now. Just give me back the key to the apartment, unless you need some more time to move out." Like any good attorney, he knew the answer to that question before he asked.

Izzy continued to ignore him. "I can get my play workshopped and produced at a small venue for $25,000, and if it's a success you can get back like ten times that. I lined up a few actors, Broadway actors, that are willing to do it. They all think it's going to be incredible."

"Then let them put up the money."

"They're actors. They don't have any money."

"Izzy, I have enough of my own problems. Putting money blindly into financing your play is not going to happen. Not from me anyway." Knowing she'd already moved out, he added, "Someone will be there to change the lock on the door before today is over. Maybe your actor friends can help you pack up."

She then reached for her bag, riffled through it, and threw a key ring on the table. "Here are your stupid keys. You cheap lecher." With that she got up and left.

Tim hoped she was leaving him too and wished that things had worked out differently. What he really wished was that he had banged her.

CHAPTER
48

S INCE HER LAST discussion with Casey, Debbie had started searching the real estate sites on the Internet. It confirmed everything she'd heard about Florida homes. She could buy a bigger, modern apartment and still have about a million left over from the deal with Goldblum alone. With more from Harry, Debbie was sure she could live comfortably for the rest of her life.

The intercom buzzed. Debbie answered and was told by the doorman that a messenger was there with a large envelope for her. "Would you please come down and sign for it?"

Probably from my lawyer, she thought. The glowing admiration for her lawyer faded. Maybe it was when she believed that Matt jilted her. In her mind they had a date, and she got stood up. *I was so ready for him, and then he shows up with that appraiser.*

After a quick trip to the lobby, Debbie was back in the apartment, looking through the documents. The first was several pages long, most of which she did not understand. She did understand the sentence that said "One million four hundred thousand dollars," with the amount shown next to the words: $1,400,000. There were yellow stickers attached next to each line that required a signature. She saw where Harry needed to sign as well.

The next document was an outline of the settlement that reflected the terms her lawyer had discussed with Harry's attorney. Proceeds from the value of his building, the car, more cash. *Maybe these lawyers are okay.*

Another document was very easy to understand. It was an invoice for legal fees. Amount due, $10,000. *Unbelievable. I already paid them 5,000!*

Instead of "hello," the first words out of Debbie's mouth were, "I don't understand some of this stuff you sent me."

On the other end of the line, Casey patiently answered, "I'd be glad to explain. Which of them needs clarity?"

"How come I'm only getting $800,000 from the sale of Harry's building? It has to be worth about four million. I should get two."

"Debbie, you're getting all of the money from the apartment."

"That's because it's mine. I've lived here my whole life. I should get all the money. When Harry bought that building, his credit sucked and he needed me to get the mortgage, and my father gave him the down payment. So I deserve half of that."

"If this went to court, unless there was something egregious, the settlement would not be that generous."

"Egregious? You mean like if he killed those guys?"

Jesus! What the fuck! I don't need this.

"Just so you know, the police already called me. They interviewed Harry to confirm his alibi. I verified that he was at a real estate closing that I was a part of."

"And I want the down payment back too, fifty thousand."

"We can ask for anything. What they'll agree to is another story. If we don't reach an agreement, though, it will go to court, and the likely outcome is that all the assets will be divided equally."

"That's what I'm saying. I want half of what he's got. Plus the fifty thousand. And everything else you put in your letter."

"What about the the apartment?" Casey asked.

"That's mine completely."

"You know, Debbie, I hear this a lot. What's mine is mine and half of everything you have is mine. I will push to make the deal a little better, but no promises. It's tilted in your favor as is."

"I saw your bill too. For that kind of money, you should be able to get me what I want."

It was time for Casey to regain control of her client. Time was working against Debbie because of the year-end deadline. Casey wanted to get this over with, and quickly. She was going to lower the hammer.

"Okay, Debbie, if that's what you want. It may take some time, probably a year or two. Just be prepared for the additional legal fees. Also, keep in mind that there is an expiration date for you to get the money from Goldblum. There's no guarantee you'd get an extension. Further, you never know how the court will rule." Casey took a pause and then went for the jugular. "Are you prepared to go through this for an extended period, both financially and emotionally? Are you prepared for the possibility that the outcome may be less generous? Are you willing to accept that my fees will increase substantially?" The last one was a trump card. It always brought clients to their senses.

It took Debbie a few moments to absorb everything she just heard. She was running out of money as it was. *How am I going to live for the next year? I don't have enough money to pay the legal fees I have now. Who knows how much more it will be in a year?*

"When do you think I can get all the money? I need it just to pay your bill."

"Debbie, it's a great deal, and you made a great decision. I will check with Harry's attorney, who has to have the same discussion we just had. If Harry agrees, we can wrap this up in a matter of weeks."

"Thank you, Casey. I'll sign and return all of these. You will have to wait for your check, though. And I want the fifty thousand back that my father gave him."

Why did she have bring up the murders? She must have been the killer. Did Harry have a part in it? God, please don't let her bring that up again. Casey dialed Matt Bernstein's extension and told him, "I'm a little tense. Get in here."

CHAPTER
49

"You gotta be fucking kidding me." Harry was sitting across from Ramos, listening to the proposed settlement agreement with his wife. "That's a joke, right?" He continued to rant. "I paid her rent, I paid for her shopping, everything since we were married, and if she ever stuck her hand in her pocket to pay for anything, it was my money. Instead of a lawyer, she should see a shrink, because she's out of her fucking mind."

Ramos used the same argument about the courts with Harry that Casey used with Debbie, but to no avail. He was adamant. Ramos insisted that the best he could expect was an equal division of the assets, unless she was involved in some felonious activity.

"You mean like if she murdered those two Russians?"

"What are you talking about?"

"Those murders. The two Russian guys on Long Island."

"Oh, that. Your wife was the killer?"

"I didn't say that she was. I said *if.*"

"If she was, you should go to the police. If she wasn't, why does it matter?"

"I was just saying..."

Ramos cut him off. "Harry, anybody can say anything about anyone else. Suppose she said the same thing about you? Someone makes a statement like that, they have to be prepared to back it up. Sort of like saying the Jets couldn't beat Slippery Rock State University. You can say it, but you don't know unless they play."

Ramos didn't want to hear anything about anything else that had to do with Harry Rosen. Although something told him Harry or his wife was involved. Why would Harry bring that up in particular? With a pending divorce and a few million dollars involved, he wouldn't be the first husband wanting to take out his wife. Or the first to do it.

Ramos didn't want to get involved, and he believed there was something to Harry's "what if" statement. There was one thing he liked about Harry: he paid in advance. He disliked everything else.

"Let's get back to this settlement. Here's what's going to happen, plain and simple: you're each going to get half of the total combined assets."

"That's totally not going to happen…"

Once again, Ramos cut him off. "It is going to happen, and because your wife is not working, she may be awarded alimony. How are going to feel when you have to write her a check every month?"

"There's no way that's going to happen."

"Oh, it's going to happen. And if it doesn't, there are going to be liens and judgments. Try getting a loan with that on your credit report."

The air was coming out of Harry's balloon. "I can't believe how one-sided this is."

Ramos sensed the resignation. "This is a fair deal, and you're rid of her. The few bucks you'll pay up-front and the car lease is nothing compared to what you might otherwise pay."

Harry's last gasp was that he would think about it.

When Ramos told Harry that if this went any further, he'd need an additional retainer of five thousand, Harry relented.

Harry left the office. As soon as Ramos heard the door slam shut, and Harry *did* slam the door shut, he called Casey.

Ramos happily said, "It was grueling, but my client is on board."

"That's great, Bill. We're only fifty thousand away."

"I'm sorry. I didn't get that."

"My client wants another fifty, and it's a deal."

"Another fifty and it's a deal. You make it sound like it's tip money. Something for the doorman at Christmas. I'm dealing with Harry fucking Rosen. You met the guy. Fifty cents, fifty thousand, fifty million, it doesn't matter. It's going to kill this deal."

"That's a pity. I guess we're never going to have that lunch at the Carlyle," Casey said with a sigh, then authoritatively added, "Call me when the modified document is signed. I've already sent it by email."

"Motherfucker." It was too late for Casey to hear. She had already hung up.

CHAPTER

50

B Y THE TIME Tim got back to Perry Street, the work crew was pretty much finished setting up the apartment. There was some furniture that didn't fit, and the foreman asked if he wantedit back in the house uptown. "No. Keep it. Sell it. Whatever you want to do with it." Tim then took some cash out of his pocket and counted out three hundred. "Here, split this up with your guys, and before you knock off for the day, stop at the house and change the lock on the second floor. Good work."

"Thanks, boss. That's very generous. The new keys are on the table. Tested them out, and they work. Any problems with anything, let me know."

"You got it. See you tomorrow."

The men emptied out, and Tim surveyed the new decor. He liked what he saw: a compact version of the previous layout. "Time to get to work." He sat at the table and called the players he wanted at the game, as well as the dealer, hostess, and security. Same game, same time, different place. No questions were asked, and most were happy because they didn't have go all the way uptown.

He laughed as he wondered if he should leave a note on the door at what was now the game's previous location: "game cancelled." As funny as he thought that was, it wasn't fair to the players he didn't invite into the relocated game. Tim decided to outsource that to Harry.

Harry was at the gym when he got the call. His plan was down the drain, but the end result was the same. Now that he didn't have a partner and all of his rules, Harry was ready. The new place was set up. All he needed were to let the unchosen, as he thought of the players Tim did not invite, know where the game was and find the people to work it.

Susan walked by. "What's with the phone? You're supposed to be working your abs. They're in there, and one day the whole world will see them."

"This is big. It's the opportunity I've waiting for for a really long time."

"*You're* big. Much too big, and your abs are my opportunity. You need to get to the 'after.' I and every one else who sees you now have seen plenty. Put the phone down."

"Let me ask you something: why do I pay you?"

"Because you're about two Happy Meals away from a heart attack."

"I'm working on something now that can put me into some serious cash."

"Serious cash will not prevent a heart attack."

"Hey, Susan, you like getting paid. I like being able to pay you, so give me some space here to get some work done."

"It's not a deal on that listing of yours I just showed, is it? I think my guys are going to make an offer."

That momentarily diverted Harry's attention. A property sale, his own card game, and a soon-to-be-ex-wife all in the same day. *This is what heaven must be like.*

"Let me ask you a crazy question: you've got a lot of clients here. You think any of them know anything about poker?"

Susan quizzically said, "You mean like if you get the nuts on the flop, should you check and hope someone raises, or immediately go all in?"

"I guess you've watched it enough on TV."

"Yeah. And on online. And in casinos. And in some private games."

"Really? Why are you doing this?"

"It was too addictive, and a very unhealthy lifestyle. Plus I went broke."

"I'm putting a game together at my new place and need a dealer. Maybe you know somebody?"

"I do. How about me?"

How much more good luck can I have today? He gave Susan all the details about the game then asked, "Are you sure you're up for it?"

"Believe me, I am. I wish I had a big enough stake to get in, but I'll settle for dealing it, assuming you'll pay me. I'm not going to work only for the tips."

"No problem. Be there by six. I'll need some help setting up."

"Let's finish up, and we can both get ready."

After a quick shower, Harry fervently worked the phone, telling of the new, safer, location, and higher stakes. He got assurances from ten people that they would be there. If Harry could jump, he would jump for joy. There was going to be a big turnout and big money.

It's funny how circumstances change your thinking. At first, he figured maybe the game pays for the rent. Now? Maybe he gets a place for the winter in West Palm Beach, close enough to the airport that he can fly in for the game and be back in the warm sun the next day. This was the stuff his dreams were made of.

Susan got to Harry's new place and remarked, "I like what you did with it." It was all she could think of to say not to offend him. Tasteful or fashionable were not evident here. Harry went for functional. Two functions, anyway: playing cards or watching TV.

"Thanks. I figure I'll get some movie posters or something for the walls when I get a chance. I'm thinking like ones from *The Hustler* and *The Cincinnati Kid*. Keep up the theme."

"Paul Newman. Great actor. I loved him in *The Sting*. Where can I put my coat?"

"I didn't think about that. Just throw it on the bed."

"Just throw it on the bed? You're going to have people walking in the door with thousands of dollars, and you're going to tell them to throw their coats on the bed?"

"Why not?"

"Because they'll expect more. A little class. Have you got an empty closet and some hangers?"

"A closet yes, in the hall. Hangers, no."

"Harry, do you have any suits or shirts?"

"Of course."

"Are they on hangers in your closet?"

"Yes."

"Then take those off the hangers and put your fucking suits on the bed. Then give me the hangers. We'll use those and your empty closet."

Harry got to work piling the clothes on his bed. Susan watched and gathered up the empty hangers. She put them on the rod in the hall closet and used one for her coat. Harry was standing behind her and said, "Whoa," when she turned around.

"Like what you see, big boy?"

He had never seen her in anything but sweatpants and tee-shirts. Who could imagine she'd look this good? A slinky, low-cut black dress that ended well short of her knees showed most of the spectacular rack that Susan had barely, just barely, hidden.

"I do like what I see. And I'm seeing a lot. You think they'll be able to focus on the game with you dealing?"

"Better tips if they're looking at my nips."

Harry was staring. In a sharp tone, Susan said, "Up here, Harry, my eyes are up here."

Startled, Harry could only manage a meek, "Sorry."

"Before I get started, it's gonna be five hundred, and I leave at midnight. If I stay past midnight, it's another five hundred, whether the game goes another five minutes or three hours."

Harry handed over the money without comment. He did sneak a quick peek when she counted the money.

"It's going to be great. Don't worry about a thing. Now where's the food?"

Harry, still recovering from the excitement of seeing her barely-covered breasts, was reduced to short answers. "In the kitchen."

Catering, to Harry, meant putting out a platter of finger sandwiches, a tray of pigs in a blanket, and a camping cooler filled with iced-down cans of beer and soft drinks. He couldn't understand why Tim would have shrimp, champagne, wine, and some other stuff that a hostess would serve. Sure, it was great, but Harry believed the players came to play cards, not eat. And they could help themselves.

"This is your idea of food? What's the buy-in for this game, twenty bucks?"

"The buy-in is twenty-five hundred."

"So these guys are walking in with that kind of money and you're going to give them a pig in a blanket? You want them to come back. It's like a wedding. Everyone always remembers the food."

Susan picked her bag up from the poker table, fished out her phone, and started dialing. "You're going to love this stuff." He heard her say that she had to feed twelve people and wanted a half tray of eggplant parm, a half tray of chicken marsala, three orders of stuffed mushrooms, and a small salad. Putting her hand between the phone and her mouth, Susan said, "That's for you, Harry." She told them to deliver it around nine.

"Gee, I can hardly wait until nine," Harry said sarcastically.

"Neither can I, Harry. Neither can I."

CHAPTER
51

E ACH TIME A player arrived, the reaction was the same when Susan answered the door. First, they nearly had to glue their eyes back into their sockets. Then, when she offered to take their coats, it brought a "thank you" and a bill, usually a ten or a twenty. Some followed that with innuendo about another tip they had for her, maybe after the game. Susan would smile and coyly remark, "You never know, anything can happen."

Harry took the dealer's seat after the crowd filled the table, throwing fifties and hundreds toward him. Harry counted each bill, making sure they amounted to the agreed buy-in of twenty-five hundred, and in return he passed stacks of chips across the table. It was hard not to notice the gold Rolex on Harry's wrist each time. Two envelopes stuffed with cash were now in Harry's jacket pocket. All ten men were seated. They were surprised when Harry got up and introduced Susan as the dealer.

"Okay, people, if you need to know how the game is played, you should cash out and leave now." It drew a few laughs, and nobody left. Susan, with some difficulty, kept her editorial comments to herself. She dealt the game professionally and kept it moving. No complaints.

A few hours later, the intercom buzzed. "Must be the food. I hope you guys are hungry and like Italian." Harry pressed the button that would open the lobby door. A couple of guys walked up behind the delivery man, who was struggling with two large shopping bags. One of them said, "Let me help you with that door." He walked in front of him, held it open, and let him pass by. The two guys stopped and let him get a few steps ahead. Harry walked back to watch the game, especially to keep an eye on Susan. He wanted to make sure she was raking money out of the pot. When he heard the footsteps, Harry said, "I'll be right there, just put it on the table."

The delivery man walked in, and just a few steps behind were the two men. One closed the door behind them. The other pulled out a gun and calmly told everyone that this was a robbery. "No noise. Do what you're told so it doesn't become a murder. Let's see all those up hands up in the air. If I see a phone in any of them, you've made your last call," the gunman told the crowd.

His partner in crime, now armed with his own gun, pointed at Harry and asked if he liked the poker references his partner made. "Hands up. Last call. Get it? Hands, call?"

Harry stood silent, his pants starting to feel damp. "Yeah, I get it."

Now standing next to Harry with his gun barrel pressing against Harry's cheek, he told his partner to collect everyone's cell phones. Dumping the contents from a bag containing the recent food delivery, the accomplice went around the table and filled the bag with phones.

"Where's yours, hot stuff?" he snarled at Susan.

"In the closet. My coat pocket."

Wanting to make sure that she didn't have anywhere to hide a device, he ordered her to stand up and turn around.

Satisfied, he told her to stay put.

As if Harry wasn't scared enough, the gunman next to him told him to open his mouth. He put the gun in Harry's mouth and calmly told him, "I'm going to take this gun out of your mouth, and either words telling me where the money is are going to come out, or a bullet is going in. Understood?"

Harry nodded. "My jacket. Left inside breast pocket."

The gunman moved the two fat envelopes from Harry's pocket to his own. Being at least a half foot taller than Harry, the gold watch on Harry's wrist was inches away from the robber's nose. The robber clumsily removed that and added it to his pocket. Pointing to the rear, he barked at Harry, "Where does that door go?"

On the verge of collapse, he could only answer, "The outside patio."

"You, delivery guy. Open the door. Everyone outside."

After all of them were outside, the two robbers locked the door and calmly walked out the front, but not before they stopped at the buffet table and picked up some finger sandwiches to go.

When the fear and panic subsided, the crowd on the patio wanted back inside. The entire episode lasted less than five minutes. Harry had aged twenty years. Someone tried the door. It was locked.

"How do we get in, Harry?" someone asked.

He was unresponsive. Susan then asked, "Harry? Harry? Are you with me?"

He could only nod.

"Do you have the house keys?"

Again, Harry nodded.

"Jesus," Susan said, getting frustrated.

She started riffling through his pants pockets. They were wet. Determining why, she shouted, "Oh, gross!" but kept on until she found the keys. A turn of the key that fit the lock and a push on the door got them all inside. Harry was Sphinx-like and had to be led in.

Demanding to be paid, the delivery man threatened to call the police. The players each kicked in enough to pay the check and tip him to keep his mouth shut.

A debate then arose among the players.

"Suppose he does call the cops? Harry gets arrested and the prick will never pay us."

Another chimed in, "I was up some serious cash. Who makes good on that?"

One of the losers offered, "You don't know that the game was going to end that way."

Still another suggested they keep playing, "Why not? The chips are on the table where they were before we were interrupted."

"Interrupted? What, was that like a phone call? We were fucking robbed."

After the debate, it was the general consensus that if Harry made them whole, who needed the cops?

"Harry, are you going to make good on this?"

No response.

"Shouldn't we put a paper bag over his head and have him breathe into it?"

"Nah, that's for hyperventilating. He's hardly ventilating."

This brought a big laugh from all. Harry came to when someone undid his belt and dropped a handful of ice cubes down his pants.

"What the fuck!" Harry yelled.

"No bullshit, Harry. Are you good for the money, or do we call the police?"

With a sigh, Harry replied that he was good for it, but he needed some time. "I got a deal working that's gonna close any day now."

After the card players filed out, Susan took her coat from the closet and walked over to Harry. "Come over to the gym tomorrow. A good workout will help...and stay away from all this food. It'll kill you."

"It'll kill me," Harry mumbled as she left.

I had a gun to my head, but the chicken marsala is going to kill me? I don't think so. He grabbed the tray and started eating.

CHAPTER
52

H ARRY WOKE UP in a cold sweat. He was living in an apartment he could not afford and owed twenty-five thousand he didn't have to guys he suspected knew how to collect.

It was 11:00 a.m. when the intercom buzzed. This time Harry asked who it was. "Cleaning service." He hit the button that opened the lobby door. When he heard the knock, he looked through the peephole in the door before he opened it.

Despite the cool fall morning air, Harry had been sitting on his patio in a bathrobe. Not yet ready to get dressed, he made himself another coffee and went back outside.

It was Saturday, and there was a full schedule of college football. Harry thought about betting a few games. *Just a few to pick up some spending money.* He looked to see which were going to be on TV and then read the sports pages for any info about those games. Twenty minutes later, Harry was on the phone with Tim.

"Good morning, Harry." This was a workday for Tim, and he was not looking to spend much time on small talk.

"Hey, big guy. I got a few that I like today."

"Go ahead."

"Alabama, Texas, Florida, Ohio State, and Notre Dame. Two grand each."

"Okay. Bama, Texas, Florida, the Buckeyes, and the fighting Irish. Spreads are in today's *Post*. Two thousand each," Tim echoed back.

"You got it."

"Hey, Harry, before I hang up. How did it go last night?"

THAT MOTHERFUCKER. HE WAS BEHIND THE WHOLE THING!

"You Irish fucking prick. I never figured you for the type of guy to pull that crap."

"What the hell are you talking about?"

"*My* game. Or what used to be my game. It was held up last night. One of your guys put a fucking gun to my head."

"Jesus, I had nothing to do with any of that. Firstly, I don't know where you live, and secondly, I'm the guy that put the game in your lap."

"Give me a break. You were pissed that I was starting to make some money and going off on my own."

"Believe me, Harry, I was not involved. Maybe you ought to look at everyone else who was there. Probably an inside job. Did you go to the police?"

"No, I didn't fucking go to the police. Am I like the king of the morons?"

Tim laughed. "Sorry, Harry, but that was funny."

"Hilarious. I'd be laughing myself, except for the fact that I'm out twenty-five g's."

"Maybe I should cancel your action. I don't want any problems having to collect if you lose."

"You're not gonna have any problems. First, my picks are locks. They can't miss. Besides, you got a big payday coming. I'm expecting an offer any day now. And the shoe is going to be on the other foot. You're gonna owe me some serious moolah."

"Okay, Harry, your action is on. Goodbye and good luck."

The cleaners did their job and left. They had thoughtfully wrapped most of the food and put it in the refrigerator. Harry discovered that when he went looking for the tonic water to go with the gin. He grabbed a handful of the pigs in a blanket and heated them in the microwave. A minute later, they were done. Three minutes after that, Harry finished his breakfast.

Wearing sweatpants and a hoodie, he walked to the gym. *The treadmill has a TV screen. I can get a run in and watch the game at the same time.* Harry thought himself a genius for that.

Which player set him up? This seed planted by Tim was germinating. The more he thought about it, the more it made sense. Harry didn't really know any of them well. Not that it mattered. He was helpless to do anything.

At the gym, Harry grabbed a towel and removed his hoodie. Beneath it, he was wearing a tee-shirt bearing the image of a leprechaun holding a beer with the words "Fighting Irish" beneath. Notre Dame was a de facto home team for New York college football fans. You didn't have to be Irish or Catholic to root for them. Most people who saw the shirt laughed.

Two miles on the treadmill was enough. He saw Susan laughing and talking to two familiar-looking guys in the back of the gym. Walking toward them, he suddenly felt a jolt of fear and froze in place. Susan noticed Harry only several steps away. There was something unnerving about the two men, although Susan did not seem the least bit uncomfortable.

"Hey, Harry, come on over. I'd like to introduce you to a couple of my friends. This is Freddie, and this is Eddie." Susan figured that Harry wouldn't remember their faces because of the fear struck into him by the gun.

By reflex, Harry stuck out his hand. "Nice meeting you."

The first of them to respond, Freddie, took Harry's hand and shook it. Harry noticed the Rolex. It was his. They were the stickup men. While the terror of the previous night replayed in his head, he managed to stammer, "Nice watch."

"Thanks. I'm thinking about selling it. If you're interested, I'll let you have it for five thousand."

Scared and dumbfounded, Harry managed to answer, "It sounds like a great deal. But I'm a little short of cash right now."

Eddie jumped into the conversation. "You know, Harry, it is a great deal, and you really should buy it. I'll bet it would look great on you. Freddie, give him the watch to try on."

Before he could answer, Eddie grabbed Harry's arm, and Freddie put the watch on Harry's wrist.

"See, it does look good," Eddie said to his cohort.

Freddie agreed. "It looks great. You like it, Harry?"

Harry nodded.

"Okay, it's yours. You'll bring us five thousand by the end of the week." Eddie added, "And you know that we know where you live."

The two watch salesmen left.

Susan, acting as if nothing had happened, said, "Harry, funny you should stop by. My clients have an offer on your listing."

"You set me up. What the fuck?"

"Do you want to hear the offer or not?"

"I trusted you. Paid you top dollar. And you have those two goons fucking rob me and put me out of business."

"It's a really great offer, Harry."

"They could have killed me."

"All cash. No contingencies."

"As if that's not enough, they walk up to me like nothing happened, then shake me down for another five thousand."

"Will you stop whining? It's a great offer. One point eight, and they close in thirty days."

All the hostility left Harry's mind immediately. Everything Susan said finally registered. He did the math in his head quickly. This was going to be a six-figure payday.

"I'll give him a call. If he doesn't take that deal, he'd better pack his bag and reserve a room at Bellevue."

"Like I said, I think it's a great offer, and you're right — he'd have to be crazy not to take it."

"When I find out, you'll find out. By the way, the money for my watch is gonna come out of your end."

"Harry, go fuck yourself."

CHAPTER
53

Late that Sunday morning, Tim walked in the bedroom carrying a glass filled with champagne and orange juice in each hand. He placed one of them on the nightstand next to Casey's side of the bed. He sat down, leaned over, and whispered in her in her ear, "Time to get up."

Saturday night was celebratory. Harry conveyed to Tim the news about the offer, and they'd spent the day screwing, shopping, drinking, eating, drinking, and screwing. They especially enjoyed the drinking and screwing. Though not in that order.

Her eyes opened, and she groaned about a headache, it being too early, and that there was no need to shout — the bad result of a very good previous day. She then saw Tim sitting there naked with a drink in his hand.

"Good morning, gorgeous. Here you go. Hair of the dog."

She sat up and took note of both his being naked and the drink he was holding. She took a long, lustful look at him, but took the glass and said, "This was a tough decision. I never thought I'd make this choice, big boy."

Tim picked up his glass and offered, "Cheers."

Casey sipped her champagne. "Hard to believe that deal would pay off that handsomely."

"I'm now a believer. A convert to the First Church of the Real Estate Investors."

She raised her glass. "Well, Brother Tim, to our first successful venture. May there be many more." Casey took a big slug from the glass.

Tim took another sip before saying, "You're not going to believe this," and went on to tell her about how Harry was robbed and terrorized. "If it happened to him, it can happen to me."

"What are you going to do about it?"

"I'm going to sell the place on Perry Street."

Casey was always suspicious about its true use and wanted to believe it was for Tim's business. She remembered her history with that apartment.

If it was still a love nest, the current occupant would be out. A jealous thought that maybe, just maybe, she had been suppressing all these years.

Casey wondered aloud, "Why?"

"Like I said, if it happened to him, it can happen to me."

Less suspicious, since she believed it might actually be used for business, Casey told her husband, "Sorry, but you can't use this apartment as an office. Not as long as I'm a member of the bar. You'll need another place to work, and make sure I don't know about it."

"I'm thinking about getting out of the business altogether."

Casey was shocked. "You've been at it a long time, and from what I can guess doing pretty well."

"I think if I focus on this real estate business, it would be more profitable. I made more on this deal than I did all told last year."

"Beginner's luck?"

"I'm going to find out."

"Let's talk about it over brunch."

Tim brought the mimosa into the bathroom with him. Ten minutes later, he was showered and dressed. Carrying the now-empty glass, he thought about pouring another. *Good champagne. It makes a good mimosa.* Since this was a workday, he rejected the idea.

The full slate of football games was going to keep Tim answering calls from bettors with strong opinions about the outcome of the games played later. At five minutes to one, just before kickoff, Tim turned off his phone. It was much like the shopkeeper that locked the door and hung up the sign that said "closed."

The NFL scheduled a second slate of games that started at four in the afternoon. He would open up again at three thirty. Bettors who suffered losses would look to get even, and those with winnings would seek to increase their fortunes. In other words, everybody he dealt with in the morning was going to call again.

A long, hot shower shook the cobwebs out of Casey's head. Able to think clearly about the sudden windfall, she had her own ideas about how to spend the money. Tim wouldn't care unless he needed her to help bankroll the next project. She would broach the subject later.

It was good timing. Casey walked into the living room dressed and ready to go. "Let's eat. Your choice. Any place you like as long as they serve crepes and don't have a TV."

"That narrows it down. Maybe we could try the Carlyle. Ever been there?

What the hell? Why would he say that? It took a great effort to maintain her composure. *Did that fucking Cuban excuse for a lawyer say something to Harry, and Harry blab to Tim?*

She suddenly recalled, "We had dinner there. Remember? Woody Allen played the clarinet in that jazz band."

"Oh, right. Care to try it again?"

Shit. He didn't buy it. He knows. Damn it. Okay, act natural. Deny. Deny. Deny. The truth is a last resort. Casey followed her own advice and said calmly, "I don't know. Do you really feel like going all the way uptown? There are plenty of great places around here. I'll sacrifice the crepes if I have to."

Why is she so squirmy? And give up on the crepes so easily? Everything is a negotiation with her. Always. Now, at the drop of a hat, no crepes? Something is going on. "Okay by me. How about that cafe over on Irving place?"

"Great idea. If your workday is over, let's go."

CHAPTER
54

WHEN DEBBIE HEARD that Harry was not going to pay the extra money to settle their divorce, she was irate. Her lawyer explained that there were two choices: they could pursue a court action, which would delay things and possibly jeopardize her agreement with the land-lord, or take less money from Harry.

Debbie was already planning a departure for sunny Florida and wasn't going to spend another winter in New York. Without the payday from Goldblum, she would need to buy a new winter coat. That wasn't going to happen.

"Tell me exactly what he said," she asked Casey.

"According to Harry's lawyer, he said to drop dead."

Her initial ranting subsided quickly. "We'll see who's going to drop dead."

Casey, thinking about the murders she was sure her client had committed, got very nervous. She picked up a pencil from her desk and started twirling it in her fingers like a baton. "Um, you're not going to do anything foolish, are you?"

"Foolish, no. But he's going to sign off on this, and nothing else."

Casey went from nervous to panic-ridden. She wanted to cover her bases and not get involved in a criminal defense for the death of Harry Rosen. "So you mean if he doesn't sign then we're going to court, right?"

"It means whatever you want it to mean."

We'll see who's going to drop dead. The more she thought about it, the more angry Debbie became. It was a long walk to Harry's office and felt even longer walking into the cold north wind. The weather had abruptly changed. Winter was on its way, and she was determined to miss the season. This year and forever after. Her fairy tale ending was being in Florida with a seven-figure bank account and without Harry.

The door to Harry's office flung open. Debbie headed toward his desk as he sat there staring as if hit by a taser.

"Harry, this is very simple. Here are some documents you need to sign now."

Somewhat composed, Harry got his words out as matter-of-factly as he could. "I'm not signing anything until my lawyer takes a look at them."

She ignored him and passed several pages, conveniently opened to the signature page, across his desk. "This one is a release for your interests in the apartment." She took a pen from Harry's desk and scribbled on an envelope lying nearby. There was ink in the pen, and she passed it in Harry's direction. "Sign it."

"Like I said, I have to consult with my attorney."

Everything that both of them had repressed over time came gushing out like lava from a volcano.

Debbie started. "I have had twenty-three years of you and your bull-shit, and that's more than anyone deserves."

"What are talking about? I could say the same thing too. All your carping. Nothing I ever did was good enough for you."

"Like what? What did you ever do for me, Harry? What? Name one thing."

"I paid the rent every month so you could sit around and watch TV all day."

"I stayed home because you thought it would be an insult to your manhood if I worked. Maybe you were worried I might see what I was missing by being married to you. And the rent you paid. If you had to pay for an apartment that wasn't rent-controlled, you wouldn't have been able to afford a frozen fish stick, let alone a lobster dinner."

"It's not like I was eating alone. You knew how to order pretty good too. God forbid you shop anywhere and use a coupon."

"I spent too much money. Is that what you're saying? You get a check for one of your big deals, and it turns into a closet full of men's clothes. Maybe I end up with a coffee mug that says 'World's Best Wife.'"

"I'm gonna tell you something, Debbie. The sex was great. All three times."

"Did you ever look in the mirror? Who could sleep with you? It would be like one of those people who get trapped in a collapsed building after an earthquake."

"Just get the fuck out of my office. I'm not signing shit. I'm going to the mat on this. Know what you're gonna get from me? *Nothing.* Got it? Nothing. Don't let the door hit you in the ass on the way out."

Both of them out of steam, but still angered, sat staring at each other. Debbie looked Harry square in the eye and in a calm voice said, "They say the pen is mightier than the sword. Is it mightier than a .38 special?"

Harry quizzically tilted his head as she looked in her purse and lifted out the gun. Debbie casually said, "There are two left in the barrel." She gripped it in her right hand and pointed the gun toward the ceiling. She leaned back in the chair. "Well, is it Harry? Is the pen mightier than the gun?"

"You know all I gotta do is call the cops and they nail you for those two Russians."

"What Russians, Harry? The ones you hired to kidnap me? Do you want to go that way? Or do you want to sign?"

"Go ahead and shoot. I go to the hospital and you go to jail. I get everything."

"Unless you go to the cemetery."

It was the second time in his life that Harry was on the business end of a gun barrel. Both had occurred in the last week. He tried to retain his composure. What he really wanted was not to wet his pants.

"Debbie, come on. You don't have to do this. We can negotiate through our lawyers. Let them work it out. There's no reason why we can't get along."

"Harry, before I make a decision on whether I pull the trigger, I'm going to ask you a question. What fucking planet are you on? You psychotic, delusional idiot."

"I'm trying to be reasonable. Is there someplace in between where we can make a deal?"

"Make a deal. A hot deal. A big deal. That's your whole life. Sign the papers so I can move on with what's left of my life." Debbie removed the divorce settlement from her bag and put it on top of the other papers. Again, open to the signature page.

Harry was becoming less intimidated by the gun in Debbie's hand. *Who said you couldn't negotiate at the point of a gun?* "Okay, I understand your point of view. You feel like you've had the short end of the stick for a long time. But consider this: maybe I have too. It goes both ways, you know. So let's assume that we've both..."

A gunshot interrupted. He felt a wave of air as the bullet passed over the top of his head. Harry no longer retained his composure. He reached for the pen and signed both documents.

"One more thing, Harry. I need some cash to tide me over. Can you spare two thousand?"

He stood up, the crotch of pants visibly wet, and counted out twenty hundred-dollar bills for his almost-ex-wife.

"Thanks for making a good decision, Harry." She threw one of the bills back to him and added, "Go get yourself a new pair of pants."

CHAPTER
55

THE STALL IN the restaurant bathroom that was down the hall from Harry's office was unoccupied. He removed his pants and placed them under the air dryer that was typically used for patrons who washed their hands. Several minutes later, his boxers were in the garbage receptacle, and Harry was going commando.

Walking back to his apartment, Harry didn't realize how cold it was. He left the building without his coat and the door unlocked. Some ten blocks later, the cold air penetrated the fog in his head. He walked past a pub and kept going. A second thought turned him around, and he yanked the door open.

There were plenty of empty barstools. All of them, actually. The burly bartender stopped emptying the cardboard box filled with bottles to tend to Harry.

"What can I get you." It was a statement, not a question.

"Gin. No, make it tequila. Patrón if you got it. Neat."

Two quick slugs and the glass was empty. Harry was getting up when his phone rang. *Tim. Jesus H. Christ. What else can go wrong today?* He muted the ringer and let the call go to voicemail. He sat down and ordered another.

Before the bartender finished the pour, Harry's phone was ringing again. *Motherfucker.* He had to take the call sooner or later and decided to answer. If you need a root canal, eventually you go to the dentist. May as well get it over with.

"Hey, how's my newly minted millionaire?"

"Pretty good, Harry." *It looks like you're helping in more than one way.* Tim didn't want to rub it in. "I got a figure for you from last week."

"Shouldn't be too bad."

Tim was at home sitting in a wing chair. He took a sip of coffee before he answered. "Depends on your definition of 'not too bad.' Four winners, eight losers at two g's each. You're minus ninety-six hundred."

"Fucking Giants."

"You weren't the only guy on the wrong side of that one. Do you want to settle this on Wednesday?"

"How about if you take it out of my end when we close on your deal?"

"I can wait. The lawyers are trying to set it up for next week. It'll be an early Christmas present for both of us."

"Terrific. I'll call you soon."

Some Christmas. Harry figured that after repaying the poker players, buying back his watch, paying Susan a commission, settling with Debbie, and his gambling losses, he'd have enough to keep himself afloat for a couple of months.

Harry chugged down the tequila, paid for the drinks, left a ten for the bartender, and walked out.

CHAPTER

56

O NE BULLET IN the barrel. Back in her apartment, or what was soon going to become her former apartment, Debbie emptied the shell casings out of the handgun. *Suppose someone finds them? Maybe the police?* She put on a pair of rubber gloves and wiped down the casings, the bullet, and the gun. All except the gun went into the trash, which then went directly down the chute in the hallway, into the compactor, and off to the dump. Good luck finding the evidence.

Back downstairs, she flagged down a cab and gave the driver the address to Casey's office. The traffic was horrible, and Debbie became more and more tense during the constant stop-and-go. Irate drivers with the green light in their favor were honking at a bus blocking the intersection. Frustrated, she told the driver to let her out.

Perfect. A McDonald's. Debbie walked to the counter and placed a to-go order. She carried the paper bag into the ladies' restroom and removed the hamburger and fries. Debbie took a bite of the hamburger and threw what remained into the trash, along with the fries. She used a napkin to grab the gun and take it out of her pocketbook and into the bag that previously contained the food. Debbie left the ladies, went into the dining room, and dropped the bag into the garbage can near the front door.

The time it took to walk the last few blocks to the offices of the Cassidy Law Firm went quickly. The receptionist wanted to know if she had an appointment. "I don't."

The receptionist gave her an icy smile and the words, "Please have a seat. I will see if she's available." This created even more tension for Casey. The brief wait seemed endless.

"Follow me, please."

It was a short walk to a sparsely furnished, windowless meeting room with a table, four chairs, and a telephone hanging on the wall next to a refrigerator. She wasn't getting the royal treatment.

The door opened, and Matt Bernstein walked in and took a seat. "Casey is tied up and asked if I could assist. I'm sorry we don't have a more comfortable room available right now."

Put off by her earlier encounter, where her expectations were severely disappointed, she was all business. "I have the signed agreements for you."

"Very good," he said as she was passing them toward him and added, "Now all we have to do is get Mr. Rosen's signature as well.

"He already signed them."

"He did? That's unusual. We didn't hear from his attorney."

"Harry and I spoke privately, and afterward he signed."

Totally misreading her, he tried some consolation. "I'll move these along and get this all buttoned up for you. You may be distraught now, but as you get further past this, you'll see how much better your life is."

"Matt, when I get the money my life will be much better."

"The apartment will likely settle within the next week or so. You should prepare to vacate. The rest when Harry gets the money. He will have to refinance or sell the building. That's a couple of months or more."

"Let me know when I can pick up a check." Debbie got up and left.

CHAPTER
57

I T WAS THE longest week. A lot of people were going to be very happy by the end of the day. The house sale was going to close, and Casey scheduled Debbie to come in for her check. The money for the apartment was in her account. She also wanted Ramos there as well. Harry was going to re-sign the documents in front of her, with his attorney. As long as Harry would be there for the real estate closing, she might as well end the entire matter. Besides, there was no way Harry was going to leave without paying her client. And there was no way Debbie was going to leave without paying her.

As the crowd arrived, they were ushered into the largest conference room in the office. Unsurprisingly, Harry and Tim were there first. There was no way that Casey would chance Harry exploding without a suppressor, and that was Tim until Ramos arrived for part two of this saga.

The buyers entered with their attorney and a not-so-unattractive realtor named Susan something or other. Even Casey took notice.

There wasn't much small talk. Harry sat quietly as the papers were passed along the table and duly signed and notarized. Invoices were gathered, and Casey's paralegal prepared a closing statement and a list of checks to be written.

If the week that passed since this was scheduled seemed like a year, the hour that passed since the closing started seemed like a decade. Finally, the wire transfer the sellers arranged for was confirmed to be in Casey's escrow account. The paralegal left the room, and the fifteen minutes she was gone felt like a century.

There were smiles all around as everyone got their checks, except Harry.

"Did you forget someone?" Harry wanted to know.

"Stand by for a moment, Mr. Rosen. We will get to that."

Handshakes and departures followed, except for Harry.

Casey left Harry alone and found her husband waiting outside the door. Two big smiles as they looked at each other. "A job well done, Mr. Cassidy. Don't head for Brazil until we divide up that check." There were half a million reasons for them to be smiling.

Tim suggested, "I have a great idea. Let's make it a special night. I'm going to see who's playing at the Cafe Carlyle and try to get a reservation."

Fuck. This can't be a coincidence. "It's a great idea. I love it."

"Maybe we should get a room too? Stay uptown and make a night of it."

Shit. Shit. Shit. It took all she had to maintain her composure. "You know it would take me longer to pack an overnight bag than it would to get home. Besides, there's nothing we can do at the Carlyle that we can't do at home."

"Good point. Bring your A game tonight. I'm stoked." He put his arm around her, pulled her closer, and squeezed her ass as he hugged her. "See you later." Tim turned and walked out.

Back in the conference room, Harry again asked for his check.

"Your attorney didn't call you? Mr. Ramos will be here shortly, as will my client, Mrs. Rosen."

"With all due respect, this is bullshit. One thing has nothing to do with the other."

"Mr. Rosen, I cannot speak with you without your attorney present." She left Harry alone in the conference room.

"Could I at least get a coffee while you hold me hostage?" Harry yelled to Casey's back.

Without turning to Harry, Casey told the person nearest to her to take care of Harry's request.

It was only a matter of minutes before the coffee, Ramos the attorney, and Debbie the soon-to-be ex-wife got there. Casey brought a folder with her and showed the contents to Ramos. She told him how her client brought these to her and wanted him to have copies as well. Then she added, "I'd like the signatures notarized."

Ramos looked at the signatures, then at Harry. He showed him the pages where he signed and asked if that was his signature.

"Yes," Harry answered.

Ramos continued, "And did you sign it knowingly and of your own free will?"

Harry hesitated and made eye contact with Debbie. She momentarily glanced down at her bag, wishing the gun wasn't in a garbage can somewhere. All eyes on Harry, especially the piercing glare of Debbie, he answered, "Yes."

The formalities continued until Casey was satisfied that nothing could come back to haunt her at a later date. She then handed Harry his check, with a copy to Ramos.

Harry looked at the check. He knew what was coming, but the reality of receiving the significantly reduced amount because of payments to Susan, *that bitch,* and Debbie, *that fucking bitch,* made him blurt out, "A bullet would have been cheaper."

Although Debbie's check was in the seven figures, she saw the bill for legal services and commented venomously, "Forty thousand, Casey? Harry's right, a bullet is cheaper."

Is she threatening me? Jesus. I'm pretty sure she's got two murders under her belt. Are there more? Will there be any more? Will it be me?! Maybe she's only pissed about the fee? Hoping that was the case, Casey turned her dial to attack and directed the comment to Ramos. "My client wants the rest of the settlement in sixty days. If we have to come after you, we will. Sell the building, mortgage the building, we don't care. If you don't, I'll prepare a new deed giving my client sole possession." Casey thought that the tirade was a forty-thousand-dollar performance.

Ramos asked Harry if he understood that.

Already standing with his coat on, Harry answered, "Yeah. I got it. And I hope you all have a really great day and don't rot in hell."

CHAPTER
58

T HE ELEVATOR DOWN stopped at several other floors on the way. This did not help Harry's temperament. Angry was three notches down from where he was. Finally reaching the lobby, the elevator doors opened and he pushed his way from the back of the crowd to make his exit.

How much worse is this day going to get? Tim was waiting for him.

"Hello, Harry."

"Hiya, Tim. You had a pretty good day, huh? I told you that deal was gonna be a home run."

"It was. I'm glad you made out okay too. I know you want to settle up with me, and I thought I'd wait for you and we could walk over to your bank."

"You know I'd be glad to do that, but I'm supposed to meet a potential seller about a listing. It could be another great investment for you."

"Enough, Harry. We go to the bank. You deposit your check and get back enough cash to pay me. Very simple. You play, you pay."

"All right, all right, I get it. Let's go. I'm telling you, though, one day you're gonna owe me and I'm gonna squeeze you like a lemon."

"I hope to see that day, because the way you're going lately, the Cleveland Browns will be playing the Detroit Lions in the Super Bowl." Tim was pretty sure that Harry knew neither had ever been to the big game.

"Very funny. Even I would never bet that."

"You and your wife, is it over?"

"Yeah, it's over."

"What's next for Harry Rosen?"

"I gotta sell my building and give her another big load of money. Probably work out of my new apartment. But you shouldn't worry. I'll have enough left over to support you. Maybe I can claim you as dependent on my tax return." Harry started to cheer up, realizing that he'd still have a couple of million left from the sale. "You know I'm going to be a multi-millionaire soon."

"And how does that change your life?"

"Are you kidding? No wife and a pile of money? I'll have all these hot young girls chasing after me like crazy."

"Harry, that's not all it's cracked up to be." The specter of Izzy came to mind. "You'll end up with child support, alimony, and an empty wallet. Be careful."

"You know what? These women get away with murder."

CHAPTER
59

I T WAS CHRISTMAS Day. The sun was shining, and the Caribbean Sea was a glorious blue. They flew in the previous day. A few hours to Puerto Rico, and then a short charter flight, and they were in paradise.

Casey was lying on a lounge chair next to the pool at the villa they rented in St. Bart's. Tim had just finished mixing two mimosas when a phone rang. It was Casey's. He brought it to her with the drink.

"Hi, Sis, Merry Christmas."

"The same to you and Tim. I'm sorry you couldn't make it this year. I hope you're having a fun time."

"We are. How are you?"

"We are all fine. I will send you an email with some photos and updates, but I'm a bit embarrassed by your generosity. I don't know what to say. I mean, Air Jordan sneakers for each of the boys, and the big-screen TV, and the Instant Pot. It's just too much."

"You were always good to me. Now that I can, I'm happy to give a little something back."

"All I can say is thank you. Merry Christmas and Happy New Year."

Tim watched her put the phone down and raise her glass to her husband. "Merry Christmas, and God bless us all, Big Tim." Tim clinked her glass. Before he could get in a swallow, his cell beckoned.

It was Harry. "Hey, Happy Hanukkah."

"Yeah, okay, sure. Are you taking action today?" he wanted to know.

"Since when is it illegal to book bets on a holiday?"

Tim took Harry's bets, as well as the others who called to do the same, and wish him a happy holiday too.

CHAPTER
60

WHAT A LONG, strange trip it was for Debbie Rosen. She drove the thousand or so miles in her Mercedes from New York to Delray Beach. This was not the same sleepy West Palm Beach suburb of a previous generation. Bars and restaurants lined Atlantic Avenue from the beach to Federal Highway. Pawnshops ceded their storefronts to upscale eateries. In the month or so since she arrived at her version of the Garden of Eden, Debbie had purchased a condo with a water view, joined a beach club, and figured out where to get half-price drinks in the afternoon and half-price dinners before six. She had arrived.

Meeting people was easy. There were so many from New York that the introduction was typically, "Where in New York? Oh, the Upper East Side. Do you know...?" And from that point, it was, "We're going for cocktails later. You should come."

The week between Christmas and New Year's packed the entire county. Anyone who owned a second home was using it and likely had friends or family visiting.

Her beach posse was more like a sorority at spring break, only a tad older. They determined that an early departure was in order so they could get seats at the bar. Any bar, anywhere in town so they could walk home. Older and wiser in that regard.

Margaritas were the order of the day, and then the evening. Music playing, blasting really, jostling crowds, and voices that needed to be loud to be heard. Debbie felt an elbow in her back that knocked her slightly off balance. She turned suddenly and was immediately met with an apology and the offer of a drink, even if hers hadn't spilled.

They introduced themselves, spoke about the weather, and ordered another round. More talk about food and restaurants, then yet another round. The conversation turned to real estate, followed by one more round. By this time, Debbie was working on her fifth when she asked, "What kind of work do you do?"

"I'm a cop. A detective, actually."

"And you said you're from New York?"

"Long Island."

"Oh, have I got a story for you. I was once kidnapped there."

Made in the USA
Middletown, DE
04 November 2019